Veloci-Rapture
End Time Thriller

Veloci-Rapture
Copyright © 2023 Randel Ulysses Ready

ISBN: 9798866044153

All rights reserved. This book or any portion thereof may not be reproduced or used in any manner whatsoever without the author's express written permission except for the use of brief quotations in a book review.

This is a work of fiction. Names, characters, businesses, places, events, and incidents are either the products of the author's imagination or used in a fictitious manner. Any resemblance to actual persons, living or dead, or actual events is purely coincidental.

Scripture quotations are from:
1) KJV—King James Version.
2) NKJV—New King James Version ®, Copyright 1982 by Thomas Nelson. Used by permission. All rights reserved.
   3) Scripture quotations marked (NLT) are taken from the Holy Bible, New Living Translation, Copyright 1996, 2004, 2015 by Tyndale House Foundation. Used by permission of Tyndale House Publishers, Carol Stream, Illinois 60188. All rights reserved.

Veloci-Rapture

End Time Thriller

Randel Ulysses Ready

Table of Contents

Insanity Escape 1
God, CO2, and You 8
The Day Everything Changed 17
Where's Samantha? 29
Great Balls of Fire 39
Tribulation Force 53
The Chronicle 66
Two Witnesses 74
The Chronicle Continues 86
Explosive News 97
Hamburgers, Brats, and Corn Cobs 104
The Samson Option 114
Grand Opening 129
Operation Lightning Strike 140
A Tale of Two Cities 153
Destination Babylon, New York 168
Wiley Coyote 186
Quick Thief 197
Daniel's 70 Weeks Prophecy 203
Six Mega Signs 209
Congratulations 217

Chapter One

Insanity Escape

The star-filled night sky gave way to the early morning sun as it glistened off the water, and the twins woke to the wailing sounds of a mother loon and her chicks swimming on the lake.

Jason rolled out of his sleeping bag, slipped on his shoes, and unzipped the tent door. He grabbed a few sticks, placed them on the campfire embers, and rekindled the flame. He cracked open a half dozen eggs, tossed several sausage links into the frying pan, and placed it on the campfire grill.

"Man, that sure does smell good," Jamie said as he exited the tent and sat on a log beside the fire. Jason handed his brother a steaming cup of coffee, "Good morning."

It was a gorgeous summer weekend in the Wisconsin Northwoods, where the twin brothers had gone to celebrate their eighteenth birthday, hiking, canoeing, and camping on the Eagle River chain of lakes. "Hey, Jason, what do you say that after breakfast, we grab the canoe and hike over to Crystal Lake? The lady at the bait shop said the fish are biting."

"Sounds good to me!"

The twins finished breakfast, retrieved the 15-foot canoe from the vehicle roof rack, tossed in the fishing equipment, and walked the narrow trail to the lake shore. Jason climbed into the canoe's bow, and Jamie shoved off. Jason was fishing for Panfish, and Jamie was trying to catch one of those legendary Northwoods Muskies. It is said that it takes 10,000 casts to catch one of those monsters that can grow over four feet in length and weigh over 60 pounds.

Jason noticed a bald eagle perched atop a tall white pine tree. Jamie looked up, and the eagle took flight, spreading its massive black wings and gliding to the lake's surface. Her sharp-clawed feet plunged into the clear water, and she flew back to her nest with a small fish gripped in her talons. The mama eagle swooped down several times so close to the canoe that the twins could feel the breeze from her wings as she flew back to her nest with another fish to feed her chicks.

So far, the eagle had caught more fish than the twins, but it wasn't long before the fish started biting. Jason reeled in fish after fish, but Jamie didn't catch a single Musky.

Jamie glanced at the blue sky. The sun was at its zenith, indicating that it was lunchtime. "I'm hungry," his stomach growled. "Let's go get something to eat." So, the boys paddled back to shore, pulled the canoe onto the sandy beach, and hiked back to the camp, eating blueberries along the way. "I sure hope we don't run across a bear. You know how much bears love blueberries," Jason said.

Jamie lifted his right eyebrow, "Yeah, especially since you forgot to pack the bear spray, Dum, Dum!"

The last thing the boys wanted to do was run into a bear. A black bear, especially a mother bear with cubs, can become a homicidal maniac in a matter of seconds. She will attack anything she perceives as a threat to her cubs.

The twins were about a hundred yards from the camp when they were startled by a thrashing sound to the left of the trail. The tall ferns and brush obscured the view, but something was moving around in them.

"What do you think it is?" Jason whispered.

Jamie stared into the ferns, "I can't tell..."

Was it a bobcat, a deer, or a bear? It was anyone's guess, but the twins weren't about to stick around to find out. So they hightailed it back to the camp as fast as they could.

Jamie arrived first, breathing rapidly as he sat on the campsite picnic table. A few seconds later, Jason arrived, leaning on the Old Indian as he caught his breath.

"Man, I'm starving!"

"Me too," Jamie said.

Jason grabbed the lunch cooler from the Old Indian and sat it on the picnic table. The twins quickly scarfed down the sandwiches, chips, and Coke. Jamie burped as he pointed to the Old Indian, "Jason, you forgot to close the hatch door."

The Old Indian is what the boys named their 1985 Jeep Cherokee. It was rough around the edges but ran well and took them wherever they desired to go.

Jamie was determined to catch a Musky, it was time to pull out the big gun: *The Titan Dive and Rise Lure* that his sister, Jenna, had given him for his birthday. Jason strapped his 15-inch Crocodile Dundee bowie knife to his belt just in case they ran into a bear on the way back to the lake. It probably wouldn't stop an angry bear, but it was better than nothing.

"Let's go," Jamie said. Ten minutes later, the twins were in the canoe, paddling to the steepest shoreline and darkest lake water. "This looks like a good fishing spot." Jason agreed, "Yeah if I was a Musky, this is where I'd be!"

Jamie tied the Titan lure to the fishing pole line, raised the pole, and with a quick flick of the wrist, the lure flew 75 feet through the air, splashing into the water. He cranked the pole's reel, pulling the six-inch lure through the water. The Dive and Rise Lure tempted the Musky's appetite by plunging headlong into the abyss and surging back to the surface.

Suddenly, something attacked the bait, almost pulling the pole out of Jamie's hands. He momentarily let the fish run with the bait and slowly began reeling it in. After about a 10-minute fight, the fish surfaced next to the canoe. It wasn't a Musky, but it was the next best thing—a good-sized Northern Pike.

A hundred casts later, still no luck. Jamie's hopes of landing a legendary Musky were fading as quickly as the sun was setting. Jamie said a silent prayer, and let the Titan lure fly. It landed two feet from a dead tree lying in the water.

A few seconds later, the buzzing sound of the reel's fishing line indicated that a fish had taken the bait and was on the run. Jamie stood slowly, being careful not to capsize the canoe as he fought the big fish. The fish took a deep dive and then surfaced flying out of the water! "Wow! Did you see the size of that thing?" Jamie shouted.

It was a Musky, and it was a big one!

Twenty minutes later, the exhausted Musky surfaced. Jason helped his brother pull the monster into the canoe, being careful not to place his hands near those razor-sharp teeth. The twins weren't sure how much it weighed, but it was heavy and 47 inches long!

The boys paddled back to the sandy beach shore and took a few snapshots of the big fish. After a quick and refreshing swim in the lake, it was time to filet the fish catch, head back to camp, and cook supper before the setting sun hid behind the forest trees.

It had been a great day of fishing on Crystal Lake. Jamie was thrilled to have reeled in a Northern Pike and to catch that big – bragging rights – Musky, and Jason filled the ice chest half full of Sunfish, Bluegill, and Small Mouth Bass. Jamie started the campfire, and Jason did the cooking. After eating a delicious fried fish dinner, the twins sat around the campfire, roasting marshmallows and reminiscing about the good old days.

The Wisconsin Northwoods was ideal for relaxing, revitalizing, and leaving your troubles behind. Of course, at eighteen years old and fresh out of high school, the twins had no significant worries (at least, that's what they thought…)

Jamie looked at his watch, stood, and yawned, "It's almost midnight. I'm going to hit the sack."

"Yeah, I guess I should, too," Jason said.

The boys rolled out the sleeping bags and grabbed the pillows. The moon was full, and the enchanting sound of howling wolves echoing across the lake lulled the boys into dreamland.

At 3 AM, Jason woke to the sound of a breaking branch and a rumbling growl. The campfire light revealed the silhouette of a large bear sniffing around the tent. Jason whispered, *"Jamie, wake up, there's a bear outside!"*

He didn't answer. Jason flicked on the night light. Jamie wasn't in his sleeping bag. He wasn't in the tent. Jason ran his fingers through his hair, *"Where on earth is he?"*

The bear walked slowly around the tent, pushing its nose against the tent fabric, *"Stupid me, I should have put the donuts in the Jeep. Bears love donuts more than blueberries."*

The bear stopped in front of the tent door. Jason's brow lifted, and his eyes enlarged as he watched the shadowy figure of the six-foot-tall bear standing on his hind legs sniffing the air. The ground shook as the big bear's front feet landed back on the ground.

It let out a loud, devilish growl, and with one swipe from each claw, the tent door was shredded into pieces! The bear took a step, poking its head inside the tent. Jason threw the box of donuts at the bear. It caught one and spit it out—the bear's eyes were fastened on Jason—it wasn't hungry for donuts!

Thoughts of being eaten alive whirled through Jason's mind. *What should I do, run? No, don't run. Any sudden movement will provoke an attack. Just lie still; if the bear realizes I'm not a threat, it may go away.*

The bear took another step, pushing its massive 600-pound body inside the tent. Jason grabbed his Crocodile Dundee bowie knife and pulled the sleeping bag over his head. The bear stepped onto the sleeping bag and took two more steps. Its front legs stood on Jason as it sniffed and growled. Its weight caused Jason's chest to constrict until he could hardly breathe.

The bear raised its paw, and with one quick swipe, its sharp, daggered claw ripped the sleeping bag from Jason's face. Jason lifted the knife and rammed it into the bear's side, but it didn't faze the bear. The bear's thick fur armor coat was nearly impenetrable. He rammed the knife into the animal's side again and again but to no avail. It just made the bear angrier.

The bear snarled, displaying its ravenous teeth and fangs. He could feel and smell the animal's breath as they stared eye to eye. Hot drool dripped from its powerful jaw, splattering Jason's face.

I'm at the mercy of a monster!

The bear let out a blood-curdling roar and opened its mouth wide. Jason grabbed hold of the animal's bottom jaw with both hands and pushed up with all his might, trying to keep the monster's fangs and teeth from biting off his face or ripping out his throat.

The bear shook his head, attempting to break Jason's grip. Jason couldn't let go. It was a life-or-death situation. He had to buy some time. *Perhaps Jamie will come to the rescue, burying the campfire axe deep into the bear's brain!*

Jason fought relentlessly to keep the bear's bite at bay, but it was a losing battle. The adrenaline rush was wearing off, his strength was waning, and his grip was loosening. Images of his Mom, Dad, and Jenna crying at his funeral flashed before his eyes as blood-red drool ran between his fingers and streamed down his arms.

Jason's body trembled, and his mind raced. His hopes of surviving vanished when he realized why the bear's drool was blood red. Jamie wasn't coming to his rescue because his brother was dead.

Tears slid down his cheeks as he squeezed his eyes shut, *"Oh Lord, please don't let it be. If someone has to die today, let it be me."*

Jason's heart pounded.

He could hardly breathe.

He drew a difficult breath and screamed, *"Please help me, Jesus!"*

With a jerk of terror, his eyes snapped open, and he gasped for air. The bear was gone; God had heard his prayer. Peace flooded Jason's soul as the sound of his snoring brother penetrated his ears. It was a dream. Thank God, it was just a dream!

Chapter Two

God, CO2, and You!

The Wisconsin Northwoods was a great place to escape the sexual, cultural, and political insanity that was spreading through the American landscape like wildfire. It was also one of the few wildlife camping areas that hadn't been affected by the changing climate. Devastating droughts, atmospheric rivers, flash floods, mudslides, hurricanes, tornadoes, and wildfires have, over the past few years, displaced, disrupted, and destroyed thousands of homes, businesses, and lives.

In one way or another, climate change disasters were affecting everyone on the planet. Mother Nature is sick and is vomiting out the inhabitants around the globe.

Who's to blame for climate change?

Well, according to the climate change, Gods and Goddesses: YOU, ME, and EVERYONE but them!

Before the twins graduated from Hideaway Falls High, the school principal invited an Evolution and Climate Change expert to speak. The title of his sermon was GOD, CO2, AND YOU.

The first half hour of his speech was spent attempting to convince the students and teachers that God doesn't exist and that the Creation account in Genesis was just the figment of someone's storytelling imagination.

The second half-hour was spent trying to persuade the students that the greatest threat to humanity was not terrorism, illegal immigration, nuclear weapons proliferation, or even World War Three—but climate change. He said that the world had reached a critical point in history, and the only solution to save the planet from inevitable extinction was the following:

1. Reduce the planet's population. The ideal population for sustainable life and development is two-thirds fewer people than we have presently. This means that the earth's population must be reduced by 5.2 BILLION PEOPLE!

2. Destroy Capitalism. The problem with Capitalism is that it gives individuals the ability to gain wealth. Wealth enables people to purchase cars, trucks, boats, motorcycles, jet skis, ATVs, RVs, and aircraft. Plus, wealth provides the means for the average hard-working individual to live where they want, travel where they wish, and fulfill the American dream of owning a home. All these luxuries and activities produce a carbon footprint that is destroying our planet.

3. Reduce Carbon Dioxide (CO_2) Emissions to near zero and eliminate nitrogen-based crop fertilizers, which are greenhouse gases responsible for the rise in global temperatures and destruction of the stratosphere's ozone layer.

4. Reduce the number of Methane Farting Farm and Ranch Animals by 75 percent.

The expert spoke confidently and authoritatively, but Jamie and Jason weren't buying it! Undoubtedly, the twins weren't thrilled when the school cafeteria replaced roast beef, hamburgers, and hot dogs with synthetic lab-grown meats and buns made from cricket flour. The twins, however, were not climate change deniers. They realized something was responsible for the unprecedented numbers of natural disasters wreaking havoc around the globe. They just didn't believe that automobiles and farting pigs and cows were the cause.

The twins first became skeptical of the climate change narrative when a few years ago their science teacher, Mrs. McFarland, replayed the 2006 documentary *An Inconvenient Truth*. The twins and the class watched Al Gore flying in a helicopter as he witnessed a 700-foot Arctic glacier melting and collapsing into the ocean. It was that particular scene that kickstarted the Global Warming Climate Change hysteria that spread around the world. From that point forward, every climate-related disaster was blamed on climate change.

The trouble with the documentary was that the collapsing 700-foot-high Arctic glacier wasn't even real. The twins had recognized the video footage during classic movie night with the family. The melting glacier was a computer-generated graphic from the 2004 science fiction movie THE DAY AFTER TOMORROW! The twins informed Mrs. McFarland about it. She checked into it and discovered they were right. The movie was a sham and a scam!

The Expert's Climate Change lecture was over; it was time for the Question and Answer session. Jamie's hand went up first. "Yes, young man, what's your name and question?"

"My name is Jamie Rhodes, and my question is this. How does evolution explain the archeological discovery of fossils of fish and sea creatures on mountaintops in continents around the globe?"

The expert rubbed his chin and scratched his head. "I'm not sure. I've never been asked that question before. I guess that millions of years ago, a worldwide flood covered the mountains, and when the water receded, the fish and sea creatures got stuck on the mountaintops."

Jamie laughed, "Mr. Expert, you're right. There was a worldwide flood, not millions of years ago, but in 2348 BC. That's why God told Noah to build the Ark!"

The auditorium erupted with laughter.

The expert was embarrassed; he didn't know what to say, so he played along, rolling his eyes, saying, *"I sure didn't see that one coming!*

"Next question!"

Several students stood with raised hands, but the expert's eyes were drawn to the pretty girl in the third row with long red curls and a short skirt. "Young lady, what's your name and your question?"

"My name is Sierra McFarland. I've been asked out on dates by many boys, but none of them were half monkey and half human! If evolution is true, why don't we see the transition from monkeys to humans happening today? Doesn't the fact that the missing link is still missing disprove evolution?"

He thought for a long moment and then answered, "Well, perhaps Bigfoot is the missing link. Just because Sasquatch hasn't asked you out on a date doesn't prove that he doesn't exist!"

Everyone laughed except for Sierra. She shook her head and whispered, *"What an idiot!"*

"Okay, that's enough questions about evolution. Who's got a climate change question?" The expert scanned the students with raised hands. Jamie stood waving his arms, beckoning, *Pick me, Pick me!*

The expert pressed his lips together and shook his head. No way he was going to let that redneck smart-ass student ask any more questions. He raised his gaze, noticing a student standing at the back of the auditorium. He pointed, "The student with the red baseball cap, what's your name and your question?"

The student respectfully removed his cap, "My name is Jason Rhodes." The expert's eyes widened, and he slapped his forehead when he realized the smart-ass student had a twin brother!

"Mr. Expert, I was wondering how global warming can cause extreme dry weather and droughts in some states and simultaneously cause record-setting rainfall and floods in others?"

The expert answered, "Global warming is not the only factor influencing extreme weather events. The effects of climate change can vary depending on the location, season, and natural climate patterns. Some regions may experience more dry weather and droughts, while others may experience more wet conditions and floods.

"Does that answer your question?"

Jason nodded his head up and down, shook his head left to right, and shrugged his shoulders, "Yes. No. Not really!"

The expert cleared his throat and adjusted the microphone, "Next question!"

"The student with the big black afro, what's your name and your question?"

"My friends call me Jamar Jumping Jack Johnson, and my question is this. How can global warming cause the *North Pole Ice Cap* to shrink and simultaneously cause the *South Pole Ice Cap* to grow larger as it has in recent history?"

You could hear a pin drop as the students and teachers waited for the response… … …?

The expert couldn't think of a persuasive answer, so he gave the politically correct response that any good government-funded climatologist would give. "I'm not sure, but climate change is settled science. And if we don't do something about it, it will soon be too late to save the planet!"

Sierra McFarland wasn't about to let the climate change expert get off the hook that easily. She stood asking loudly, "How can global warming cause record-setting heat waves and droughts in the summer and record-setting cold temperatures and blizzard conditions in the winter? Those two weather events are polar opposites. How can global warming be responsible for both?"

The expert squinted his eyes, and his face reddened as he glared at Sierra, "Young lady, sit down! I didn't call on you!"

That command didn't sit well with the students or Sierra's favorite teacher, Mrs. McFarland, Sierra's mother. She was one of the few teachers who wasn't afraid of the politically correct cancel culture. She stood and her voice rose, "Well, Mr. Climate Change Expert, since you refuse to answer Sierra's question. I will answer the question on your behalf!

"Global warming cannot be responsible for both extreme hot and cold temperatures. It is a scientific contradiction, and no doubt, is why the climate change alarmists changed the name from Global Warming to Climate Change. That way, no matter the weather event, they can blame it on climate change, be it a drought or a blizzard!"

The school Principal stood shouting, "Mrs. McFarland, that's enough, sit down!" She ignored him and continued, "America's leaders love to add that three-word tagline—God Bless America—at the end of their speeches. Perhaps instead of asking God to bless America, we should start thanking Him for already blessing us! Why would God bless America with such a vast abundance of oil, natural gas, coal, livestock, and other natural resources if He didn't want us to use and enjoy them?

"Imagine how many lives in third-world nations could be rescued from poverty, disease, and starvation if America shared our clean coal technology and provided countries with inexpensive gas to run farm implements, drill water wells, and grow their economies. Instead, they send us idiots and liars to deceive our students!"

The auditorium erupted; students were hollering one question after another. Some supported the expert, and others supported Mrs. McFarland. Someone hurled a shoe. The expert ducked, the shoe barely missing him. He ran for the exit, mumbling, *"Sheesh, this is a tough crowd!"*

The school Principal stood motioning for the students to be quiet and then grabbed the microphone, "Everyone, go to your next class immediately!" The twins, Sierra and Mrs. McFarland were sent to the Principal's office and warned to keep their comments and questions to themselves. Mrs. McFarland was accused of being not woke enough to teach and was fired for challenging the "settled science" of climate change."

Mrs. McFarland stormed out of the Principal's office, slamming the door! Sierra turned to the Principal, giving him the stink eye. *"Settled science, yeah, right! The climate change theory is about as scientific as Darwin's evolution theory that NO ONE, PLUS NOTHING, EQUALS EVERYTHING. Which is a scientific impossibility!"*

The Principal frowned, pointing at the door, "One more word out of you, and I will expel you and the twins. Now get out and go to your next class!"

Unfortunately, instead of entertaining ideas like assisting third-world countries with American ingenuity and resources, those comments and questions got students in trouble, videos canceled, authors silenced, and employees fired. Why? What was the climate change head honcho—*The guy in the red suit with a pitchfork, long tail, and black horns*—trying to hide from the world's citizens? What in the world does the statement, *'The earth's population MUST BE REDUCED BY 5.2 BILLION PEOPLE'* even mean?

The PC police monitored everything from phones to videos and articles to books. YouTube videographers and podcasters had to intentionally mispronounce and misspell words to trick social media algorithms and search engines so they didn't get canceled and so citizens could find their videos, blogs, and articles. *So much for Free Speech!*

Like most teenagers, the twins often said silly things and made stupid mistakes. But unlike the potheads that grew up in the 70s and 80s—which now run our schools and country—the twins were bright, had a grip on reality, and were unafraid to speak the truth. They believed that God, not man, was ultimately in charge of the changing climate. Understanding that global temperatures were predominately affected by the sun's activity, not man's. The more frequent and larger the solar flares, the hotter the earth's temperatures. The less frequent and smaller the solar flares, the cooler the earth's temperatures.

The twin's father, Pastor John Rhodes, says the reason natural disasters are becoming increasingly unnatural in frequency, intensity, and duration has nothing to do with *GLOBAL WARMING* but everything to do with *GLOBAL INIQUITY!* A city, state, or nation can become so sinful that God will visit that land and cause it to vomit out the inhabitants.

> "Do not defile yourselves with any of these things; for by all these the nations are defiled, which I am casting out before you. For the land is defiled; therefore, I visit the punishment of its iniquity upon it, and the land VOMITS out its inhabitants. You shall therefore keep My statutes and My judgments, and shall not commit any of these abominations, either any of your own nation or any stranger who dwells among you (for all these abominations the men of the land have done, who were before you, and thus the land is defiled), lest the land VOMIT you out also when you defile it, as it VOMITED out the nations that were before you" (Leviticus 18, verses 24 to 28).

"The word "ABOMINATION" speaks of sins that are so filthy, repulsive, and detestable that it makes God, so to speak, sick to His stomach. Those sins are listed in the biblical book Leviticus, chapters 18 to 20.

"God's Word is replete with examples of nations that He destroyed because of their wickedness. God is patient, giving every nation space to repent, but will intervene in judgment when its citizens refuse to repent. The fact that the vomiting of the inhabitants has become a worldwide phenomenon is not just a sign that God is displeased with the behavior of the nations but is a sign of the end of the age!

"Jesus, the apostles, and the Old Testament prophets used the metaphor "birth pangs" to describe how the end times will come upon the world. Just as when a pregnant woman's delivery time draws near, the birth pangs become more frequent and intense. In like manner, natural disasters are becoming more frequent and severe because they are a sign that the earth will soon give birth to the New World Order, as revealed in the prophetic pages of Scripture. It's time for Christians to stop calling weather-related disasters Climate Change Events and call them what God's Word calls them: BIRTH PANGS!"

Chapter Three

The Day Everything Changed!

The morning fog began to lift as the rising sun gradually illuminated the Northwoods camp. This time, it wasn't a nightmare, nor the sounds of chirping birds and wailing loons that woke the twins. Instead, a strange ruckus just outside the tent caused sleeping eyes to open suddenly.

Jamie sat up, "What's making all that racket?"

"I don't know. I sure hope it's not a bear!"

Jamie held his finger to his lips, "Keep quiet; I'll peek out the window. He pulled on his shoes and began tying them.

Jason's brow creased, "Why are you putting on your shoes? You can't outrun a bear."

"No, Jason, I can't outrun a bear, but I can outrun you!"

"Thanks a lot, Jamie. Leave me behind to get eaten!"

Don't worry, Jason. If a bear wants to eat you, it will first have to eat me. Put on your shoes. If it's a bear, we'll run for the Jeep."

"Good idea!"

Jamie tilted his head sideways, "Don't tell me you forgot to put the fish cooler in the Jeep last night!"

Jason lifted his right eyebrow, "Uh-oh, I guess I did forget to do that!"

"Seriously, Jason, bears can smell fish a mile away!"

Jamie quietly unzipped the tent window flap and peeked out.

Jason sucked in a deep breath, "Is it a bear? I hope it's not a bear. I hate bears!"

Jamie rubbed the sleep from his eyes and looked again, "Well, it's not a bear."

Jason expelled a relieved breath, "Good, what is it then?"

"It appears to be a gang of masked bandits. One is sitting on the picnic table drinking a bottle of Coke, and the other five are enjoying Sushi for breakfast."

Jason thought for a second, "Do you mean Raccoons?"

"Yes, raccoons, and they sure are cute!"

"I got to get this on video," Jason said as he quietly unzipped the tent door, trying not to scare the critters. He captured the adorable chittering little thieves on video, clanged a couple of pots and pans together, and watched the raccoon family scamper into the forest.

Jamie raised an eyebrow and shook his head as he looked at the overturned ice chest and half-eaten fish lying in the sand. "Jamie, I hope you're not mad at me for forgetting to put the fish cooler in the Old Indian."

Jamie rubbed his chin and smiled, "Nah, I'm not mad. The Raccoon Crime Family will make a great YouTube video. I bet we'll get a million hits!" Jason nodded, "I can't wait to show the video to Jenna. She's gonna go nuts watching the masked bandits feasting on our fish smorgasbord!"

The twins' fifteen-year-old sister Jenna was maturing into a beautiful young lady but was still a tomboy at heart. She loves the great outdoors, but when it comes to spending time with her brothers or boyfriend, the boyfriend wins every time.

The last day of camping in the Wisconsin Northwoods had arrived. It was time to take down the tent, pack the camping gear, and head out. The twins planned to rush home, shower quickly, and then get to church in time to hear their father's Sunday morning sermon. The first service every Sunday at Faith Calvary Chapel was dedicated to end-time eschatology, of which both boys were avid fans and seldom missed the service.

The boys retrieved the fifteen-foot-long canoe from the lake and secured it on the Jeep Cherokee's roof rack. Jamie opened the back hatch and tossed in the camping gear while Jason dowsed the campfire.

"I think we're good to go," Jason said as he flipped a quarter into the air — Jamie called it — "Heads!" Heads it was, so Jamie chose to drive, and Jason rode shotgun.

Jamie turned the key, the Old Indian coughed, sputtered, and blew a smoke signal out the tailpipe...Vroom. Jamie put the shift lever in gear and headed down the gravel road. After ten miles of kicking up dust, he took a right onto the blacktop highway heading south.

Jamie grabbed a CD from the windshield visor and slid it into the player. The twins were big classic rock fans, and Creedence Clearwater Revival was their favorite band. The song *Bad Moon Rising* began playing. Jamie drummed his fingers on the steering wheel, and Jason played the air guitar and sang the lyrics.

I see a bad moon rising; I see trouble on the way.

I see earthquakes and lightning; I see bad times today.

Don't go 'round tonight; It's bound to take your life; There's a bad moon on the rise.

I hear hurricanes blowing; I know the end is coming soon.

I fear rivers overflowing; I hear the voice of rage and ruin...

It was a three-hour trip back home to Hideaway Falls, but it didn't seem long before familiar landmarks indicated that the twins were almost home. Suddenly, a speeding pickup truck going the opposite direction veered across three lanes, jumped the curb, and skidded across the grass median, heading straight at them.

"Watch out!" Jason shouted.

Jamie swerved in the nick of time, avoiding a head-on collision!

The out-of-control truck slammed into the concrete structure of the overpass bridge. The twins jumped out of their vehicle and ran as fast as they could to the smoldering truck to rescue its occupants before it burst into flames. Jamie grabbed hold of the door handle; it wouldn't open—the door was locked. He spotted a rock lying in the grass, picked it up, and smashed the window. He reached inside, unlocked, and opened the door. Thick black smoke billowed out of the cab. As the smoke cleared, Jamie made an astonishing discovery—no one was inside!

"Look around," Jason shouted. "The driver must have been thrown out!" Jamie just stood there, frozen in time, his eyes wide and staring.

"Jamie, snap out of it; help me find the driver!"

Jamie didn't move a muscle. Jason grabbed his shoulders, shaking him, "Jamie, what's wrong with you? You look like you've seen a ghost!" He drew a shaky breath, "Jason, don't you realize what has happened? The truck's doors are locked. The windows are up. The driver's seat belt is fastened, but there is no driver!"

The hairs on the back of Jason's neck stood on end, and chills slid up and down his spine as he realized what his brother was trying to tell him. The driver was not thrown from the vehicle; he couldn't have been because the windows were up, the doors were locked, and the seat belt was buckled.

Deep inside, the twins understood what the phenomenon of the missing driver meant—but both were afraid to acknowledge it.

Shaken to their core but physically uninjured, the twins ran back to the Jeep. The phone was ringing. "Hello, this is Jason." The voice on the telephone inquires, "Jason, are you and Jamie okay?" It was their older brother, Dusty, the news reporter.

"Yes, we're both okay! We're going home to check on Mom, Dad, and Sis."

"Great, let me know what you discover," Dusty said.

"Dusty, what about your wife, Samantha? Is she…"

"I don't know. Sam is at church, and she never takes her phone to church. I will be driving there shortly. I can't wait to find out if she is all right and what in the world is going on. It appears that tens of thousands, perhaps even millions of people, have vanished from the face of the earth!"

Jason sucked in a deep breath and exhaled slowly, trying to calm his nerves. "Dusty, I think you know what has taken place."

"Don't jump to conclusions, boys. It may not be what you think it is! I'm about to go live on air; turn on your radio."

Moments later, local programming was interrupted: "This is a National Emergency Broadcast. I'm Dusty Rhodes, reporting from World News Headquarters in Babylon, New York. I apologize if my voice sounds a little shaky. I'm stunned, as I'm sure you are too, by the vast number of cataclysmic events being reported worldwide. At about 9 a.m. Eastern time, several passenger airplanes, some carrying 200 or more passengers, fell from the sky, causing neighborhoods to burst into flames in cities from coast to coast.

"Tens of thousands of vehicle crashes are being reported by local police agencies in cities across our nation and around the globe. Hundreds of people have been injured and killed in massive interstate pileups involving dozens to hundreds of cars, semi-tractor trailers, and buses. Hospitals and emergency centers will soon be overwhelmed with mass casualties. If you are a retired doctor, nurse, or paramedic, America needs your help. The police and fire departments request that everyone else stay home and stay inside until further notice.

"I repeat, this is a National Emergency. If you are a firefighter or paramedic, contact your local World News Network Station for more information on how you can help. I will be giving updates at the top of every hour. Stay tuned, and stay safe!"

A few minutes later, the twins pulled into the parking lot of Faith Calvary Chapel. Jamie slammed on the brakes. The twins exited the vehicle and darted to the church. Their Uncle Jack was standing at the base of the church stairs. "Uncle Jack, is Mom, Dad, and Jenna inside?" Jack was speechless. He just shook his head and pointed to the door.

The twins shot up the steps and entered the church. What they saw confirmed their worst suspicion. The Christian rapture had happened, and they had been left behind! The parking lot was full of cars, but the church was mostly empty. About 75 percent of the 200-member congregation was missing in action.

The twins scanned the sanctuary. Their gaze fell on a lady slumped over on the front row pew. At first glance, it appeared the lady was praying, but as the twins blinked away unshed tears, they realized that the lady was their mother and she wasn't praying but was unconscious!

Jason rushed down the aisle and embraced his mother, gently shaking her, "Mom, wake up. Please wake up." Mom's eyes began to open, and then, with a quivering lip, she asked, "Boys, you're okay. You're here?"

"Yes, Mom, we're here. Where are Dad and Jenna?"

"They're gone—Dad and Jenna are gone—they're both gone." Mom started sobbing almost uncontrollably but caught her breath and explained: "Jenna and I were listening to your father's sermon when he smiled at us, and suddenly, his countenance changed. His face shone like the sun, and his clothes became white as snow. I watched your father lift from the floor and ascend rapidly through the roof. Dad vanished into the heavens, and so did Jenna.

"God took them; I'll never see them again."

Jason wrapped his hands around Mom's hands, "Yes, you will, you will see them again. Don't you remember the bible study we had with Dad? Jesus is returning to earth, and when He does, Dad and Jenna will be with Him."

"Mom sighed, "That's right, boys, I remember. What about Dusty? Have you heard from him?"

"Yes, he's fine. I just spoke with him on the phone. He couldn't connect with Samantha. So he's driving to her church. He will let us know what he finds out."

As Jason consoled Mom, Jamie heard the voice of one weeping. Turning to his left, he noticed a distressed young woman sitting on the floor, rocking back and forth. A baby bottle lay beside her, and she was using the baby's blanket to wipe away her tears. It was Sarah, a friend and classmate.

Jamie walked over to Sarah, swallowed back his emotions, and sat beside her. He gently pulled the blanket from her eyes. "Sarah, it's me, Jamie. Where's your baby?"

"My baby is gone. My little darling is gone. All the children are gone— Jesus took them all to heaven. Sarah could barely speak; she mumbled in a desperate whisper, *"My husband, my husband, is gone too. I'm all alone; I don't know what to do."*

Sarah lost her Mother and Father in a house fire just a few years ago. Now she lost the love of her life, her husband and child. "Don't worry, Sarah, God hasn't abandoned us. He would like nothing better than to reunite you with your family." Jamie grabbed her trembling hand as he rose from the floor, "Come on, Sarah, let's get you something to drink, and I will tell you more about Jesus' plan to restore your family."

Jason and his mother, Macy, wandered through the church, assisting and comforting the left-behind congregation. There were a lot of wet faces and more than a few broken hearts. Jason, however, was stunned to hear several church members blaspheme the God of Heaven.

A middle-aged woman picked up her Bible, threw it across the room, and ran out the door screaming, "I hate you! I hate you! God, I hate you!" A deacon complained, "I served in this church for over 20 years and donated thousands of dollars. If anyone deserved to go to heaven, it's me!" Another said, "I was baptized here, I sing in the choir, and you left me behind. What kind of a Savior are you?"

Jason's heart burned with righteous indignation. He stood, raised his hand, and pointed his finger toward heaven. "Who are you to judge God?" Someone answered, "Jason, who are you to judge us? God doesn't love you any more than he loves us. He left you behind, too, didn't He?"

Jason responded, "It's true Jesus did leave us behind, but it's not God's fault. It's your fault, and it's my fault. Jamie and I could have been killed in a car accident on the way here, but God spared us. I am alive, Jamie is alive, and you are alive. God has given us another opportunity to get right with Him before it's too late. I will miss my father and my sister Jenna, but I praise Jesus that He did not leave them behind!"

Jason surveyed the congregation, spotting Tom and Sally Johnson. "Mr. and Mrs. Johnson, where are Johnny and Elizabeth?"

Mr. Johnson pressed his lips together, and tears spilled from Sally's eyes as she explained what had happened. "Well, Jason, I was listening to your father's sermon when he appeared to transform into a heavenly angel as bright as the morning star. Then, a moment later, your father, Johnny, and Elizabeth vanished into the heavens."

Jason pointed to the empty wheelchair in the aisle, "Mr. and Mrs. Johnson, I'm so sorry for your loss, but take heart. I'm sure little Johnny is in heaven right now—trying out his brand new legs—jumping and running as fast as he can!"

Tom and Sally nodded with a slight smile and sat down. Jason continued, "I'm sure you remember the three times that Elizabeth and I dated. Elizabeth is one of the sweetest girls I ever met and fun to be around, but do you know why I never asked Elizabeth on a fourth date?"

"No, I don't know, and I'm sure Elizabeth also wondered the same thing," Tom answered.

Jason cleared his throat, "Well, I never asked Elizabeth out again because the date always included a conversation about Jesus. And truthfully, I heard enough about Him at church. Elizabeth, however, wasn't like me. She could never stop talking about Jesus. I had intellectual knowledge about Jesus, but Elizabeth had a personal relationship with Him. She loved Jesus more than anything or anyone!"

Jason refocused his attention on the congregation, "Perhaps you remember Jesus' story about the two men who went to church to pray. One was a religious man, and the other a dishonest businessman. The religious man stood and prayed. *'God, I thank thee that I am not as other men: Extortioners, unjust, adulterers, or even as this businessman. I fast twice a week and give tithes of all I possess!'* The businessman stood in the back, considering himself unworthy to even look toward heaven. He smote his chest and said, *'God be merciful to me a sinner.'*

"Jesus said that one of the men went home justified that day. Which one was it, the religious man or the dishonest businessman?"

Silence, dead silence!

Jason looked intently at the congregation, "Jesus said that it was not the religious man but the unworthy sinner that got saved that day. Like the religious man in Jesus's parable, I had thought my church attendance, participation in church rituals, and mental acquiescence to the gospel facts made me a Christian. I was wrong, so very wrong.

"It's been said that the distance between Heaven and Hell is just eighteen inches. That's the distance between the head and the heart. I now understand what the apostle Paul meant when he stated that to win Christ, he first had to count all his self-righteousness and religiosity as worthless as human dung!"

Jason sunk to his knees, "I'm going to ask Jesus, right now, to forgive me and to save me, and if any of you desire to do the same, you can pray along with me."

Some left-behind church members walked out the door, shaking their heads in unbelief and disgust. Those who remained repented and believed the Gospel.

Someone began singing, *"Amazing Grace, how sweet the sound that saved a wretch like me."* Then several more joined the chorus, *"I once was lost, but now am found, was blind but now I see."* Soon, everyone rose from their knees and began singing and praising the Savior!

The Purpose of the Rapture

There was just one explanation for the phenomenon of the vanishing driver and missing church members. It was something that the twins had heard their father preach about dozens of times. It is an event that millions of Christians look forward to with eager anticipation. This imminent future event is what theologians call the "Rapture" or the "Catching Away." It is described in First Thessalonians chapter 4, verses 16 to 17.

> "For the Lord, himself shall descend from heaven with a shout, with the voice of the archangel, and with the trump of God, and the dead in Christ shall rise first, then we which are alive and remain shall be caught up together with them in the clouds, to meet the Lord in the air, and so shall we ever be with the Lord."

The twins understood a lot about the subject of the Rapture. Their father was head Pastor of the prophecy institute at Faith Calvary Chapel. They understood the significance of the prophetic signs that indicated the Rapture was quickly approaching our world. But they never imagined in their wildest dreams that it would be them that was left behind!

Often times, it takes a personal tragedy to awaken us to our spiritual shortcomings and the uncertainty and brevity of life. Not everyone is as fortunate as Jason and Jamie in avoiding life's head-on collisions. Accidents and illnesses claim the lives of over one hundred fifty-five thousand people daily. That's six thousand four hundred fifty-eight every hour, or one hundred seven every minute.

Unfortunately, for many, death will become the arresting officer that drags them to their prison cell, called hell. And the shocker is that according to Jesus, many among these damned people will be professing Christians. Jesus warned,

> "Not everyone who says to Me, 'Lord, Lord,' shall enter the kingdom of heaven, but he who does the will of My Father in heaven. Many will say to Me on that day, 'Lord, Lord, have we not prophesied in Your name, cast out demons in Your name, and done many wonders in Your name?' And then I will declare to them, 'I never knew you; depart from Me, you who practice lawlessness!' (Matthew 7 verses 21 to 23).

The people who will hear Jesus pronounce those eternally damning words, "Depart from Me!" are nominal Christians, not real ones. They are deceived. Just as Dusty, Jason, Jamie, and their mother, Macy, were. For this reason, Scripture admonishes everyone who professes faith in Christ to examine themselves—making sure that they are not mere professors but actual possessors of saving faith.

The purpose of the Rapture is two-fold. The first purpose is to resurrect all Christians, those who had previously died, and to rescue those alive before God's wrath is unleashed upon a sinful, unrepentant, and unbelieving world.

In a moment, in the twinkling of an eye, Christians will be transformed from mere mortals into immortal beings. Each Christian will receive a new body fashioned after Jesus' resurrected body—no more subject to aging, illness, or death. A supernatural body capable of transcending space and time in a moment and empowered to do things that even Superman couldn't do!

> "Behold, I tell you a mystery: We shall not all sleep, but we shall all be changed—in a moment, in the twinkling of an eye, at the last trumpet. For the trumpet will sound, and the dead will be raised incorruptible, and we shall be changed. For this

corruptible must put on incorruption, and this mortal must put on immortality. So, when this corruptible has put on incorruption, and this mortal has put on immortality, then shall be brought to pass the saying that is written: "Death is swallowed up in victory. O Death, where is your sting? O Hades, where is your victory?" (First Corinthians 15 verses 51 to 55).

The second purpose of the Rapture is to fulfill Jesus' promise found in John chapter 14, verses 2 and 3.

"In my Father's house are many mansions, if it were not so, I would have told you. I go to prepare a place for you. And if I go and prepare a place for you, I will come again, and receive you unto myself; that where I am, there you may be also!"

At the Rapture, Christians will meet Jesus in the air and then be personally escorted by Him to their new home in heaven. Then, at the end of the Tribulation period, Christians will return with Jesus Christ to set up the Kingdom of God on earth. A time when Jesus Christ is King, and Christians will rule and reign with Him for 1,000 years. Then, this old planet and universe will be destroyed and replaced with new heavens and a new earth.

That, beloved, is just the beginning of a never-ending adventure that God doesn't want you, me, or anyone else to miss out on!

Chapter Four

Where's Samantha?

Sunday, 9:45 a.m., 45 minutes after the disappearance. Dusty dials Samantha's number—still no answer. Dusty's friend and cameraman, Mike, hangs up the phone and walks over to Dusty's desk. "Everything is fine with my family. Everyone is accounted for. What about Samantha?" Mike asked.

"I'm not sure. I'm driving to the church she attends right now. Wanna ride along?"

"Sure."

Dusty and Mike walked briskly down the stairs to the parking lot. Dusty pushed the unlock button on his 2024 Ford Bronco. It was about a twenty-minute drive. Dusty pulled onto the four-lane highway, which was littered with wrecked vehicles. He weaved and navigated around the vehicles, police cars, ambulances, and debris as thoughts about Samantha flooded his mind. Not even six years had passed since he and Samantha had tied the knot.

He pulled down the windshield visor where he had tucked away a picture of his bride that he had snapped while on their Honeymoon Cruise to Jamaica. Samantha's white dress contrasted with her chestnut hair and tan skin. Her bright smile and chocolate eyes were mesmerizing. Tears began to well as he considered the possibility that she had been raptured into the heavens. Dusty felt like screaming and crying simultaneously, but he was not the type who wears his heart on his sleeve. He wasn't about to let Mike see him bawling like a baby. So, he decided to focus his attention on something to laugh about rather than cry about.

"Hey Mike, I've got a story to share with you that I think you'll get a kick out of. Wanna hear it?"

"Sure. Coming from you, it's got to be good!"

"Guess where Samantha and I went on our first date?"

"I don't have a clue."

"Come on, take a guess!"

"A movie?"

"Nope."

"A carnival?"

"Wrong again."

"Sky diving?"

"Not even close."

"Okay, I give up. Where did you and Samantha go on your first date?"

"It was at Sam's church, and was the most fun I've ever had!

"Samantha's parents were very protective and insisted that our first date be at the First Pentecostal Church of America in her hometown. It's the same church that we'll be arriving at shortly. I don't know if you're familiar with Pentecostal churchgoers, but unlike my father's church, they don't just sit in the pew saying Hallelujah and Amen. Well, at least not at Sam's church!

"Samantha informed me that Pentecostal churches are Continuationists. They believe that the first-century gifts of the Holy Spirit, speaking in tongues, prophesying, casting out demons, receiving divine revelations, and other miracles, have not ceased but continue today. She told me she hadn't discovered her spiritual gifts yet but said perhaps I'd discover mine. Anyhow, I was up for it, and here's what happened.

"Samantha and I were running a few minutes late, and by the time our shadows darkened the church door, the band was already playing, and the choir was singing. The congregation was on their feet, lifting hands and swaying to the music. Some were speaking and singing in heavenly languages. I couldn't understand a word they were saying, but the pastor had the gift of interpreting tongues. So, later, he preached a sermon based on what the tongue speakers spoke.

"Well, you know me. I wasn't about to miss out on the fun! So, I stood up, snapping my fingers and shuffling my feet. I don't know what came over me, but when I opened my mouth, the words that came out were, *'Do wah diddy diddy dum diddy do; Do wah diddy diddy dum diddy do.'* I was grooving to the music and swaying to the beat.

"A few minutes later, the pastor pointed at me and commanded, 'Son, come on up here!'

"I walked up the staircase onto the stage, and the pastor asked me my name and welcomed me to the church. He looked toward heaven and began speaking in the tongues of angels: *'Sha-baba, la-so-Tora, so-Tora, sha-baba, sodamora.'* He laid his hands on my head and repeated: *'Sha-baba, la-so-Tora, so-Tora, sha-baba, sodamora.'* Then, bam it happened!"

Mike glanced at Dusty, "What happened?"

"I crashed to the floor, banging my head. I think for a moment the pastor thought I was injured or dead because I heard him say, 'Can you hear me, son? Son, can you hear me?' I slowly opened my eyes, and he helped me to my feet. He pressed the microphone to my lips and asked, *'Son, how are you feeling?'*

"To everyone's relief, I said, Except for a slight bump on my head, I never felt better!"

The pastor began praising the Lord, and the congregation cheered. The band started playing, and I was grooving and swaying to the beat, singing *Do wah diddy diddy dum diddy do.* The band was rockin' and rollin', and then the choir joined in. Before you know it, the entire congregation was snapping their fingers and shuffling their feet, singing *'Do wah diddy diddy dum diddy do; Do wah diddy diddy dum diddy do!'"*

"You're joking, right Dusty?"

"No, it really happened!"

"So, Dusty, you're telling me that you discovered that you, too, have the gift of speaking in tongues?"

Dusty pressed his lips together for a moment, trying not to giggle. "No, Mike, I don't have the gift of tongues today, and I didn't then. Like I said, I didn't want to miss out on the fun. So, I improvised! The words *'Do wah diddy diddy dum diddy do'* actually are the lyrics from the hit 1960s song by Manfred Mann. I don't know if the congregation thought I was singing in tongues or if they just played along, but it was crazy fun!"

Mike rolled his eyes and shook his head, "You just confirmed my suspicion about you. You are certifiably a Nut Job!"

"Hey, that was ten years ago. I was just eighteen — we all do crazy things at that age!"

Mike nodded, smiling, "Yeah, I could tell you some crazy stories myself, but I'll save that for another day."

Dusty turned the corner and pulled into the First Pentecostal Church parking lot. He shouted, "There's Sam's car!" He slammed on the brakes, shoved the shifter into Park, and grabbed the door handle. Mike grabbed Dusty's shirt, "Hold on for a second. I have something to say before you go in.

"I know you love Samantha more than anything and would like nothing better than to hold her in your arms again. But from what you told me about the tribulation events. If Jesus has taken Sam to heaven, you shouldn't be upset but thankful."

Dusty stared out the windshield as he considered Mike's advice. He turned to Mike, "I suppose you're right. Thank you for reminding me; you're a good friend."

Upon opening the church door, Dusty was shocked to discover that apostle Jackson had also been left behind. The pastor appeared just as surprised to see him. "I'm so sorry, Dusty. Samantha is not here. She was raptured. One of the church members informed me that Samantha and her Mother and Father were sitting in the pew directly in front of him. Suddenly, it was as if a great light penetrated their bodies. He watched Sam and her parents defy gravity and ascend rapidly through the church ceiling and into the heavens!"

The news of Samantha's vanishing left a gathering lump in Dusty's stomach as he realized his beautiful bride was gone. He took a deep breath, releasing it slowly, "So you're telling me that the rapture was not a secret invisible event as portrayed in the left behind movies, but was a visible eyewitness event?"

The pastor wiped away an escaping tear, "Yes, just as the apostles watched Jesus ascend into the heavens. In like manner, I watched my wife, Jasmine, ascend. In a moment, in the twinkling of an eye, she was transformed from a mere human into an immortal shining star. She never looked so beautiful and radiant—a second later, she was gone!"

"Apostle Jackson, did you lose many in the rapture?"

The pastor swallowed hard at the question, "My best estimate is that about 25 percent of the congregation was raptured. That's difficult for me to digest. I mean, I never, in my wildest dreams, would have imagined that 75 percent of my congregation would be left behind. Of course, I never thought I would be one of them, but here I am!

"Please don't call me apostle, Dusty. I'm not worthy of the title. I evidently thought I was someone that I'm not." Just call me Joshua."

Dusty laid a comforting hand on the pastor's shoulder, "Don't be so hard on yourself. We are all in the same boat. Your left-behind congregation needs you more than ever, Joshua. The winds of rage and ruin will soon be upon us. If we allow Jesus Christ to be the Captain of our Soul, He will assist us in navigating the deep and dark waters of the tribulation.

"The critical thing to remember is that Jesus Christ is still our hope. He is the life jacket that we must put on. We all need to do some soul-searching and discover the truth of what Jesus meant when he stated, 'You must be born again!' I know Samantha had discovered that truth, and so must we if we hope to see our loved ones again and escape the fires of hell.

The Pastor nodded as he cleared his throat, "I couldn't agree more, Dusty."

"Joshua, I would like to introduce you to my friend and cameraman, Mike. If you don't mind, I would like to interview a few congregants about the vanishing. People need to hear the truth because, as you know, Jesus warned that millions will be deceived by the lies of the Antichrist and the false prophet that will soon debut."

"Sure, I will be in my study doing some soul-searching and praying. If you need me, knock on the door."

"Okay, Joshua, thank you, and let's stay in touch."

Listening to the stories of the left-behind congregation who lost loved ones in the rapture was heartbreaking. No one said anything for the first few minutes on the drive back. Mike broke the silence. "Dusty, what's going to become of us that have been left behind?"

Dusty hesitated for a moment as he gathered his thoughts. "Well, Mike, if we become true believers in Christ, we will likely be hunted down and killed for our faith, but we will gain eternal life. If we don't become true believers, we probably will fall for the lies of the Antichrist and take the 666 mark of the beast. It will make life easier for a while, but God will send His angels to separate the sheep from the goats at the end of the tribulation. The sheep will be granted entrance into the Kingdom of God, but the goats will be cast into the lake of fire along with the Antichrist and False Prophet. Where they will be tormented day and night forever and ever!"

The hairs on Mike's arms stood on end as he listened intently. "I don't know about you, Dusty, but I will do whatever it takes to become one of Christ's sheep—come hell or high water!"

"Mike, I don't think that's a baa baa baaaaad idea."

"Dusty, can't you stay serious for one minute?"

"Sorry, Mike, it's just my stupid way of coping with tragic events. Would you rather hear me cry or bleep like a sheep?"

Mike shook his head, "If you're going to mimic animal sounds, you should practice. Your sheep bleep sounds more like a stuttering chicken than a sheep!"

Dusty laughed. Then Mike started laughing out loud until his side hurt. "Dusty, I see what you mean. Laughter is good medicine."

"Mike, I'm not as stupid as I look. Just ask my twin brothers; they tell me that all the time!

"Seriously, Mike, I agree with you. There is nothing more important than becoming a born-again believer. Exactly how I can be transformed from a goat into a sheep is still a mystery, but I plan on finding out. I know that church attendance, water baptism, communion, and speaking in tongues don't make anyone a Christian. If it did, you, me, and pastor Joshua would be in heaven right now instead of sweating bullets down here."

Mike's brow wrinkled, and he rubbed his chin whiskers, "Wait a minute, something is not adding up. On the way to Sam's church, you told me the story of your first date with Sam at her church. You said pastor Joshua laid his hands on you and spoke in tongues."

"That's right, so what's your point?"

"Well, Dusty, I know that the difference between true Christians and false Christians is that true believers have the Holy Spirit living inside them. Those who did were raptured, and those who didn't were left behind. Since tongues are a gift of the indwelling presence of the Holy Spirit, pastor Joshua never spoke in Holy Spirit-inspired tongues. He thought he was an apostle and had the gift of tongues but was deceived on both accounts. The strange words he spoke over you were about as authentic as your *'Do wah diddy diddy dum diddy do'* tongue-speaking rant!'"

Dusty nodded, "Good point."

Mike, if you remember, on the way to Sam's church, I mentioned that Pentecostal churches are Continuationists."

"Yeah, I remember."

"Well, Faith Calvary Chapel, where my father pastored, is a Cessationist church. They believe that the office of apostleship, the gift of tongues, and most of the supernatural gifting of the Holy Spirit ceased when the twelve apostles' lives ceased in the first century."

Mike raised his brow, "Who's correct, the Continuationists or the Cessationists?"

"I'm not sure. I had planned on researching the subject but never got around to it."

Mike glanced at Dusty, "I will be happy to research the topic. It's time to dust off the old Bible anyway. I have many questions, and I think God has the answers."

Mike was the perfect person to research the topic of tongues and the gifts of the Spirit. He had the memory of a savant and an exceptional ability to make sense of complex subjects. "I have one more question for you, Dusty. If you don't mind."

"Sure, I don't mind. We're both trying to figure this thing out."

"Pastor Joshua stated that seventy-five percent of his congregation was left behind. That's a bunch! Why do you think so many missed out on the Rapture?"

"Personally, Mike, I think the main reason so many were left behind is that millions of Pentecostals and Charismatics were told they could become Christians by reciting the Sinner's Prayer. I'm not saying that no one has ever gotten saved reciting the prayer. I am saying that reciting the Sinner's Prayer does not guarantee Salvation.

"When Jesus and the apostles were asked what they must do to attain eternal life. They never told anyone to recite the Sinner's

Prayer—not even once. Jesus and the apostle's message always was to repent and believe in the Lord Jesus Christ. If the command to repent was not given directly, it was alluded to in the passage narrative. The Gospel message always was repent and believe, and thou shall be saved.

"My father always preached that faith and repentance are two sides of the same coin. You cannot have one without the other. For salvation to occur, both must be present in the sinner's heart. Millions have said the Sinner's Prayer but still live like the devil. That is because true repentance had never taken place. I know this because I was one of those people!

> *"The LORD is near to those who have a broken heart, And saves such as have a contrite spirit."*

According to God's Word, saving faith comes through a repentant heart, not reciting a prescribed prayer. That's why I believe the Sinner's Prayer makes far more false converts than real ones."

"That was some preaching, Dusty. I'm dumbfounded how you could know so much about God's Word but miss out on the Rapture!"

Dusty bit his lip, then answered, "You know what they say, 'It's not how much you know but who you know that counts!'"

Mike nodded, "Isn't that the truth?

"Say, Dusty, do you have any CD copies of your father's sermons? I have many unanswered questions about the future and Salvation."

Dusty opened the vehicle's console lid—it was packed. "Take your pick!"

Mike searched the CD labels. He grabbed three with intriguing titles:

Is Hell Forever?
The Gospel According to Jesus.

Mike read the title of the third CD out loud: *Will the Rapture Happen Soon?* He chuckled, then tossed it out the window, *"We won't be needing that one!"*

Dusty turned on his signal and pulled into the World Network News parking lot. It was time to hang it up for the day, contemplate all that had happened, and prepare for the Tribulation events foretold in the book of Revelation.

"Thanks for coming with me, Mike."

"Yeah, no problem. What time will we be leaving for the United Nations tomorrow?"

"Eight O'clock sharp!"

"Okay, keep the wheels between the ditches."

"You too. See you soon."

Chapter Five

Great Balls of Fire

It was a short forty-nine-mile drive from World News Network headquarters to the United Nations Building in New York City. Dusty and his team had arrived early, were set up, and anxiously awaited the arrival of the head of the United Nations Security Force. The disappearance event had turned the world upside down. In the United States alone, millions had vanished. The entire world was in desperate need of an explanation!

Why are we still here?
Where did everyone go?
Was it an alien abduction?
Will the vanishing happen again?
Those were the questions the world was asking.

The moment the world was waiting for had come, "Good morning, I'm Dusty Rhodes, reporting from the United Nations Headquarters in New York. In a few moments, we will hear from the man who made history just a few days ago when he confirmed *The Covenant of Land-for-Peace* that promises to establish a unified Israeli-Muslim State. In exchange, after nearly 2,000 years, the Israelis will once again be able to worship God in a rebuilt Jewish Temple in the Holy City of Jerusalem.

"Without further ado, please welcome the man, the legend, Sergius Alexander!"

A tall, ruggedly handsome man approached the podium. He adjusted the microphone and began to speak in a comforting but commanding voice, "Good morning, everyone. I'm Sergius Alexander, the Superior General of the United Nations Security Force. I'm sure you are wondering what caused millions of citizens to vanish from the face of the earth.

"I spoke with the religious leaders of the three great Abrahamic faiths: Christianity, Islam, and Judaism. They all assured me that what has happened, although heartbreaking for many families, will ultimately result in the greater good of all of humanity. This may surprise you, but the disappearance event was God's way of purging the earth of the haters, the evildoers, and the deceivers! "The prophet Muhammed foretold about the event in the Quran, chapter 39, verses 68 and 69, stating:

> "And the Trumpet will be blown, and all who are in the heavens and on the earth will swoon away, except him whom Allah will. Then the trumpet will be blown a second time and behold, they will be standing, looking on. And the earth will shine with the light of its Lord Allah when He will come to judge among men."

"The Christian Scriptures also predicted the disappearance event in the Gospel of Luke, chapter 17, and the Gospel of Matthew, chapter 24:

> "I tell you, in that night there shall be two in one bed; the one will be taken, and the other shall be left. Two shall be grinding at the mill; the one will be taken, and the other left. Two shall be in the field; the one will be taken, and the other left."

"Make no mistake, according to both the Holy Quran and the Holy Bible, the people that vanished from the earth were not raptured into the heavens, as some speculate, but were swooned away to judgment!

"It's estimated that about Four Hundred Sixty-Five Million of the so-called "born again" Christians and their children were taken in the event. Those taken were of the pseudo-Christian sect that insists that Jesus Christ is the only path that leads to God and that all other paths lead to hell. They were deceivers, fabricators, and twisters of the truth!

"In this, my good friend, the Vicar of Christ, the Pope, agrees. The Pope believes, as do I, that all religions reveal God's truth, but no particular religion owns all the truth. All paths, therefore, inevitably lead to God. There will never be world peace until the world realizes that all religions worship the same God!

Suddenly, a Newsmaxx reporter stood to his feet, shouting, "Liar, Liar, Liar! Jesus is the way, the truth, and the life, and no man can come to God except through HIM! I never understood that before, but I now believe it. The Holy Bible states that we are either a child of God or a child of the devil. It is apparent, Mr. Alexander, that you are not a child of God but rather the prodigy of the evil one!"

An associate of Sergius Alexander stepped to the podium, fastening his piercing eyes on the Newsmaxx reporter. The associate extended his hand, and a small fire danced on his palm. He took a deep breath and blew on the flame, sending it into the air. The swirling flame hovered over the audience. It grew larger and larger and larger and hotter and hotter and hotter. Then in a loud voice, the associate commanded the roaring fireball to devour the dissenting Newsmaxx reporter, and it did—consuming the screaming man in flames!

Dusty's eyes grew wide in stunned amazement.

Was this a magic trick?
Were my eyes playing tricks on me?
Was this really happening?

The smell of burning flesh permeated the atmosphere, and the man collapsed onto the marble floor. This was no trick, no sleight of hand, no illusion. The only thing that remained of the defiant reporter was his charred skeleton and smoldering shoes!

Moments later, the entire U.N. assembly stood and applauded, and Sergius Alexander stepped back to the microphone. "Representatives of the United Nations Assembly and citizens of the world, we must not let this cancerous form of Christianity come back to life. God has done us a great favor in removing this dangerous form of evangelical Christianity that has metastasized throughout our world. It is our responsibility to kill any resurgence of this evil disease. We are on the verge of a new world order of peace and prosperity, and we cannot allow these instigators, deplorables, and haters to infect our world again. I propose that all nations pass new laws making this counterfeit evangelical Christianity illegal!

"My heart goes out to those of you who have lost loved ones in the disappearance, but mark my words once the dust has settled from the initial impact. This event will go down in history as the beginning point that will usher in a time of peace, prosperity, and celebration unlike the world has ever experienced!

"My Press Secretary will be available shortly to answer any questions.

"Thank you, and good day!"

A spike of nervous excitement roiled in Dusty's stomach as he realized from the prophecies in Daniel and Revelation exactly who Sergius Alexander and his associate were. He felt like shouting, *"Sergius Alexander is the ANTICHRIST! His associate is the FALSE PROPHET!"* Dusty knew, however, that he best keep his mouth shut. After all, he had just witnessed a reporter's life and career go up in flames, literally!

Sergius Alexander and his sidekick left the podium, turned, and walked straight toward the reporting team. As they approached, Dusty noticed that he was in the crosshairs of the Antichrist's eyes. His heart began beating a hundred miles per hour. He tried to conceal his anxiety, but the adrenalin rush made it nearly impossible.

A moment later, Dusty was standing face to face with the sons of perdition. He inhaled sharply, not knowing what to expect. The Antichrist extended his right hand, "You're Dusty Rhodes, World News Network reporter, right?"

Dusty expelled a relieved breath, extended his arm, and shook his hand, "Yes I, I, am, Sir."

"I'm Sergius Alexander, and this is my friend and associate, Eli Isaa. I was wondering if you and your reporting team would like to attend a meeting in Israel next week. I'm meeting with the Prime Minister and the Israeli Defense Force Commanders. Something big is going down in Israel, and I want you to be the reporter!"

"Mr. Alexander, I appreciate the offer, and it would be an honor to attend the meeting, but I must first get the trip approved by my boss, Robert Diamond, at World News Headquarters."

"I'm sure it won't be a problem. Give me your boss's number, and I will get his approval."

Dusty scribbled his boss's number on the back of his business card and handed it to him. Mr. Alexander tucked the card in his shirt pocket, and the diabolical duo walked away!

The Trip Back

It was time to wrap it up and return to World News Network headquarters. The reporting team loaded the gear into the van. Mike climbed into the driver's seat, Dusty rode shotgun, and Alan, Nicole, and Olivia took a seat behind.

Olivia and Nicole are in their mid-twenties; both are pretty and have long brown hair. Olivia is sweet, thoughtful, and optimistic. Nicole, well, not so much. If you were in a barroom brawl, she's the one you'd want on your side.

Mike is a nice-looking 30-year-old black man with a photographic memory, a big heart, and great humor. If you asked Mike how tall he is, he'd say 6 foot 5—standing on a chair. The truth is, Mike is the same height as Dusty, 5 foot 11 inches. That's why, Mike says, Dusty and he are such good friends—they always see things eye to eye.

Alan is the newest reporting team member. His appearance often causes people to do a double-take. He has a bushy black beard, wears a Kufi skullcap, and sometimes wears a long-sleeved robe called a thobe. All are single except for Dusty.

The motley crew is best described as tough, independent, and seriously goofy. When it comes to getting the job done, this mishmash of personalities somehow manages to work together like the pit crew on a NASCAR race team.

The reporting team's religious affiliations are Christian, Muslim, Catholic, and atheist. Which made for an interesting conversation on the way back. Mike kicked off the conversation. "Was that unbelievable or what? The poor Newsmaxx reporter didn't stand a chance!"

"No kidding, that flame-thrower dude scares me half to death!" Olivia said.

Nicole twirled her hair between her fingers, "Yeah, but Sergius Alexander seems to be a nice man, smart, and good-looking too!"

"Nicole, please don't tell me you fell for Sergius's bull-spit speech?"

Nicole rolled her eyes, "Well, Mike, he did quote from the Bible, didn't he?"

"He did, but those Scriptures were taken totally out of context. The Christians were not swooned away to judgment but were raptured into the heavens. There is no doubt about that!"

Nicole shot back, "Well, Catholics don't believe in the rapture!"

"Nicole, you don't have to believe in gravity, but try walking off the top of a building, and you'll quickly discover the truth!"

Dusty intervened. "Mike, I'm impressed. You almost sound like a real Christian!"

"Well, Dusty, that is because I am a real born-again believer!"

"Seriously, Mike, when did that happen?"

"Well, last night, when I was doing bible research on the topics you and I had discussed, I came across the passage about Jesus' crucifixion. Then I remembered that a friend gave me the *Passion of Christ* DVD a few Christmases ago, produced by Mel Gibson. So, I unwrapped it and popped it into the DVD player. I cracked open a cold brew and proceeded to watch the movie.

"I must say, it was the most disturbing film I ever saw—the mockery, beating, and whipping left every inch of Jesus' body dripping in blood. The crowd was screaming crucify him, crucify him.

"The Roman soldiers led Jesus away to be crucified. They spat on Him and placed a crown of thorns on His head, then struck the crown, driving the thorns into his scalp. Then the soldiers bowed before Him, mocking and chanting: 'All Hail King of the Jews! Hail, the King of the Jews!'

"The sadistic soldiers tied Jesus to a post and whipped Him. The whip had nine tails. Each tail was laced with sharp pieces of metal and bone. Every crack of the whip dug deep into His back, ripping and tearing out chunks of flesh and muscle. Then, they placed a heavy wooden cross on Jesus' raw and bloodied back and forced Him to carry the instrument of torture and death to the top of Mount Golgotha. Then the centurions stretched out Jesus' arms and drove large spikes through His hands and feet and planted the cross of Christ between the crosses of two criminals!

"Soon after, the sun hid its face, the sky darkened, and the thunder roared as the sinless Son of God hung between heaven and earth. Three hours later, Jesus cried loudly, *'My God, my God, why hast thou forsaken me?'* In pain and agony, Jesus lifted His head and cried out a second time—*It is finished!*

"The earth quaked, the rocks split, tombs opened, and the bodies of many saints came to life!

"When one of the centurions that stood by saw the earthquake and what took place, he was terrified and said, 'Truly this was the Son of God!'

"Suddenly, it dawned on me that if God the Father abandoned His Son when the world's sins were laid upon Him, my sins must be darker than I ever imagined. Time and time again, week after week, month after month, and year after year, for most of my life. I had transgressed God's laws and broken His commandments. Indeed, if anyone deserved hell, it was me!

"Then I realized why Jesus cried, 'It is finished.' It was because he had finished the redemptive work that He came to earth to do. The ransom price that God required for payment of sin had been paid in full. I then remembered the verse I learned in Sunday School as a child. "For God so loved the world, that He gave His only begotten Son, that whosoever believes in Him should not perish, but have everlasting life."

"God's amazing grace required just one thing for me to do to receive the forgiveness of sins and the gift of eternal life. That was for me to trust the Savior, and I did. Instantly, the heavy burden of remorse and guilt I had felt moments before was replaced with unspeakable joy! I now know and am certain that I am a child of the living God!"

Dusty's face lit up, and he began grinning from ear to ear. "Mike, that was an incredible description of Jesus' crucifixion. In fact, your testimony has made a believer out of me!"

Mike glanced curiously at Dusty, "Are you telling me that you just now got saved?"

"Yes, Mike, I just got saved!"

"Hallelujah! Praise the Lord!" Mike said.

Nicole grasped the back of Mike's seat, shaking it violently. *"You know, fellas, that kind of talk can get you arrested or even killed!"*

"Thank you for your concern Nicole, but I don't think God's desire for the redeemed is to become secret agents—but rather bold witnesses of the good news!" Mike said.

Olivia scooted close to Mike and Dusty, "We've been friends and coworkers for a long time. We don't always see eye to eye, but you needn't worry about me—I won't squeal on you. The way I see it, regardless of our religious or non-religious beliefs. We're all in this together: All for One, and One for All!"

"I feel the same way," Alan said. "I'm a moderate Muslim. I don't believe the later Quranic war verses abrogated the earlier peace-inspiring verses, as do the jihadis. I don't believe it is okay to lie, steal, rape, and kill non-Muslims in the name of Allah. So, you don't have to worry about me reporting you to the authorities or beheading you!"

Mike lifted his brow, "Well, that's good to know!"

"Yeah, it's hard to comb your hair without a head," Dusty quipped.

Everyone chuckled.

"Alan, may I ask you something."

"Sure, Dusty. What's on your mind?"

"I've always been curious about your first name. The name Alan is kind of strange for Muslim parents to name their child, isn't it?"

Alan smiled and answered with a slight snicker. "Dusty, Alan is not my legal name, it's al-Mahdi. The al-Mahdi is Islam's end-time superhero, and that's the reason Muslim parents often choose the name. I'm no superhero, so I prefer to be called Alan or Al, and besides, it's easier for most Americans to pronounce and remember."

"I see," Dusty said. "Tell me, what is this end-time superhero going to do?"

"Islamic eschatology teaches that the al-Mahdi will appear in the last days. He will be accompanied by Jesus. The Islamic Jesus, however, will not return to rescue the Jews and Christians as portrayed in the Bible but will return as a radical Muslim. He will come to assist the Mahdi forces and punish the unbelievers. Together, they will break the crosses—destroy Christianity, kill all the Jews, and establish worldwide Islamic rule!"

"Man O Man, Alan, do you realize that Islam's end-time superhero's mission to destroy Christianity and kill the Jews is the identical mission revealed in the book of Revelation as that of the biblical Antichrist and the False Prophet?"

Alan's eyes widened, and he leaned forward. "So, Dusty, you're telling me that Islam's end-time superheroes are Christianity's end-time villains—the enemies of the God of the Bible?"

"That's precisely what I'm saying. Satan apparently plans to use Islamic end-time prophecy to deceive Muslims into receiving the Antichrist and False Prophet with open arms. The amazing thing is this was prewritten in the book of Revelation centuries before the Quran was written and Islam became a religion.

"You see, Alan, the Christian belief in the divine inspiration of the Bible isn't based on speculation or fantasy but on historical, archaeological, and prophetic evidence. While other religious books are filled with unconfirmed claims and philosophies. The Bible supports the claim that it is God's Word with fulfilled prophecy. There are about 2,500 prophecies in the Bible, and about 2,000 have been fulfilled precisely as predicted. This is to every candid mind the indisputable proof of the Bible's divine inspiration!"

Alan tapped Mike's shoulder, "Mike, may I ask you a question?"

"Sure, Al."

"Your testimony has made me curious. You said that you know that your sins are forgiven and that you are a redeemed child of the living God. Unlike you, Muslims have no inward assurance that Allah will grant them paradise. The prophet Muhammed, the founder of our faith, said that even he didn't know if Allah would grant him entrance into heaven. Can anyone really know for certain that he or she will enter the pearly gates?"

Mike smiled, "Yes, Alan, you can know beyond a shadow of a doubt that you are a child of God. The inward assurance of Salvation results from receiving the gift of the Holy Spirit that indwells every born-again believer at the moment of conversion. The Holy Spirit bears witness with our human Spirit that we've become a child of the living God.

"So the question is, Alan, whose teachings will you follow, and whom will you trust? Will you trust Islam's prophet Muhammad, who robbed and killed people, never performed a single miracle, died, was buried, and is still in his grave? Or will you believe in the One who said that you should love your neighbor as yourself, calmed the wind and the raging sea with his word, fed over 5,000 people with 5 loaves and two fish, made the crippled walk, the blind see, the deaf hear, and raised the dead?

"Will you trust in the one who didn't even know if he would make it to paradise? Or will you trust the One that died, rose from the dead, and ascended into the heavens? Proving to be who He claimed to be—the incarnate Son of God—God in human flesh!"

Olivia interrupted, "The Rapture occurred just as Jesus foretold. I've seen the Antichrist and the False Prophet with my own eyes. I've heard Mike's testimony and the story of Jesus' sacrifice. I believe the Bible is God's word. I want to be saved right here and right now. What must I do to be saved?"

Dusty looked over his shoulder at Olivia, "Scripture states that all one must do to be saved is to repent and believe the Gospel. To repent means to change your mind about the direction you have been going and turn to God. Romans chapter 10, verses 9 and 10, states, "That if you confess with your mouth the Lord Jesus and believe in your heart that God has raised Him from the dead, you will be saved. For with the heart one believes unto righteousness, and with the mouth confession is made unto salvation."

"So I ask one and all, whose teachings will you follow, and whom will you trust for your eternal future?"

Tears streamed down Olivia's cheeks. "I'm so sorry, Lord Jesus, I was an atheist fool, but no more. I believe and confess that you are my Lord and my Savior."

"What about you, Alan?" Dusty asked.

After a long silence and careful consideration, Alan answered: "I will place my trust in Jesus. I don't care if my family disowns me or even if they kill me. I believe and am sure that Jesus Christ is the Son of the living God!"

Alan got up from his seat and kneeled beside it. "I don't even know how to pray to the Christian God. Will one of you pray and thank Jesus for me?"

"Alan, you're a child of God now. God wants to hear from you. Just speak to him as you would speak to your earthly father. You can pray out loud or silently. It doesn't matter; God will hear you!"

Nicole looked at Alan, then glanced at Olivia, Mike, and Dusty. She rolled her eyes, and shook her head, *"Oh, for Pete's sake. Now I have to work with a bunch of Jesus freaks!"*

Everyone laughed!

Mike turned on the signal and pulled into the World News Network parking lot.

Dusty's phone rang. "Hello, this is Dusty."

"Hello Dusty, this is Robert Diamond. Is your team with you?"

"Yes, they are, Mr. Diamond."

"Good, put your phone on speaker."

"Hello, team! I wanted to congratulate you on a job well done. The filming, sound, lighting, and reporting were stellar. Thanks to you, the ratings have shot through the roof. It was the most-watched live broadcast in World News Network history!

"Lastly, I wanted to tell you to pack your bags—you're going to the Holy Land! I spoke with Sergius Alexander and have approved the meeting in Jerusalem. You'll be traveling first class onboard the company jet. Don't bother coming to work the rest of the week. You and your team deserve a few days off with pay."

"Awesome! Thank you, Mr. Diamond."

"You're welcome, Dusty."

"My secretary will email you the itinerary when she confirms your reservation. That's all for now. Have a good night."

What a turn of events. What started as a scary and nightmarish day became one of the best days imaginable for everyone except Nicole. It was time, however, to hang it up for the day and head home. The happy team exited the van one by one saying, *"Good night, Elizabeth. Good night, Jim Bob. Good night, Mary Ellen. Good night, John Boy."*

Dusty couldn't keep from grinning as he heard the team parody the nostalgic goodnight wishes from the hit 1970s TV show *The Waltons*. Each episode ended with those good night wishes. When Dusty, the twins, and Jenna were children and were goofing off instead of going to sleep. Their father would shout up the stairs, 'Good night, Elizabeth, Good night, Jim Bob, Good night, John Boy.' It was Dad's subtle way of saying, 'Don't make me come up there!'

Dusty walked across the parking lot, opened the door on his Ford Bronco, and headed home. It was a short drive from World Network News Headquarters. He pulled into the garage and unlocked his apartment door. Tossed a pizza in the oven, and flipped on the local news.

The news report confirmed the Antichrist's statement that the disappearance would usher in a time of worldwide celebration. The media was ecstatic. The talk show hosts were ecstatic. The Acronym people were dancing in the streets, and the abortionists were carrying signs *'To hell with the Christians'* and *'Praise Sergius Alexander!'* The Hollywood celebrities, the atheists, the liberals, the witches, the Luciferians, the Masons, and the Marxists, were all celebrating the vanishing of the Christians. The world had gone insane!

Dusty wished he could move back home to Hideaway Falls, Wisconsin, away from the crazed and deceived masses, but understood that divine providence was at work. It was no coincidence that the Antichrist had invited him to a top-secret meeting in Israel. The thought of being within a hundred yards of the Antichrist and his flame-throwing sidekick was a scary proposition, but now that he knew God had his back. It was more like looking forward to a thrilling adventure.

Dusty knelt beside the sofa and prayed, "Lord Jesus, thank you for saving me! Thank you for saving Mike, Alan, and Olivia. Please tell Samantha the good news and that I love her. I pray that you'll open the eyes of the deceived as you opened mine. Thank you for blessing me with a great job, and a wonderful team. And please watch over my family!"

Amen.

Chapter Six

Tribulation Force

The aroma of freshly brewed coffee and sizzling bacon silently announced that it was time to wake up. Jason climbed out of bed, put on his jeans, and made his way to the kitchen. A stack of French toast drizzled with butter and maple syrup was sitting on the table, begging to be devoured.

"Good morning, Mom; it smells delicious."

"Good morning, Jason. Go wake your brother and tell him to hurry up before breakfast gets cold."

A few moments later, the twins and Mom sat around the table. Jamie noticed two extra plates and silverware placed alongside them. "Mom, are we expecting company?"

Mom glanced at Jamie and then at the plates and empty chairs. A tear formed in the corner of her eye, "Oh my goodness, I guess it's true old habits are hard to break. I miss your father and Jenna so much."

Realizing that he had just stuck his foot in his mouth, Jamie quickly changed the subject.

"Mom, why did you get up so early?"

Mom cleared her throat and took a sip of coffee. "The news is reporting that grocery store shelves are emptying fast. The rapture has caused a serious supply chain disruption. When the doors open, we must be one of the first in line at the supermarket. So, we'll leave as soon as we finish breakfast."

It was about a ten-minute drive to the local Piggly Wiggly Grocery. The Rhodes family arrived an hour earlier than the store was scheduled to open. The line of customers awaiting the store opening extended from the front door to the middle of the parking lot. They stood in line for about twenty minutes, but thankfully, the store manager decided to open early.

The doors swung open, and a human stampede of shoppers entered the store. Mom and the twins grabbed shopping carts and headed in opposite directions. People were pushing, shoving, and grabbing food from the carts of others. The security guards were kept busy trying to quell the onslaught of shoplifters. When it was all said and done, the Rhodes family headed to the car with five bags of groceries—enough to tide them over for a week or two.

The twins began loading the grocery bags into the back of the Old Indian. Three young men approached quietly behind. An unfamiliar voice said, *"You're putting the groceries in the wrong vehicle!"* The twins turned, facing the man. "You must have us confused with someone else. These are our groceries. I have the receipt right here," Jason said.

The man's eyes narrowed, and his voice deepened. "You don't understand. Those are not your groceries; they are mine. If you don't do as I say, you'll never go grocery shopping again!"

The twins looked intently at one another, both thinking the same thing. There are three of them, but beating the snot out of them shouldn't be a problem!

The twin's plan of attack quickly changed when the gang leader reached behind his head and pulled from a concealed sheath a two-foot-long Samurai Sword. "Well, boys, what are you going to do, die or live to fight another day?" The twins' eyes grew big as saucers—not from fear of the impending threat—but because they saw their

Uncle Jack sneaking up behind the two thugs standing about six feet to the leader's rear.

Uncle Jack is a monster of a man. He stands six-foot-five and is built like a tank. He reminds the twins of bodybuilder Lou Ferringo, the star of the classic TV show *The Incredible Hulk* — except Jack isn't green.

Jack took one step closer and reached forward grabbing the necks of the two thugs. He lifted them six inches into the air and then slammed their heads together. Jack released his grip, and they both dropped to the pavement like a sack of potatoes!

Hearing the commotion, the leader spun around, noticing his unconscious buddies lying on the ground. He shouted a few nasty words at Jack and began brandishing his sword back and forth like a villain in a Jackie Chan movie.

"Woooooooo — You're scaring me," Jack said in a mocking tone.

There was no way Uncle Jack was about to back down. "Well, punk, I'll ask you the same question you asked my nephews. *"What will you do, die, or live to fight another day?"* The punk snickered, "You don't even have a weapon. I will carve you up like a turkey on Thanksgiving Day!"

Jack cracked his knuckles, "If you insist. It's your funeral!"

The punk brandished his sword a few more times. Jack squared his shoulders and positioned himself to do battle. The punk lunged forward, attempting to impale him. Jack rotated his torso quickly to the left; the sword pierced his shirt but didn't draw blood. The momentum of the lunge drove the punk to the ground as he tripped over Jack's extended leg.

He sprung to his feet, facing Jack. He grasped the handle with both hands, raising the glistening sword above his head. Suddenly, Jack felt the breeze of a speeding projectile as it flew past his head and then slammed into the punk's face: WHACK! A can of baked beans dropped to the pavement, and the sword-wielding perpetrator collapsed beside it.

"Good shot, Jamie!" Jason shouted.

Jack placed his hands on his hips, looking at the twins, "What did you do that for—I was just beginning to have fun?"

Those three young men don't know how lucky they were. Uncle Jack was a former Special Forces Army Ranger hand-to-hand combat instructor. He could just as easily have broken their scrawny necks and butchered the leader with his own sword.

Jack instructed the twins, "Let's wrap this up before the police are alerted. You two load the three unconscious musketeers into the trunk of their car. I will give an anonymous call to the police, telling them what transpired and where to find the perpetrators."

After doing so, Jack got into his vehicle, and Mom and the twins got into theirs and headed back home. Mom slid toward the front seat, "Jamie, I guess you and Jack taught those three clowns that crime doesn't pay."

"You can say that again, Mom. Crime doesn't pay. It costs. That can of beans cost Samurai Sam a broken nose and a few missing teeth."

Jason laughed, "It's a good thing baked beans don't require much chewing!"

Jamie glanced back at Mom, "I told you baseball training camp was a good investment."

Mom smiled, "Yeah, I guess you were right. You're the best baked beans pitcher I ever saw!"

"Does that mean I don't have to pay back the $100.00 training camp fee?"

"No, Jamie, it means you owe me $100.00 plus $5.00 for the can of beans," Mom said as she winked at Jason.

Jamie pulled into the driveway, and Jack's truck pulled in behind. Mom exited the back seat of the vehicle. "Jack, I'm surprised to see you so soon. I'm glad you're here because I never got to offer you my condolences. Eva was a wonderful person. She seemed more like a sister than a sister-in-law to me."

"You know, Macy, Eva kept warning me that the rapture was imminent. I should have taken her more seriously. There is something good, however, that came out of the emotional rollercoaster of that day. I surrendered my life to Christ!"

"Jack, that's wonderful news!"

"Macy high-fived her brother, "Anyway, Macy, I followed you home because I have a couple of ideas I'd like to run by you." Macy handed a bag of groceries to her brother. "Let's go inside. I'll brew a pot of coffee, and we'll talk."

After putting away the groceries, everyone pulled up a chair at the kitchen table. "Okay, Jack, tell us what's on your mind?"

"Well, how I see it, Macy, it's no more business as usual. I believe our little adventure today was a preview of coming attractions. I fear gangs will soon be roaming the streets, kicking in doors as food shortages worsen. I think establishing a Tribulation Force Freedom Center would be a good idea. A place where I can teach the tribulations saints survival skills and self-defense techniques. A place where Christians gather to brainstorm, strategize, and seek refuge when the spit hits the fan.

"I know that all three of you are well-versed in the Scriptures that pertain to the tribulation's events. The Tribulation Force Freedom Center will be a place where you and the twins can educate the flock on what's coming next and how to prepare for it. It will give everyone a strategic survival advantage.

"What do you think about the idea, Macy?"

The twins looked at their mother, "Come on Mom, say yes!"

Macy ran her finger around the rim of the coffee cup, stood, and slowly paced around the table. She stopped behind the boys, running her fingers through the twins' thick brown hair. "Jack, I think that is a great idea! Where do you propose we set up the Tribulation Force Freedom Center?"

"Well, Macy, I was thinking Faith Calvary Chapel. The reinforced steel doors, the shatter-resistant windows, and the alarm system make for a safe and secure location. Plus, there is plenty of room, a kitchen, sleeping quarters, and a big freezer in the basement."

Macy's eyes brightened, "Sure, why not? I will send out a Sunday invitation to the left-behind congregation, and boys' you can assist Uncle Jack in getting things set up. Jason has the key to the chapel, and you guys can start on the project today if you wish."

The twins high-fived one another, and Jack stood and gestured with a quick salute, "Yes, mam, it will be our pleasure!" He took one step toward the door and turned around, "Macy, I do have one more question."

"What's that, Jack?"

"Can you give me an idea of what will happen over the next few years?"

"I can answer that question, Uncle Jack," Jason said. "I've been reviewing Dad's end-time sermon notes and have good and bad news to report. The good news is that the New World Order envisioned by the United Nations, the World Economic Forum, and the Antichrist will be destroyed at Jesus' Second Coming.

"The bad news is that between now and then, multitudes will be killed in biological, chemical, and nuclear wars. The stars will fall from the heavens, poisoning a third of the oceans, rivers, and lakes. A third of all the fish and water creatures will die. Mighty earthquakes and massive tsunamis will destroy a third of all the ships and wash away cities and islands. Terrible famines and deadly plagues will ravage the planet. The sun will intensify, scorching the earth's inhabitants. Flaming asteroids will pummel villages and cities. Demonic locusts will torture the unsaved for 5 months—and half of the world's population will be killed!"

Jack removed his cap and ran his hand over his head, looking at Macy, "Great... then we have nothing to worry about!"

Jack walked to the door, the twins following with silly grins!

Let's Go for a Ride!

"Macy, I'll have the boys back before dark."

Mom stood in the doorway, watching the three walk to the driveway. "Those boys are just like their father, always up for an adventure. May Heaven help us!"

"We'll take my truck, "Jack said.

The twins walked around the truck, looking it over. "Wow, Uncle Jack, you bought a new Cyclone 700!"

"Yeah, I purchased it just a few weeks ago. It's got 700 horsepower and 672 foot-pounds of torque. The optional three-inch lift accommodates those big 37-inch on-off-road tires. Plus, it has massive six-piston Brembo front brakes to increase stopping power, an off-road auto-leveling suspension to handle any terrain, and a high-performance exhaust that roars like a lion!!

"Let's go for a ride!"

Jamie rode shotgun, and Jason climbed into the back seat. Jack turned the key, and the Cyclone's beating heart rumbled out the tailpipes.

"Man, that does sound sweet!" Jamie said.

Jack exited the driveway and pulled onto the street.

"Where are we going?" Uncle Jack.

"To my place, I need to pick up a few tools."

"Do you still live in the same house?" Jason asked.

"Not the same house, but on the same ranch. If you remember, my place is about ten miles outside the city limits."

"I remember, but it's been a few summers since I've been there."

"Man, these seats are comfortable," Jamie said as he pushed the power lumbar button. "I sure wish I could afford a truck like this. I've been saving up for a new vehicle for a few years. If my calculations are correct, I should be able to afford a new Cyclone 700 when I'm about 87 years old."

Jack laughed, "Yeah, your Jeep Cherokee has seen better days, that's for sure. Those are some nasty rust holes in the fenders…doors…hood…roof…and tailgate."

"Uncle Jack, you don't know the half of it. That rust almost got me arrested," Jamie said.

"Arrested! What on earth are you talking about?"

"Well, Uncle Jack, I was driving home from a bowling tournament a few weeks ago, minding my business, when suddenly, a little dog jumped out in front of me. I briefly slammed the brake pedal to avoid hitting the dog and then glanced in the rearview mirror to see if it had made it across the street. The dog was fine, but I noticed something round and shiny chasing me down Main Street."

Jack glanced at Jamie curiously, "Something round and shiny was chasing you down the street. What in the world was it?"

"I was wondering the same thing. So I quickly slowed down to get a closer look, and suddenly, a shiny chrome bowling ball whizzed right by me. The ball drifted to the left and bounced off the tire of a parked car, rolling across the road right in front of a police car. It hit the front wheel of a parked motorcycle, and six Harley-Davidsons fell over like dominos. I can tell you the biker gang members didn't look too happy—they love their Harley motorcycles more than their tattoos, wives, and girlfriends!

"Finally, the bowling ball stopped after rolling down the gutter another 100 feet. The police car made a quick U-turn with lights flashing! I thought the cop was coming for me, but thankfully, he stopped to investigate the round, shiny object that almost took out his squad car's front grill!

"On the way home, I started thinking about that chrome bowling ball because I thought I was the only one in the county who owned one. Guess what, Uncle Jack? It turned out that the chrome bowling ball chasing me down Main Street was my own stupid bowling ball."

"Seriously, how'd that happen?" Jack asked.

"Well, when I briefly hit the brakes to avoid missing that little dog, my bowling ball rolled off the back seat and broke through the rusty floorboard of the Jeep. I was going about 30 miles per hour, so when the bowling ball hit the pavement, it was traveling that fast, too! That's when I looked in the rearview mirror noticing the shiny round object following me. So I slammed on the brakes, and my chrome bowling ball zoomed right past me!"

Jack laughed, shaking his head, "That's the craziest story I've ever heard."

"Sure, Uncle Jack, it's funny now, but it wasn't funny then. That stupid bowling ball darn near got me arrested and thrown in jail!"

Jack was an intense individual and a man of few words, but his nephew's goofy, fun-loving attitude magically transformed his personality into a carefree spirit of good times. After losing his wife Eva in the rapture, the twins' company was just what the doctor would have ordered.

Jack pointed out the front window, "See that stop sign ahead. My place is exactly one mile from there." Jack approached the crossroad and stopped. He tossed a hundred dollar bill on the floor in front of Jamie's feet. *"You can have that, Benjamin. If you can pick it up!"*

Jamie bent forward and reached down to pick up the one-hundred-dollar bill.

Jack floored it! The Cyclone launched like a rocket, driving the twins back into the seats. Jamie wasn't about to give up. He strained with all his might, bent over, and was within one inch of grabbing the money when Jack pushed a button on the visor. Once again, the accelerating G-Force nailed the twins to the back of their seats.

Jack glanced at the twins. Their eyes were as big as pancakes! He let off the accelerator, laughing so hard he about wet his pants. "I must confess something to you, boys. See that little green button up there on the visor? That button releases a shot of Nitrous Oxide, producing an additional 300 instant horsepower!"

Jamie removed his cap and threw it on the floor, "That's not fair, Uncle Jack. I was so close to being a hundred dollars richer that it's ridiculous."

"Don't worry, you can keep the hundred dollars. Just be sure to split it with your brother."

"Thanks, Uncle Jack," the twins reverberated.

Jack turned on his signal and stopped in front of an iron gate. Pushed a button, and the gate swung open. "Cool. No more getting out of the truck, removing the padlocked chain, and manually swinging open the gate. Huh, Uncle Jack?"

"Nope."

"You've got a black top road that goes all the way to the house too!"

"Yep."

"Is that your new house?"

"Sure is."

Jack turned onto his Terra-lock brick driveway and parked alongside his old truck. The boys exited the right side, and the twin's mouths dropped open a half inch as they stared at Jack's new house.

"Come on, boys, I will give you a tour!"

The boys trailed behind on the brick sidewalk that meandered through a beautiful flower garden that Eva had planted that spring. The twins caught up to Jack just as he sat on the porch bench.

"That's an awesome bench!" Jason commented.

The bench's thick oak seating slab was supported on each end by carved wooden bears standing on their hind feet with teeth showing and claws extended. "I special ordered the bench from a world-renowned chainsaw artist who lives in Minocqua. It was Eva's birthday present."

Jack tapped the bench, "Take a seat. The bears don't bite."

Jack pointed, "See that line of trees off to the right, just beyond the creek. On the opening day of deer hunting season last year, I shot a 10-point buck from right here while enjoying a cup of coffee."

"That must be 250 yards. Did you shoot it with an AR-15 assault rifle?" Jamie asked.

"I have a few AR-15s; they're fun to shoot, light, accurate, and the high-capacity 30-round magazine makes it a great defensive weapon. That's why the anarchist politicians hate them so much. But for deer hunting, I shoot a Wetherby 300 Magnum rifle. It's got a lot more knockdown power than an AR-15. It took just one shot to drop that big buck in its tracks!"

Jack walked to the front door, disarmed the security alarm, and entered the vestibule that led to the Great Room. The twins walked behind, looking up at the huge custom-made Deer Antler Chandelier that hung from the vaulted ceiling. Northwoods-styled hand-carved furniture and rich leather sofas and recliners decorated the hardwood flooring. A massive stone fireplace towered through the second and third-floor balconies. A double-barrel shotgun hung above the mantle, and a black bearskin rug laid in front of the fireplace.

"Man O man, Uncle Jack, what do you do for a living, rob banks?" Jamie asked.

Jack raised his left eyebrow, *"Yep, but don't tell anyone!"*

Jamie looked at Jason and whispered, "He's kidding, right?"

Jason shrugged, "Maybe?"

Jack looked at his watch. "We gotta get going; we have a lot of work to do. It will take a little time to convert Faith Calvary Chapel into the Tribulation Force Freedom Center."

"But Uncle Jack, you didn't finish giving us the tour of your home!"

"It will have to wait for another day. I was thinking of having a cookout on Saturday. Do you think Macy would like to come?"

"If Mom doesn't have to cook, I'm sure she will be happy to attend," Jason replied.

"Okay, let's get going." Jack pulled a set of keys from the front pocket of his blue jeans. "Which one of you wants to drive your new truck?"

Jack tossed the keys in the air; Jamie jumped the highest. He read aloud the note attached to the keys: *Happy Birthday, boys. Better late than never!*

The twins looked at one another, with teeth glistening, "Seriously, Uncle Jack?"

"Yep. I don't need three trucks. Just be sure to take good care of Mad Max."

Mad Max was the nickname Eva gave Jack's truck. It reminded Eva of the trucks in the Mel Gibson Mad Max movies. The twin's new truck was a jet-black 2022 GMC Denali Extended Cab with only 14,000 miles. It sported a 6-inch lift kit, monster tires, a front-mounted wench, quad chrome-tipped Borla exhaust, and six spotlights rode atop the chrome roll bar.

"It's yours if your mother approves."

The boys sighed, "Uncle Jack, we're 18 years old."

"Yeah, but you still live at home, she's your mother, and she always will be! Don't worry, boys. Your mother will be thrilled that you no longer have to drive that old rusty bowling ball bag."

After a few hours of work, the Tribulation Force Freedom Center was good to go. Jamie and Jason took turns driving their new truck on the way home.

The twins pulled into the driveway. Mom heard the exhaust rumble and met the twins at the front door. "Mom, Uncle Jack gave us his old truck, Mad Max!"

"Wow, that sure was nice of him."

"Wait 'till you see his new home. It must have cost a million dollars! He's having a cookout Saturday and wants us to join him."

"Sounds good to me."

"Mom, can I ask you a question?"

"Sure, Jamie what's on your mind?"

"Uncle Jack didn't really rob banks, did he?"

Mom rolled her eyes, "No, Jack didn't rob banks. Eva's father is quite wealthy, and when Jack and Eva got married, he gave them a very generous wedding present."

"Cool! What does Eva's father do for a living?"

Mom thought briefly, "If I'm not mistaken, I think her father, Mike, owns a pillow factory."

Chapter Seven

The Chronicle

It's late Thursday morning. Macy is listening to music on the Alexa speakers. The music is interrupted, and Alexa announces: "Someone is at your door!" The Ring Doorbell Camera reveals who it is. Macy's eyes brighten, and she walks briskly to the front door, throws it open, and gives her son a big welcome-home kiss. "Dusty, I'm so happy to see you. What a wonderful surprise!"

"It's great to see you too. My boss gave me a few days off so I thought I'd come for a visit. Where is everyone?"

"At church, assisting Uncle Jack in converting Faith Calvary Chapel into the Tribulation Force Freedom Center. It's almost lunchtime; they should be back any minute."

"Great, I haven't seen Uncle Jack in a while. How's he handling life without Eva?"

"We have each other's shoulder to cry on when needed, so we're surviving. What about you, Dusty?"

"I miss Samantha, but knowing that one day we'll be reunited is comforting."

"Reunited?" Mom said curiously with a big smile, "So, you're telling me you got saved?"

"I did. I'm a true believer now!"

"That's wonderful! But don't leave me in suspense—tell me about it!"

"Well, Mom, I was deeply soul-troubled after losing Samantha in the rapture. I was terrified that I would end up in Hell. I wanted to get saved in the worst way. I read the Bible every chance I got. I told Jesus I believed in him but had no inward assurance that I was a true believer. I prayed several more times, but nothing changed. I was at my wit's end. Finally, I told the Lord I believed but asked Him to help my unbelief.

"A few days later, the crew and I returned from the United Nations broadcast in the Company Van. Mike, my cameraman, informed us that he got saved while watching the Passion of Christ movie. He recapped the story of Jesus' crucifixion and when he got to the point when the Roman soldiers were pounding spikes through Jesus' hands and feet. I thought, 'HOW CAN THESE PEOPLE BE SO EVIL AND DECEIVED?' Not only were they crucifying an innocent man, but God incarnate—the Son of God!

"Then, I perceived that, in essence, I was just as deceived and guilty as the Roman soldiers. It wasn't the nails in Jesus' hands and feet that fastened Him to the rugged cross—it was my sins, iniquities, and transgressions. In my mind's eye, I saw the hand holding the hammer that drove in the nails, and that hand was mine! I prayed silently, asking Jesus to forgive me for doubting Him—and He did. At that very moment, I felt the Holy Spirit washing away my sins as He indwelt my soul! Words cannot describe how wonderful it is to know my sins are forgiven. I deserved judgment, but God gave me mercy. I deserved Hell, but God has promised me Heaven. What a Savior, what an awesome God."

Mom embraced Dusty, and said, "This calls for a song of rejoicing." Mom walked into the living room and sat at the piano, and Dusty stood alongside. She began playing and singing.

When We All Get to Heaven,
What a day of rejoicing that will be!

When we all see Jesus,
We will sing and shout the victory!
Onward to the prize before us,
Soon His beauty we'll behold!
Soon the pearly gates will open,
We shall tread the streets of gold!

Mom glanced up at Dusty. Tears were flowing down his cheeks. "Ooooh, my goodness, you better go splash some water on your face. If Jack and the boys notice you've been crying, they will tease you forever!"

"The wind blows where it wishes, and you hear the sound of it, but cannot tell where it comes from and where it goes. So is everyone who is born of the Spirit."

A few minutes later, the twins and Jack were seated in the living room. Dusty walked in wearing a smile and was greeted with high-fives and a big bear hug from Uncle Jack. Jack lowered Dusty back onto the floor, and smiled, "My nephew rubbing shoulders with the Antichrist, who would have ever imagined?"

Jamie punched his older brother's shoulder. "Yeah, bro, don't trust that monster!"

"Don't worry, I'm not afraid of the big bad wolf. It's his partner, the human blow torch, that freaks me out. I think the big bad wolf likes me. He must because he invited me to attend a top-secret meeting in Israel. He said something big was about to happen and wanted me to be the reporter. So, I'm flying to Jerusalem next week!"

"Cool!" said the twins.

"How are you doing, Uncle Jack?"

"So far, so good, Dusty.

"We're going to have a little end-time brainstorming session after lunch. I hope you will join us."

"Sure, that should be fun."

The Great Sea Beast

After filling their bellies and clearing the table, Jack kicked off the end-time brainstorming session. "I would like to know more about the Antichrist and False Prophet. Their Mission, Mode of Operation, and that kind of stuff? What can you guys tell me?"

Jason raised his hand, "Well, Uncle Jack, I've been pouring over my father's end-time sermon and have discovered some extraordinary details. As you know, the prophetic books of the Bible are rich in symbolism. God often uses symbols to reveal things to whom he wishes and to hide them from others. Jesus often spoke in parables for the same reason." Jason explained.

"One day, the disciples asked Jesus, 'Why do you speak unto them in parables? Jesus told them, 'Because it is given unto you to know the mysteries of the kingdom of heaven, but to them, it is not given.' For those who desire to know the truth, God reveals it. Those that don't, He leaves blind, deaf, and dumb!

"Fortunately, many symbols in Revelation are interpreted in the text or elsewhere in Scripture. So, it's not as perplexing as it first appears. For instance, we are told in Revelation chapter 12 that the "dragon" is Satan. In chapter 17, the angel informs John that the beast he saw rising out of the sea was not a real seven-headed monster. Instead, the beast's "heads" represent kingdoms, and the "horns" on the heads represent kings. Here is what John wrote:

> "And I stood upon the sand of the sea, and saw a beast rise up out of the sea, having seven heads and ten horns, and upon his horns ten crowns, and upon his heads the name of blasphemy. And I saw one of his heads as it were wounded to death; and his deadly wound was healed. And all the world wondered

after the beast. And they worshipped the dragon which gave power unto the beast: and they worshipped the beast, saying, Who is like unto the beast? Who is able to make war with him?" (Revelation 13 verses 1, 3 to 4).

"The apostle John, the Revelator of the Book of Revelation, was imprisoned on the Isle of Patmos for preaching the Word of God when he received visions of the past, present, and future. The angel of the Lord told John that the seventh head of the beast represents the final gentile world empire. The ruler of the empire is the Antichrist, who receives a "deadly wound." The Antichrist, however, according to Revelation verse 8, will not remain dead but will come back to life!

"The beast that thou saw was, and is not; and shall ascend out of the bottomless pit, and go into perdition: and those who dwell on the earth shall wonder, whose names were not written in the book of life from the foundation of the world, when they behold the beast that was, and is not, and yet is."

"When the Antichrist arises from the dead, the angel said he will *ascend out of the bottomless pit.* In other words, the Antichrist will die as a man but resurrect as the son of perdition—Satan incarnate!

"Furthermore, John stated that when he had the vision of the beast rising out of the sea, he *stood upon the sand of the sea.* Patmos Island is located on the Mediterranean Sea. Therefore, we can conclude that the Antichrist's Empire and his armies will arise from the nations encompassing the Mediterranean Sea. The same region from which the ancient Roman Empire ruled the world.

The False Prophet

Jason took a sip of coffee and continued, "There is also another "beast" that the apostle John describes in Revelation 13, verses 11 to 14."

"And I beheld another beast coming up out of the earth; and he had two horns like a lamb, and he spoke as a dragon. And he exercises all the power of the first beast before him, and causes the earth and them which dwell therein to worship the first beast, whose deadly wound was healed.

And he doeth great wonders so that he makes fire come down from heaven on the earth in the sight of men. And deceives them that dwell on the earth by the means of those miracles which he had power to do in the sight of the beast; saying to them that dwell on the earth, that they should make an image to the beast, which had the wound by a sword, and did live."

"This second beast is a man that biblical scholars call the False Prophet. The False Prophet will command that an image of the Antichrist be made as a tribute to him who received the fatal sword wound but miraculously came back to life. He will demand all to worship the image that also miraculously lives and speaks!"

"Thank you, Jason. Dusty, do you have anything to add?"

"Yeah, Uncle Jack, I do."

"Unlike Jesus, the True Prophet. Who performed fantastic miracles and led people to worship the true God. The False Prophet will deceive the world into worshiping the false God—the Antichrist. Jesus Christ is the true Lamb of God who speaks the truth of God. The False Prophet has two horns like a lamb but is a usurper who tells the lies of the dragon!

"Scripture leaves no doubt that a strong relationship exists between Satan, the Antichrist, and the False Prophet. It appears that this combination of evil is Satan's attempt to create a trinity of his own—the Unholy Trinity!"

"Thank you, Dusty. That is quite insightful. "

The Mark of the Beast

"Jamie, do you have anything to add?"

"Yes, I do, Uncle Jack." It concerns the Mark of the Beast recorded in Revelation chapter 13, verses 16 to 17.

"And he had power to give life unto the image of the beast, that the image of the beast should both speak, and cause that as many as would not worship the image of the beast should be killed And he causes all, both small and great, rich and poor, free and bond, to receive a mark in their right hand, or in their foreheads, and that no man might buy or sell, except he that had the mark, or the name of the beast, or the number of his name."

"Those two verses inform us that the False Prophet will require all the world's citizens to receive the Antichrist's mark. Anyone who refuses to obey his command, take the mark, or bow down to Antichrist's image will be unable to buy or sell and will ultimately be hunted down and killed.

Jack raised his brow, and his eyes widened. "It's astonishing that this stuff was written 2,000 years ago. I mean, it's like reading today's headlines. John's vision of the future isn't describing the ancient world of horses and chariots but the high-tech world we live in today!

"The time of the internet, video phones, and satellite television. A time when the world as a whole will be able to watch the death and resurrection of the Antichrist. A time when cash will be replaced by a Central Bank Digital Currency, thereby preventing anyone from buying or selling unless they have the mark of the beast. A high-tech world of electronic surveillance and Transhuman AI robotic technology that will enable the Antichrist's image to speak, move, and kill! "If this doesn't prove the Bible's divine inspiration, I don't know what does!"

Macy held her Bible in the air, "Jack, what you have learned is just the tip of the iceberg. Scripture has much more to say about the Tribulation and the Antichrist."

Jack glanced at the clock on the wall, "I would love to hear more, but I have a bunch of chores that need to get done. Can we continue the session tomorrow evening?"

"That's fine with me," Dusty said. "I won't be flying back to Babylon until Thursday."

Macy nodded, "I should get the dishes done anyway."

Dusty walked Jack to the door. "I hear you got a Cyclone 700. Will you let me drive it?"

Jack pulled the keys from his pocket, smiled, and answered, "No."

Chapter Eight

Two Witnesses

I will give power unto my Two Witnesses, and they shall prophesy a thousand two hundred and threescore days, clothed in sackcloth. And if any man will hurt them, fire proceeds out of their mouth, and devours their enemies: and if any man will hurt them, he must in this manner be killed. These have power to shut heaven, that it rain not in the days of their prophecy: and have power over waters to turn them to blood, and to smite the earth with all plagues, as often as they will." (Revelation 11, verses 3, 5-6).

The early morning sun peeked through the window blinds, awakening Macy Rhodes. She climbed out of bed and walked to the kitchen.

"Good morning, Mom," the twins reverberated.

A large stack of blueberry pancakes, sausage patties, and a steaming cup of coffee awaited Mom. "You guys cooked breakfast for me. Bless your hearts."

Jason handed Mom a red rose, pulled out a chair, and Mom settled into it.

"Okay, boys, what do you have up your sleeve?"

"Nothing, Mom. It's your Birthday!"

Mom glanced at the Calendar hanging on the refrigerator. "Hey, it is my Birthday! Thank you, it looks delicious."

"Where's Dusty?"

"He's still sleeping. I tried to wake him, but he grouched at me and pulled the covers over his head," Jason said. Dusty is just not the same. He's no fun anymore. He's supposed to be on vacation but only wants to read his emails, make phone calls, and listen to the news. It's like he has lost his passion for life."

"Mom nodded, "I think his heart is broken. He's having a hard time adjusting to life without Samantha. If anyone can rekindle Dusty's passion for life, it's you two. I am sure you'll think of something to make him laugh again, and when you do, I will play along."

Dusty walked into the kitchen and slouched into the chair.

"It's Mom's Birthday!" Jason said.

Dusty yawned, "Oh, it is? Happy Mother's Day."

Jason rolled his eyes, "I said, Birthday, Dum Dum!"

"Sorry, Mom. Happy Birthday."

"Hey, Dusty, after breakfast, Jamie and I are going to toss the ball around in the backyard and reminisce about the good old days. Want to join us?"

"No thanks. I need to check my emails, make a few calls, and then I'm going to watch the news."

Dusty poured a cup of coffee, walked into the living room, and opened his laptop. Mom and the twins finished breakfast. The twins grabbed their baseball gloves and ball from the closet and headed for the backyard, and Mom washed the breakfast dishes.

Memories of the boys' childhood flooded Mom's mind as she watched out the kitchen window the twins playing catch. Jason and Jamie loved physical activities and the great outdoors. When it came to sports, they were the neighborhood Allstars. Their hand-eye-foot coordination, even at 10 years old, was amazing.

Mom recalled the time the twins had a contest. Each would take turns tossing the ball into the air and swinging at it. The one that hit the ball the most was the winner.

Jamie went first. He pitched the ball several feet above his head and swung at it as it descended. Ten out of ten times, success. The result was the same with Jason, ten out of ten times success. This went on for over an hour. Finally, they gave up. It was clear there would be no winner. No one struck themselves out but sent the ball flying every time.

Dusty, on the other hand, was just the opposite. He was more of a people person. He could talk up a storm and would rather visit with friends and family than play baseball. Dusty didn't possess the physical acumen or coordination of the twins, but he made up for it with an invincible, optimistic, and cheerful attitude.

When Dusty turned 11 years old, his birthday present from his father was a baseball and bat. Every day for a week, Dusty would go to the backyard, toss the ball into the air, and attempt to hit the ball. He would pitch it up. Swing, and miss. Pitch it up. Swing, and miss. Pitch it up. Swing, and miss. Pitch it up. Swing, and nick the ball, sending it 2 feet. Pitch it up. Swing, and miss. Pitch it up. Swing, and miss.

If that had happened to the twins, they would have come into the house crying, but not Dusty. Dusty picked up the ball, skipped back to the house, and walked in wearing a grin.

"Guess what, Mom?"

"What Dusty?"

"I discovered today that I'm not very good at hitting the ball, but I think I must be the world's best pitcher!"

Mom laughed, "I think so too. You pitched a perfect game!"

Mom was jolted back into the present when Dusty shouted, "Mom, you got to see this! Moses and Elijah are on television!"

"No kidding! Hold on, I'll go get the boys!"

The twins and Mom hurried into the living room to join Dusty. Jamie pointed at the TV, "Are you kidding me, that really is Moses and Elijah!"

The camera swung to the World News Network reporter. "Good afternoon, everyone. I'm Misty Carmichael, filling in for Dusty Rhodes, who is on vacation. This is a live report from the Temple Mount in Jerusalem, Israel.

"Just moments ago, two men who appeared to have stepped out of the Bible's Old Testament pages walked the pathway to the Temple Mount. Both men are dressed in sackcloth garments. Everyone is asking one another, *'Who are these strange-looking men?'* Some are saying that they are Moses and Elijah!"

A supernatural power emanated from the two men as they made their way through the massive crowd of worshippers standing at the Temple Mount's base. One of the men carried two stone tablets engraved with the Ten Commandments in his right arm and a long wooden staff in his left hand. The other had a long white beard, was bald, and wore a wide leather belt around his waist with the inscription: *Jehovah is My God emblazoned on it!*

Suddenly, a man with a bushy black beard and curly locks shouted, *"Hey Moses and Elijah, it's too soon for Trick or Treat. Halloween isn't until October!"* Undaunted by the mockery, the two climbed the Temple Mount stairs, and when they reached the top, they turned to face the crowd.

Misty stopped at the base of the Temple Mount and turned to face the camera. "It appears that the two men are about to speak. This should be interesting. Let's listen in…"

The one, the crowd, called Moses lifted the two stone tablets that contained the Ten Commandments of God and cast them down the stairs. The tablets landed at the feet of the crowd and broke into pieces. He lifted his staff and waved it over the Jewish worshippers.

> "You stiffnecked and uncircumcised in heart and ears, you do always resist the Holy Ghost: as your fathers did, so do you! Which of the prophets have not your fathers persecuted? Slaying those who foretold of the coming of the Just One—the King of Israel and Savior of the world.

The Temple that once stood on this Mount has lain in ruins for two thousand years because your ancestors rejected the Holy One of Israel, but you desire to reconstruct the Temple of God and resume animal sacrifices that can never take away sins!

"The God of all creation does not dwell in Temples made with hands—Heaven is His throne, and the earth is His footstool. The law of God that required animal sacrifices was a shadow of good things to come, but a shadow is not a substitute for the real thing. It is evident that the blood of bulls and goats can never once and for all provide atonement for sins. Otherwise, once purged, the worshipers should have no more conscience of sins. In such sacrifices, there is a remembrance of sin. Therefore the sacrifice of animals had to be offered continually month after month and year after year because the blood of animals can never permanently cleanse the sinner's conscience.

"Therefore God sent His only begotten son, the Lamb of God, perfecting forever them that come to Him in faith. After He had offered himself the sacrifice for sins, He defeated death and is now seated at the right hand of God. Of which the Holy Ghost bears witness to the truth, as it is written in the Holy Scriptures: 'This is the covenant that I will make with them after those days, saith the Lord. I will put my laws into their hearts, and in their minds will I write them; and their sins and iniquities will I remember no more!'"

Some Jewish and Muslim hearts were touched by the spirit of truth, while others cursed and shook their fists. One of the Muslim worshipers shouted, "There is no God but Allah, and Muhammed is his prophet!" Several dozen more joined the crescendo, "There is no God but Allah, and Muhammed is his prophet! There is no God but Allah, and Muhammed is his prophet!"

Suddenly, a dark cloud appeared over the crowd. Misty the reporter looked up, "Oh, my goodness, look at the sky!" Flashes of lightning and loud rumbles of thunder shook the ground, frightening and silencing the dissenting voices.

The man with the long white beard stepped forward, his eyes aflame and his voice barking, "You worshipers of Allah and disciples of Muhammed harken unto me. You protest that the Holy Scriptures of God have been corrupted by the Jews and Christians and that the original divine message was lost. God, therefore, had to send the prophet Muhammed to reveal the actual words of God, which you declare are written in the Quran.

"Let me ask you a question. Do you really believe that the God who spoke the world into existence, flung the stars into space, and hung the earth on nothing cannot preserve the integrity of His Word? Is it, rather not your book that is full of mistruths and lies?"

A man screamed, "STONE THE BLASPHEMERS! STONE THEM! STONE THE BLASPHEMERS!"

Several dozen men picked up stones and hurled them at the two witnesses, but before the stone projectiles reached the men of God, they made an in-flight 180-degree direction change and accelerated. A moment later the sound of cracking skulls echoed off the walls as the boomeranging stones found their targets. Thirty-eight bodies fell to the ground. Many died before their bodies hit the pavement, while others convulsed in pain as life's blood drained from their skulls. Soon, all the mockers stopped jerking and stopped breathing.

One of the Temple Mount guards pulled the gun from his holster and pointed it at Elijah. Elijah formed his hand into the shape of a pistol. Thumb up and index finger pointing at the man saying, "I WOULDN'T DO THAT IF I WAS YOU!"

The man ignored Elijah's warning and pulled the trigger. The gun misfired. He pulled the trigger again, and the gun exploded, sending metal shrapnel into his face. The guard screamed as he dropped to his knees, "My eyes! My eyes!" Blood oozed between his fingers and streamed down his arms as he covered his face in shame and pain!

Six other guards drew their pistols. Elijah shook his head and wagged his finger left and right. "No, No, No, I wouldn't do that if I were you." The guards wisely holstered their guns.

Elijah turned to the crowd, "I have done this man a favor. He is blind but now sees the truth. One day, he will tread the streets of gold, but you will kindle the fires of hell! REPENT AND BELIEVE IN THE LORD JESUS, AND YOU WILL BE SAVED!"

A sunbeam penetrated the darkened sky and lit the steps. Signaling that Moses and Elijah's mission was done for the day. The Two Witnesses walked down the Temple Mount stairs. The one they called Moses lifted his staff, and the large crowd parted like the Red Sea.

Misty held out her microphone, "Are you Moses and Elijah?"

"I don't mind being called Moses," he replied as he turned to his partner. "Do you mind being called Elijah?"

"No, Moses, I kinda like that name!"

"Good, then I will call you Moses and Elijah."

Misty picked up the pace, trying to keep up, "Elijah, that was an impressive showdown."

"Yeah, Misty, some people just never learn. The Muslim nations surrounding the Holy Land are five hundred times the size of Israel. Their population is millions more, and their armies are vastly larger, but in every war, the God of Israel defeats the God of Islam," Elijah said.

"If you are Moses and Elijah, the last time you walked the earth was centuries ago. Am I right?" Misty asked.

"That's correct," Moses answered.

Misty smiled, "You two look good for your age. I bet you're impressed with today's technology. I mean the cars, helicopters, cell phones, and stuff like that."

Elijah chuckled, "Young lady, I rode to heaven on a flaming chariot pulled by horses of fire! I never died, and I am thousands of years old! I have walked the streets of solid gold and stood in the Throne Room of Almighty God. My Home in Heaven makes Taylor Swift's Mansion look like an outdoor toilet. So, no, I'm not impressed with your electric cars, windmill generators, and solar panels."

"Well, we are trying to save the planet!"

Moses grinned, "Misty, I've got news for you. You won't recognize this planet by the time God gets done with it. It's going to look like a train wreck!"

Misty's eyes widened, "Why, what's God going to do to it?"

"Read the book of Revelation, Misty, and you'll find out!" Elijah said.

"Moses, may I ask you a personal question?"

"Sure?"

"You called me Misty. How do you know my name? Can you read minds?"

"No, I can't read minds, but I can read your name tag."

"Oh, silly me," Misty said.

"Nice talking to you, Misty. Perhaps we will meet again." Moses said.

Misty eyes widened, and she squeaked, "Wait a minute, you can't go yet! I just started the interview. Don't you want to be famous?"

Misty tried to keep up with them, but running in 6-inch high heels on a cobblestone path wasn't easy. She shouted, "Where are you two going?"

"Wherever God tells us to go, that's where we will be."

Misty faced the camera, "Well, I guess that's a wrap. Stay tuned for the rest of today's news."

Dusty stood, "WAS THAT AWESOME OR WHAT?"

"No doubt about that, Misty is one foxy lady," Jamie said. "I mean, talk about eye candy! That long blonde hair cascaded over her shoulders like a golden waterfall, and those baby blues sparkled with curiosity, and her smile was enchanting."

Dusty rolled his eyes, "Not her, Dum Dum—Moses and Elijah!"

Jason glanced at Jamie, "Yeah, Dum Dum! If you ask me, I think Moses and Elijah made a memorable first impression. Their goat hair sackcloth outfits were super cool. It made them look just like Fred Flintstone and Barney Rubble. But Misty's stunning beauty, short purple dress, thin black waist belt, and matching Stiletto high heels stole the show!"

Dusty slapped his forehead, "Have you guys lost your minds? That was Moses and Elijah. We just witnessed biblical prophecy being fulfilled right before our eyes, and all you two can talk about is Misty Carmichael. Sheesh!"

"Dusty's right, boys. Moses and Elijah's performance was terrific up to the point of Misty's interview. I think Moses and Elijah were distracted by Misty's stunning beauty and winsome personality. They seemed intimidated by Misty's deep probing questions and superior intellect," Mom said.

The twins could no longer contain themselves and burst into laughter! Mom caught the contagion, and soon, laughter filled the room. Dusty shook his head, "You guys had me going for a while, but when Mom mentioned Misty's superior intellect. The ruse was up—I knew that I'd been had! "Misty is pretty, but she is not the sharpest tool in the shed."

"Dusty, it is so nice to hear you laughing again," Mom said. "I had difficulty keeping a straight face when Misty started asking Moses and Elijah questions. She reminded me of the blonde joke your father liked to tell."

"What joke was that?" Jason asked.

"I'm not good at telling jokes. Your father was the family comedian, not me."

"Come on, Mom. Tell us the joke."

"Okay, boys, I'll give it a shot."

Two blondes were staring at the Moon.

The tall blonde asks the other blonde, 'Are we closer to the Moon or closer to Florida?'

The shorter blonde answered, 'The Moon.'

'How do you know that?'

She answered, 'Well, you can't see Florida, can you?'

"Mom, don't get me laughing again. My side hurts as it is," Dusty said.

Mom rose and strolled to the center of the living room. "Dusty, I know that you miss Samantha a lot, and boys, I know that you miss Dad and Jenna, but we will be reunited one day. Meanwhile, you don't have to worry about anything, not even for one second.

"God can turn our trials into triumphs. He can turn our troubles into blessings. His protective power will keep us secure in His mighty hand until the day God calls us home. Until that time, there are a lot of souls that need to be saved. I'm sure Dad, Jenna, and Samantha are in heaven cheering us on!

"We can learn a lot from Moses and Elijah's method of evangelism. No doubt, if Moses and Elijah had preached the love of Jesus rather than the law of God, they would have made friends instead of enemies. The world isn't offended when Christians preach the love of Jesus, but when the truths of sin, righteousness, and hell are preached, many become offended."

"Moses and Elijah's approach to sharing the Gospel is noticeably different from the approach of modern-day evangelism. In light of how most pastors and Christians share the Gospel, Moses and Elijah failed because they didn't "Get a Decision." Heaven's angels, however, don't rejoice over "decisions"—they rejoice over sinners that repent!

"When Moses tossed the Ten Commandments down the steps and pointed his staff at the crowd. They understood that it meant they were guilty of breaking God's laws. The purpose of presenting the law before presenting the Savior is to tear away the fig leaves of self-righteousness so that the person can see himself as God sees him—wretched, miserable, blind, and naked—a sinner in desperate need of redemption! The Gospel is good news, but it is good news only to those who can handle the truth and respond in repentant faith.

"To preach the love of God without first preaching sin, righteousness, and judgment can be likened to tossing a lifesaver to a swimmer in a shallow pool of water. He has no fear of drowning and couldn't care less about the lifesaver. But throw a lifesaver to a man who realizes that he is drowning in a sea of sin and he will grasp it like there is no tomorrow!"

"Mom, that was some awesome preaching! You should make a YouTube video."

Mom pressed her finger to her lips, "Listen, what's that noise?" The plates in the kitchen dish-strainer were rattling. The pictures on the living room wall began swaying. Mom lost her balance and fell back onto the sofa, spilling her coffee cup.

Dusty's eyes enlarged, "It's an earthquake!"

A few moments later, the shaking stopped.

"Don't worry, it's over. I've experienced earthquake tremors like this before in my travels." Dusty said.

"An earthquake in Wisconsin, that's strange," Jason said.

Mom rose from the sofa, "I better get a towel and soak up that spilled coffee before it stains the carpet."

Dusty motioned to the twins. The three huddled and whispered so Mom couldn't hear and quickly sat back down.

Mom entered the living room and tossed a towel over the puddle of coffee.

"Mom?"

"Yes, Jamie."

"The consensus of your three sons is the earthquake was God's way of saying that He thought your preaching was awesome!"

Mom raised one eyebrow and shook her head, "Oh, that's so sweet, but flattery will get you nowhere! I know your tricks, boys, and the answer is no. No, you cannot fly to Israel with Dusty to meet Moses and Elijah! It's too dangerous, and the Tribulation Force Freedom Center Grand Opening is Sunday!"

Mom started walking back to the kitchen. The boys glanced at each other and whispered, *"How did Mom know what we were going to ask?"*

"Mom stopped and turned, facing her sons, *"You know, boys, what they say about mothers is true. We do have eyes in the back of our heads, and unlike Moses and Elijah, mothers can read minds!"*

Dusty nodded, "I don't doubt that. Not even for a second." Then he glanced at the twins and motioned, "Come on, let's go and play catch!"

Chapter Nine

The Chronicle Continues

Dusty heard Uncle Jack pull into the driveway and rushed out the door to greet him, "That's one cool truck. I hear it's super-fast.

Jack nodded, "Yeah if you see a Mustang GT running around town without doors, you'll know why! The race was fender to fender for a while, but Mustang Sally's doors got blown off when I hit the Nitrous Oxide button!"

Dusty smiled, shaking his head. "Fun times in the tribulation, who would have ever imagined."

"Yeah, Dusty, we may as well live it up while we can. I'm sure the good times won't last long."

"No doubt about that, Uncle Jack."

"You know Dusty, I learned so much at yesterday's brainstorming session. I could hardly wait for this evening's get-together."

"Yeah, me too. Let's get at it!"

Jack and Dusty joined Macy and the twins seated at the kitchen table. Jack grabbed a chocolate chip cookie and poured a glass of milk. "Macy, would you like to kick off the Antichrist study?"

"Sure."

Macy opened God's Word to the passages that her husband, Pastor John, had highlighted concerning the Antichrist and his follower's blasphemous religious beliefs. She put on her glasses and began reading,

> "Who is a liar but he who denies that Jesus is the Christ? He is Antichrist, that denies the Father and the Son. Whosoever denies the Son, the same has not the Father: he that acknowledges the Son has the Father also."

> "Beloved, believe not every spirit, but try the spirits whether they are of God: because many false prophets are gone out into the world. Hereby know you the Spirit of God: Every spirit that confesses that Jesus Christ has come in the flesh is of God: And every spirit that confesses not that Jesus Christ has come in the flesh is not of God: and this is that spirit of Antichrist, whereof you have heard that it should come; and even now already is in the world." (1 John 2, verses 22 to 23; and chapter 4, verses 1 to 3).

"Thank you, Macy. Does anyone have anything else to add?"

"I do, Uncle Jack," Jason said. "Speaking of the Antichrist, the Old Testament prophet Daniel stated,"

> "He shall speak great words against the Most-High and shall wear out the saints of the Most-High, and think to change times and laws, and they shall be given into his hand until a time and times and the dividing of time [the last three and half years of the tribulation].

> "Neither shall he regard the God of his fathers, nor the desire of women, nor regard any god; for he shall magnify himself above all. And his power shall be mighty, but not by his own power: and he shall destroy wonderfully, and shall prosper, and practice, and shall destroy the mighty and the holy people.

> "And through his policy also he shall cause craft to prosper in his hand; and he shall magnify himself in his heart, AND BY

PEACE SHALL DESTROY MANY: he shall also stand up against the Prince of princes, but he shall be broken without hand." (Daniel 7 verse 25; chapter 8 verse 25).

Jack scribbled a quick note and looked up, "I never told you this before, but when the terrorists attacked the United States on September 11, 2001, destroying the World Trade Centers and killing 3,000 Americans. My duty as an Army Ranger Instructor was to take a deep dive into the religion of Islam to understand better the Muslim mindset that prompted the attack. So, I'm somewhat of an expert on Islam.

"Astonishingly, Daniel and John's prophetic proclamations were written centuries before Islam became a religion, yet both describe Islam's religious beliefs and political ambitions to a tee! From our study yesterday and tonight, I have identified five Modus Operandi of the Antichrist that I want to share with you.

"First, according to the prophecy in Revelation, the Antichrist's preferred method of execution is beheading. Guess what? It just so happens that Islam's prophet, Muhammed, and his followers preferred method of execution is also beheading. Who can forget the brutal and gruesome internet videos of the Islamic State (ISIS) beheading twenty-one Egyptian Christians for refusing to renounce Jesus Christ? And the beheadings of men, women, teenagers, and toddlers done by the Palestinian terrorist organization Hamas when they attacked Israel in October 2023!

"Second, according to Daniel's prophecy, the Antichrist will change the times and the laws. Guess what? Muslims don't use the Gregorian Calendar to track times and dates like most of the world, but instead use the Islamic Calendar called the Hijri. Islam also has their own set of financial, religious, and political laws called Sharia. In every instance from the time of Muhammed until the present day, whenever Islam conquers a non-Muslim land. The first thing they do is to change the times and laws to a system of Islamic jurisprudence.

"Third, Daniel stated that the Antichrist will not regard the desire of women. Guess what? The same is true of Islam. Unless you've been living under a rock, everyone knows that women in Islam are often treated like second and third-class citizens. Depending on the sect of Islam, Muslim women are considered so inferior to men that often, the wife is not permitted to walk alongside the husband but must follow in his footsteps. In some countries, Muslim women cannot vote, drive a car, get an education, or leave the house without their husbands' permission. Even in Sharia courts, a woman's testimony is considered half the value of a man's.

"Fourth, the Antichrist will, by peace, destroy many. Guess what? Daniel's prophetic proclamation also fits Islam to a tee. I don't think it is coincidental that Islam is called the religion of peace. History, however, has proven that just the opposite is true. DESTROYING MANY IN THE NAME OF PEACE has been Islamic terrorists' Method of Operation throughout Islam's fourteen-hundred-year history.

"Islam is a religion of peace in non-Muslim countries where the Muslim community is primarily moderate. However, when radical Muslims gain economic, political, or military advantage, they believe it is their religious duty to conquer the land and convert the inhabitants to Islam by word or sword!

"In fact, after the death and resurrection of Christ, most of the Middle East converted to Christianity. Today, however, the Christian church in the Middle East, for the most part, has been obliterated. So far, the religion of peace has killed an estimated 270 million people!

"Fifth, from what Macy just read, the Antichrist will deny that Jesus is the Son of God and deny His death and resurrection. Guess what? It just so happens that the Muslims' Holy book boldly declares that God never had a son, Jesus never died on the cross, and He never rose from the dead."

Jason interrupted, "Uncle Jack, hold on for a moment. I think I know where you're going with this. You're thinking that Daniel is telling us that the Antichrist will declare that he is Allah, the God of the Muslims."

"Well, Jason, if the shoe fits!"

"I must admit, Uncle Jack, that the evidence favors your analysis. The similarities between the Antichrist's and Islam's political and religious ambitions are uncanny. It appears to be beyond mere coincidence, but we must be careful not to take Daniel's words out of context. The fact is that Muslims worship Allah, but Daniel stated that the Antichrist will NOT REGARD THE GOD OF HIS FATHERS…NOR REGARD ANY GOD; FOR HE SHALL MAGNIFY HIMSELF ABOVE ALL! Therefore, it is clear that the Antichrist will not declare himself to be Allah, Ashtoreth, Zeus, or any other particular god of the world's religions!"

"Yeah, Jason, I see what you mean. I guess this does present us with somewhat of a prophetic enigma. I can't imagine Muslims worshiping any God other than Allah," Jack observed.

Macy ran her finger around the rim of the coffee cup as she considered the conflicting worship conundrum. She thought momentarily, then spoke, "You guys have left out one crucial detail—the God factor!"

Jack tilted his head, glancing at Macy, "The God factor, what's that?"

"Well, Jack, Scripture informs us that God gives everyone space to repent but warns that His Spirit will not always strive with man. The time is coming when those who refuse to acknowledge Jesus as Lord and receive Him as Savior. God will send them a "strong delusion" so that they will believe the lie! Listen to what is written in Second Thessalonians 2, verses 9 to 12.

> "Even him, whose coming is after the working of Satan with all power and signs and lying wonders, And with all deceivableness of unrighteousness in them that perish;

because they received not the love of the truth, that they might be saved. And for this cause, **God shall send them strong delusion, that they should believe a lie**: That they all might be damned who believed not the truth, but had pleasure in unrighteousness!"

"It will not matter if one is an atheist, Buddhist, Hindu, Jehovah's Witness, Mormon, Jew, or Muslim. If you reject Jesus Christ, the Son of God—God incarnate, you will believe the lie that the Antichrist is God! So, from what we have learned, the Antichrist will not proclaim that he is God until the mid-point of the seven-year tribulation. At that time, he will not declare that he is the God of any particular religion but instead will proclaim himself to be the God of gods, the highest of all gods, even the God of the Bible.

"It wouldn't surprise me if the Antichrist will use the same Quranic verses that he quoted at the United Nations to convince the world that Christians were not Raptured but swooned away to judgment to convince the Muslims that he is God incarnate. I wrote that Quranic passage down, and here is what it says,

"And the Trumpet will be blown, and all who are in the heavens and on the earth will swoon away, except him whom Allah will. Then the trumpet will be blown a second time and behold, they will be standing, looking on. *And the earth will shine with the light of its Lord* **Allah when He will come to judge among men**" (Quran, chapter 39, verses 68 and 69).

"Notice that the verse does not say that Allah is coming to *judge men* but to *judge **among** men*. So many Muslims will have no problem believing that the Antichrist is Allah—the God who comes to earth to live and judge among men!"

"Thank you, Macy, that explains a lot," Jack said.

Jamie began tapping and pointing his index finger to a verse in his Bible. "I just noticed something Daniel stated about the Antichrist that I had never seen before. I think this will explain the

Antichrist and Islam's connection! Listen to Daniel's words concerning the Antichrist in chapter 11, verses 38 and 39.

> "But in his estate shall he honor the God of forces: and a god whom his fathers knew not shall he honor with gold, and silver, and with precious stones, and pleasant things. Thus shall he do in the most strong holds with a strange god, whom he shall acknowledge and increase with glory: and he shall cause them to rule over many, and shall divide the land for gain."

"This passage informs us that the Antichrist will join forces with a strange god, one whom his fathers knew not shall he honor with gold, silver, and precious stones. In other words, the Antichrist will join forces with a people whose god that Daniel's fathers—Abraham, Issac, and Jacob—were unfamiliar with.

"Daniel's ancestors were familiar with many false gods, as revealed in the Old Testament, but Daniel didn't name them. Instead, he says the Antichrist will acknowledge and increase with glory a strange god. A god that wasn't worshipped in the days of Daniel's ancestors but will be worshipped in the last days. Again, this perfectly describes the Islamic God, Allah—the God of the Muslims who wasn't introduced to the world until centuries after Daniel's prophetic proclamation."

"Thank you, Jamie.

"Now, it all makes perfect sense. The Antichrist will use radical Muslims' inherent hatred of the Jews and Christians during the first half of the Tribulation to assist him in establishing his throne in the rebuilt Temple in Jerusalem. During the second half of the Tribulation, the Antichrist will declare that he is God and demand that all, including Muslims, worship him.

"Some will not believe the lie but believe in Jesus and be beheaded. Those who refuse to repent and turn from their wickedness: God will send them strong delusion, that they should believe a lie: That they all might be damned who believed not the truth, but had pleasure in unrighteousness!"

"Am I correct?"

Dusty stood and saluted, "Uncle Jack, your assessment is spot on. I recently had a conversation with my newest reporting team member, Alan Qasim, that I think you'll find fascinating. Alan was a devout Muslim but is now a Christian. He told me that Muslims don't recognize the Antichrist and False Prophet revealed in Revelation as evil monsters but Islamic superheroes—the al-Mahdi and the Islamic Jesus. Muslims believe in the second coming of Jesus, but they are taught that when He returns, he will return as a radical Muslim. He will come to assist the forces of the al-Mahdi and shatter the crosses, kill the Jews, and establish worldwide Islamic rule.

"My point is that Muslims don't realize it, but Satan is utilizing Islamic eschatology to set up Muslims to receive the Antichrist and the False Prophet with open arms!

"Undoubtedly, we are witnessing the initial stages of the fulfillment of these end-time prophecies. The Antichrist has made his debut on the world stage. His rise to fame and power through diplomacy, mighty signs, and lying wonders has begun. Millions have already been deceived! It won't be long before the Second Horsemen of the Apocalypse begins his ride of terror foretold in Revelation 6 verses 3 to 4.

> "When He opened the second seal, I heard the second living creature saying, "Come and see." Another horse, fiery red, went out. And it was granted to the one who sat on it to take peace from the earth, and that people should kill one another; and there was given to him a Great Sword."

"Perhaps the *Great Sword* mentioned in this verse is the *Sword of Radical Islam*. Time will tell, but one thing is sure. The Tribulation Force must be prepared to battle the spiritual forces of evil. God has provided the armor we must put on to survive and rescue others from the deception, lies, and evil forces being unleashed upon our world.

"The time cometh, that whosoever killeth you, will think that he doeth God service." — John 16 verse 2

"The terrorists have no problem killing people—even women, children, and babies—because they believe the lie that that is what their God wants them to do!

"What does Jesus have to say about such evil people?"

"You are of your father the devil, and the desires of your father you want to do. He was a murderer from the beginning, and does not stand in the truth, because there is no truth in him. When he speaks a lie, he speaks from his own resources, for he is a liar and the father of it." (John 8 verse 44).

"The terrorists have been brainwashed into believing that if one dies in jihad, Allah will give him 72 virgins to enjoy in Paradise. The truth of God's Word is that the terrorist will not open his eyes in Paradise at death—but in hell. Seventy-two virgins will not be waiting to greet him, but demons to torture him!

"God doesn't want Muslims to end up in hell—Jesus' blood was shed so they wouldn't have to go there. Sharing the Gospel can transform a Christian-hating and Jew-hating person into someone who loves his neighbor just as he loves himself. Don't ever forget that!"

Macy stood, looking at her sons, "We have come so far and learned much about the future and the love of Christ. I know that your Father would be very proud of us all. I am sure there are many more golden nuggets to dig out of God's Word, but this is enough for today. The good news is that the Antichrist and his deceived masses will not succeed. We may lose some battles, but Christ and

Christians will win the war! Let's conclude this meeting with the assurance of that victory described by John the Revelator."

> Now I saw heaven opened, and behold, a white horse. And He who sat on him was called Faithful and True, and in righteousness, He judges and makes war. His eyes were like a flame of fire, and on His head were many crowns. He had a name written that no one knew except Himself. He was clothed with a robe dipped in blood, and His name is called The Word of God. And the armies in heaven, clothed in fine linen, white and clean, followed Him on white horses. Now out of His mouth goes a sharp sword, that with it He should strike the nations. And He Himself will rule them with a rod of iron. He Himself treads the winepress of the fierceness and wrath of Almighty God. And He has on His robe and on His thigh a name written:
>
> KING OF KINGS AND
>
> LORD OF LORDS!
>
> Then I saw an angel standing in the sun; and he cried with a loud voice, saying to all the birds that fly in the midst of heaven, "Come and gather together for the supper of the great God, that you may eat the flesh of kings, the flesh of captains, the flesh of mighty men, the flesh of horses and of those who sit on them, and the flesh of all people, free and slave, both small and great.
>
> And I saw the beast, the kings of the earth, and their armies, gathered together to make war against Him who sat on the horse and against His army. Then the beast was captured, and with him the false prophet who worked signs in his presence, by which he deceived those who received the mark of the beast and those who worshiped his image. These two were cast alive into the lake of fire burning with brimstone. And the rest were

killed with the sword which proceeded from the mouth of Him who sat on the horse. And all the birds were filled with their flesh." (Revelation 19 verses 11 to 21).

Jack's voice rose as he stood raising his Bible high. "What book is like this book? Whose God is like our God? He has indeed declared the end from the beginning and from ancient times the future to come. His counsel shall stand, and His prophecies will be fulfilled precisely as predicted because no one can stop an unstoppable God!"

Everyone shouted, "Praise the Lord!"

Chapter Ten

Explosive News

Dusty opened one eye as the twins shook him violently. "Wake up! Wake up! New York City has been NUKED!"

The early morning sun peeked through the window blinds. "Get up, get dressed." Jamie yanked the blankets down to the foot of the bed.

Dusty sat up rubbing his eyes, "What on earth are you talking about?"

Jamie's persistent voice broke through Dusty's sleep-fogged mind. "We need to get to a bomb shelter. China and Russia are attacking us!"

Dusty shivered, "Oh my goodness, where's Mom?"

"She's missing, we can't find her!"

Dusty sprung out of bed and ran to Mom's bedroom. She wasn't there.

He peeked in the bathroom. She wasn't there.

He scrambled down the second-floor stairs and ran into the family room, sliding halfway across the floor in his stocking feet. He sprinted down the hallway into the living room. She wasn't there.

He opened the front door and shot down the steps that led to the garage. He grabbed the doorknob—it was locked. He stood on his toes, peeking in the window. Mom's car was sitting in the garage.

He scratched his head, *"Calm down, think. Where would she be?"* He thought for a moment, *"I bet she took shelter in the basement!"*

Dusty darted back up the steps and into the house, rushed to the basement door, and opened it. The lights were off, *"Shoot, she can't be down there."*

He slammed the door, cupped his hands around his mouth, sucked in a deep frustrated breath, and shouted to the top of his lungs, *"Mom, where are you?"*

He heard Mom's voice, "Dusty, I'm in the kitchen."

He hurried down the hallway to the kitchen. Mom was standing at the stove.

"Mom, what on earth are you doing?"

"I'm fixing breakfast. Do you prefer your eggs sunny side up or well done?"

Dusty ran both hands over his head, *"Man, that was some nightmare. It seemed so real."* He turned, noticing Jamie and Jason standing in the hallway, pointing at him and giggling. His face reddened, and his voice growled, "You dirty rats, I'm going to kill you!"

The twins sprinted out the patio door into the backyard. Younger, lighter, and faster—Dusty didn't bother chasing them.

"Come on, Dusty, breakfast is getting cold." Mom said as she shook her head. "I don't even want to know what the twins did to get you so riled up, but you should have known that payback was coming sooner or later. Did you forget all the pranks that you played on the twins? You put peanut butter in the twins' shoes. You put clear plastic wrap under the toilet seat. You mixed laxatives into the twins' chocolate birthday cake. The poor boys couldn't leave the bathroom for two days! Should I continue?"

"No, Mom, you don't need to say more. You're right, I deserve payback."

"You know the twins got up earlier than normal just so they could give you a ride to the airport. I told them to go and wake you so you wouldn't be late."

Dusty smiled, "Well, I'm awake, that's for sure! I can skip the breakfast coffee.

"I've got to admit that was a good prank. I really thought New York City got NUKED!"

Mom chuckled, "Is that what they told you?"

"Yeah, and I bought it, lock, stock, and barrel!"

"Dusty, I hope there are no hard feelings toward the twins."

"No hard feelings, Mom. I had it coming."

Mom took a sip of coffee, "What do you say? Let's call a truce and eat breakfast on the deck with the boys."

"I think that's a good idea."

Mom and Dusty carried the breakfast food, plates, and silverware to the deck picnic table. Dusty motioned and shouted, "Come and get it!"

The twins looked at each other and said in unison: "I hope he doesn't mean a knuckle sandwich!"

"Come on, guys, the food is getting cold."

The twins were surprised that Dusty had taken the prank so well. They walked onto the deck, threw a leg over the picnic table bench, and began loading blackberry pancakes onto their plates one at a time, cautiously checking each pancake. Just to be sure, nothing sinister was stuck on the bottom.

"Boys, I've got to admit that was a great prank."

The twins blew on their fingernails and polished them on their shirts. "Thanks, bro, but we learned from the best."

Dusty smiled and then looked at his watch, "Oh my goodness, I need to get to the airport ASAP! The Company Jet should be touching down any minute."

"Don't worry, Mad Max will get you there on time!" Jamie said.

Dusty scarfed down a few more bites, took a sip of orange juice, and ran to the bedroom. He stuffed his clothes into the suitcase and sprinted to the front door. He gave Mom a quick hug and peck on the cheek and the trio ran to the truck.

Dusty tossed his luggage into the truck box. "I'll sit in the back seat," He said as he opened the extended cab door—it was full of the twins' junk. Jason tugged on Dusty's shirt, "You can sit in the front with us; there's room for three." Dusty slid into the center, and Jason jumped in and closed the door. Jamie turned the key, and a stampede of 500 horses rumbled out the exhaust.

Dusty shook his head, "You lucky Dogs, this is a cool truck."

Jamie put the truck in gear, "Buckle up, we're off to the races!"

"I know a shortcut that will shave off ten minutes," Jamie said as he took a sharp left and headed across the county fairgrounds. The boys jostled and bounced in the seats as Jamie navigated the truck over the bumpy and mud-puddled terrain.

Mad Max launched off the top of the dirt knoll, flying 40 feet through the air, "Yahoo! Yahoo!" Dusty shouted. Water and mud splashed thirty feet when the big tires hit a massive puddle, drenching a bicycle rider.

The man on the bike flipped up his middle finger.

Jamie stuck his head out the window and yelled, "SORRY!"

Fifteen minutes later, Mad Max pulled into the airport. The Company Jet had just landed and was taxing to the VIP entrance gate. "There's the Jet. Stop, and let me out!"

Jamie pulled into the closest parking spot, and the trio jumped out. The twins hugged their brother and watched him run to the chain link fence gate. Dusty handed his flight I.D. to the guard. The guard grinned, nodded his head, and then opened the gate.

Dusty turned and waved to the boys as he boarded the Jet. His brothers waved and shouted, "Goodbye, Dusty. Don't forget to call."

The twins watched the Company Jet fly away and returned to the truck... "Jamie, what are you waiting for? Let's go."

Veloci-Rapture

"I can't find the keys!"

"Check your pockets."

"I did already!"

Jamie pulled down the visor, but no keys. He searched the floorboard, but no keys. Jamie rechecked his pockets, but no luck.

"Perhaps you dropped the keys outside when we were saying goodbye to Dusty," Jason said.

The twins jumped back out and walked around the truck twice, frantically searching the ground. "I don't see them."

"Me neither!"

The twins glanced at each other, realizing they'd been had. They couldn't believe it; Dusty pulled a fast one on them again!

"Perhaps Uncle Jack has an extra set of keys. I will call him," Jamie said. "He's going to think we are a couple of idiots!" He called, and the phone rang, but no answer.

The twins searched the area one more time, shaking their heads. The airport guard approached, "Looking for something?"

"Yeah, my stupid brother flew off with the keys to Mad Max!"

The guard looked over the truck. "So you named the truck, "Mad Max, huh? I've got a truck that I call Black Eye. It's black like yours, but I'm sure it doesn't sound as good as Mad Max. Do me a favor and start it up so I can hear what it sounds like!"

Jamie looked at the guard with a confused look thinking, "I just told him I don't have any keys, and he asked me to start it up! *Sheesh, what an idiot!*"

The guard reached into his pocket, "Oh, yeah, I almost forgot to give you these."

Jamie's eyes brightened, "You found my keys! Where on earth did you find them?"

"Your brother, the one you affectionately call "stupid," gave me the keys and this American Eagle silver coin. He told me to let you sweat it out for a few minutes and then give you the keys along with his business card."

Jamie flipped over Dusty's business card and read aloud the one-word message: *"Gotcha!"*

The guard smiled, "That was a great prank!"

The twins nodded affirmatively and high-fived the guard.

The boys learned two important lessons that day: Don't leave the keys in the ignition, and Dusty is still Prank King!

Jamie fired up Mad Max. He revved the engine several times, putting a smile on the guard's face. It was time to head home and give Mad Max a bath and a liquid wax rub-down. Then, go to Uncle Jack's place for hamburgers, brats, and corn cobs.

Mom heard the twins pulling into the driveway, and a few minutes later, they walked through the door. "Mom, you won't believe what Dusty did." Mom cut off Jamie before he could finish the sentence, "Let me guess, He pranked you again?"

"Man, did he ever!"

"You can tell the story when we get to Uncle Jack's. I'm sure he will be interested in hearing it. Right now, I have something serious to tell you about. While you two were gone, I had a visit from a couple of police officers."

Jamie swallowed hard and asked, "The policemen didn't mention anything about a chrome bowling ball, did they?"

Mom tilted her head curiously, "Why would the cops ask me about a bowling ball? Is there something that you should be telling me, Jamie?"

"No, Mom, I was just curious because you know cops nowadays. All they think about is crispy cream donuts and chrome bowling balls." Jason rolled his eyes.

"Is that right," Mom said. "I don't recall the officer asking about donuts, bigfoot, leprechauns, unicorns, or a chrome bowling ball. Instead, the officer handed me a *Cease and Desist Order* telling me that the Mayor had issued an executive order that now makes sharing the gospel in public illegal."

"Are you kidding me? What a jerk! Someone should kick his butt!"

"Remember this, boys. God's Word tells us that our battle isn't against flesh and blood but against principalities, against powers, against the dark spiritual forces of this world. So, don't curse the Mayor, but instead pray for him."

"Good idea, Mom. Let's pray right now—before that stupid Mayor decides to outlaw cool trucks like Mad Max," Jamie said.

So, Mom closed her eyes and prayed for the Mayor, asking God to deliver him from demonic influences and for his salvation. Then Jason concluded the intercessory prayer, saying, "Lord, please teach Jamie to put his brain into gear before putting his mouth in motion!"

"Ouch! I mean, Amen," Jason said as he rubbed his shoulder that Jamie slugged.

Chapter Eleven

Hamburgers, Brats, and Corn Cobs

Macy last visited her brother Jack's place a year ago. She knew that Jack and Eva had built a new home but hadn't seen it. After hearing the twins go on and on about it, she was anxious to get there. Macy locked the door as she and the twins exited the Rhodes family home.

"Listen to this Mom," Jamie said as he pushed the remote start button on his key fob. The lights flashed, and the exhaust rumbled out the tailpipes as Mad Max came to life.

"Is that a sweet sound or what?"

"I'd say, can I drive?"

"Sure, I guess," Jamie said with a concerned look.

"Don't worry, I'll keep it under a hundred miles per hour!"

Mom wasn't kidding. She burnt rubber out of the parking lot, squealed the tires at every signal light, and passed five cars arriving at Jack's place in short order. She turned onto Jack's blacktop road, pulled onto the driveway, and parked in front of the five-car garage. She turned off the ignition and handed the key fob back to Jamie. "Thanks, that was fun!"

Jamie wiped his brow, "Man-O-Man, when you passed those cars, you were doing 98 miles an hour. You must be starving!"

Mom smiled, "I must be. The last time I drove that fast, I was 18 years old, and gas was 75 cents a gallon."

Jack heard them coming and met them on the front lawn. "Let's go out back, and I'll toss some burgers on the grill—I could eat a horse!"

"Speaking of horses, Jack. Where are they? Usually, they come running when they hear or see a vehicle," Macy asked.

Jack smiled and rubbed his belly but didn't say a word. The trio followed Jack up a couple of steps onto the deck walkway that led to the back of the house. The deck extended the length of the home and was enhanced with a sauna, whirlpool hot tub, and brick barbecue pit. Macy and the twins walked across the deck as Jack loaded the grill with hamburgers, brats, and corn cobs.

The twins noticed the backyard horseshoe pit, "Uncle Jack, I bet Jamie and I can beat you and Mom in a game of horseshoes," Jason challenged.

"Perhaps, after we eat. You two should go practice while I talk to your mom."

"Okay, Uncle Jack."

Macy placed her hands on the deck railing as she gazed across the expansive backyard, noticing ducks swimming in the pond. "It sure is beautiful in the country. I see why Eva loved it so much."

"Yeah, Eva was born in the city but was a country girl at heart. She loved to relax in the deck hot tub, sipping on a glass of wine after working in the greenhouse. You can try the hot tub later if you wish. I'm sure one of her swimsuits will fit you just fine."

"Thanks, Jack. I might take you up on the offer, but I'm curious about your greenhouse."

"The greenhouse is behind the garage. It's a short walk off the deck. I'll show it to you after we eat." Smoke rose from the barbeque pit as Jack flipped the burgers and bratwursts. He tossed a slice of cheese on half of the burgers and brushed butter on the corn cobs.

Macy slowly breathed in the cookout aroma, it was mouthwatering. Jack loaded the food onto the platter, "Come and get it, boys."

Macy lifted the bun, squirted a little ketchup on the burger, and took a bite, "Mmm, it's delicious. I never knew horse burgers could taste so good."

Jack smiled, "Horses are for riding, not eating." The horses are behind the barn while alarms are installed in the corral and inside the barn. Meat is hard to come by and, as you know, is extremely expensive. If a horse thief or cattle rustler comes onto this property, they will be in for a big surprise!"

Macy took another bite and sighed, *"I'm glad these are not horse burgers. I'm kinda fond of Old Nelly."* Jack glanced at the twins as they reloaded their plates, "Speaking of horses, will you two check on them to ensure they have enough oats and water?"

"Sure, Uncle Jack."

Jack and Macy walked down the deck steps onto the Terra-lock sidewalk that led to the greenhouse. "Oh, my goodness, Jack, a glass greenhouse!"

"Not exactly, Macy. It has the appearance of glass but is stronger and more durable. Each panel is made from triple-layer polycarbonate and capable of withstanding over 100 lbs. of snow and 140 mph winds, so I can grow fruit and vegetables all year long. It has full-length ridge vents automated by thermostat control, an Israeli-designed drip water management system, and two high capacity Carbon Dioxide generating machines."

Macy scratched her head, did you say, "Carbon Dioxide, Jack, as in CO2?"

"Yep. You won't believe the effects CO2 has on the size of the plants!"

Jack pushed open the door, and Macy entered the greenhouse. "Gee whiz, Jack, I see what you mean. I feel like I just entered Jurassic Park. I hope a Tyrannosaurus isn't lurking behind those giant tomato plants," Macy said with a giggle.

Seriously, Jack, you're telling me that your flowers and plants are so large and lush because of increased Carbon Dioxide levels?"

"You betcha."

"But Jack, I thought CO2 was bad for the environment and plant life."

Jack picked a flower and gave it to Macy, "The scientific evidence suggests otherwise, Macy. In the past, Carbon Dioxide was called the miracle molecule because it is the substance that makes God's green Earth GREEN. Greenhouse owners have known for decades that increasing CO2 levels three to five times the atmospheric levels radically improves plant health, size, and yields. That's because CO2 is not a pollutant but a nutrient that accelerates plant growth and increases the size, quality, and nutritional value of fruits, vegetables, flowers, grasslands, and crops.

"Those facts about the miracle molecule were taught in high school science classes for decades, but students today are taught that CO2 is the demon pollutant from hell that is destroying the world. The truth is without CO2, pollination and photosynthesis wouldn't be possible. Over 80 percent of flowering plants would not reproduce, most edible plants would wither, and oxygen-producing forests would eventually die and rot away."

"So, Jack, why do you think the CO2 narrative has changed from God's miracle molecule to the demon molecule from hell?"

"Well, Macy, the theory is that the global political elite believes overpopulation is the most significant contributor to climate change. If the world's population can be persuaded by the climate change cultists and the incessant fearmongering of the complicit media into believing CO2 is public enemy number one. Then, the world will go along with the suicidal plan of reducing and eliminating carbon dioxide from the atmosphere, effectively decreasing the world's population through food shortages and mass starvation!"

Macy's brow lifted, "Jack, do you really think people can be that evil?"

"It wouldn't be the first time that a government used starvation to eliminate those who posed a threat to the social and economic ambitions of the political elite. In 1929, Ukraine was a part of the Soviet Union, ruled by Joseph Stalin. Stalin wanted to rapidly create his socialist dream of collectivization, which included replacing individually owned and operated farms with big state-run collectives.

"Ukraine's independence-minded farmers resisted giving up their freedom, land, and livelihoods to the government. So, Stalin enacted laws making gardening and farming illegal without special government permits. The draconian laws enacted forced many farmers and ranchers to go out of business. Soviet officials then confiscated farmlands, crops, and livestock, and the citizens who supported his Marxist policies ransacked the homes and farms of the Ukrainian peasants. The final result was that 3.9 million Ukrainians starved to death!"

"Oh my goodness, Jack. That's horrible."

"I got news for you, sister, it's coming to America and already has in some states. The globalist goal of controlling food, energy, and money is the same as Stalin's. It's just being done on a larger scale and under the auspice of saving the planet from Climate Change.

"Most of the environmentalists are Evolutionists and Communists. They don't believe that human beings were made in the image of God but rather evolved from some premortal slime. The value of human life to them is not much more than that of a cockroach. Saving the planet from Climate Change has become their religion, and Mother Earth has become their god. Therefore, they have no problem offering human sacrifices to appease their god. One of their leaders recently commented that most of the world's population are worthless eaters—breathing in valuable oxygen and breathing out poisonous carbon dioxide!

"People are already becoming desperate. Shoplifting, stealing horses, and rustling cattle are on the rise across America. That's what prompted me to install the corral and barn alarm systems. Of course, the food shortages we've seen thus far will pale compared to when the Third Horseman of the Apocalypse is unleashed. Millions will die from starvation due to war, natural disasters, and the intentional destruction of the miracle molecule that makes all plant, animal, and human life possible.

"You know, Macy, a few years ago, I would have considered such talk a ridiculous conspiracy theory, but the fact that hundreds of miles of Carbon Capture pipelines are being laid across America's breadbasket states suggests that it is a real conspiracy. The pipelines consist of giant CO2 Reduction Machines that suck the CO2 out of the atmosphere and then transport it to underground storage tanks. I'm not sure how many pipelines are in the works, but just this one pipeline will tremendously impact the animal and human food supply that America and much of the world depend on!"

"Jack, what do you suppose the extracted CO2 will be used for?"

"Well, Macy, CO2 has multiple uses. It is used in beverages, welding, and fire extinguishers. It is used as a refrigerant and to create plastics and polymers. Plus, CO2 is used in euthanasia."

Macy frowned, "Did you say euthanasia, Jack?"

"Yes. Carbon dioxide has been used extensively for mass euthanizing during disease eradication. For instance, in 2022, an outbreak of bird flu led to the euthanization of millions of chickens and turkeys. Typically, the buildings that house the animals are sealed, and carbon dioxide is pumped in until the animals stop breathing."

Macy rubbed her forehead, "Jack, Adolf Hitler loaded people into train cars and pumped in carbon monoxide, killing multitudes. Do you think that America could get to that point?"

"I hope not, but it wouldn't surprise me if it does."

"Who controls the food supply controls the people. Who controls the energy can control whole continents. Who controls money can control the world!"

"Macy, I should have warned you. Once I get going on this subject, I cannot stop until I've said my peace and my blood stops boiling!"

"Don't apologize, Jack. I find it interesting, albeit a scary lesson on the climate change fanaticism that has invaded our society. I wish more Americans had your passion and enthusiasm in discovering the truth."

Jack smiled and motioned, "Come on, Macy, it's time to take you on a tour of my home."

Exploring the three-story log home took the best part of an hour. "Jack, your home is amazing—it's stunning! Now I understand why the twins couldn't stop talking about it."

"Thank you, Sis, but I saved the best for last," Jack said as he winked at his sister.

Macy followed her brother across the great room and down a long Terry Redlin picture-framed hallway. Her eyes widened, and her eyebrows arched as she noticed the dual black cherrywood doors at the end of the hallway. Golden door handles and frosted glass panels etched with the words *Sweet Dreams* pleasantly contrasted the tall, dark cherry doors.

Jack swung open the doors, and Macy's jaw dropped, "Is this the Master Bedroom?"

"Yes, it is Macy."

Macy strolled across the oak flooring and sat on one of the two leather recliners surrounding the stone fireplace. "What a gorgeous fireplace."

Jack flipped a switch, and flames danced between the logs. "Listen closely, Macy, and you'll hear the flames crackle like a real wood fire!"

"Yeah, I hear it. It reminds me of when we were kids sitting around the campfire on Crystal Lake."

Macy stood and walked across the room, running her finger along the brass railing that led to the master bath. She opened the door, and her eyes were drawn to a lighted makeup desk and mirror that looked like something a movie star would have. Next to it, a sauna and a tanning bed decorated the black and white marble floor tile. Macy took a few more steps, peeking around the wall that hid the bathroom essentials. Her voice rose as she noticed the walk-in bathtub, *"I have always wanted one of those!"*

Macy exited the master bath, noticing two walnut bookcases forming an archway entrance to a supersized walk-in closet filled with Eva's dresses, high heels, blue jeans, and hiking boots. "Macy, you and Eva are about the same size. I think she would like it if you helped yourself to her wardrobe."

Macy held a purple dress to her neck and swayed in front of the mirror. Jack blinked away the tears as memories of Eva flooded his mind. "You know, Macy, Eva didn't purchase her clothing at the local Target store."

"I can see that, Jack; these dresses are beautiful!"

Macy exited the closet, her gaze drawn to images of raccoons, fawns, and bear cubs carved into the walnut headboard that rose from the bed to the ceiling. She walked over and flopped down on the luxurious king-size bed. "Jack, you sure do know how to spoil a girl."

"All of this was Eva's doing, not mine," Jack said. "She designed it all. It's over the top for me, but she loved it. I haven't slept in here since the rapture. It's a shame to let this beautiful bedroom go to waste. I bet you'd enjoy Eva's Sweet Dreams bedroom creation. Perhaps you should try it out and see if it's to your liking!"

"Jack, are you suggesting that I should spend the night?"

"No, I'm asking if you'd consider calling this place your home. I know the twins would love living here, and you'd love it too. There's plenty of room, and the Master Bedroom will be all yours. You will not be my guest. It will be my home and your home. Mi-Casa, Su-Casa!"

"Well, Jack, that's a pretty tempting offer."

"Macy, things are going to get nasty real quick. I have a friend, a Border Patrol Officer, who told me that the President's refusal to close and secure the border has resulted in 129 countries emptying their prisons and insane asylums and sending them to the southern border. It won't be long before hardened criminals and nut jobs will be roaming our streets. Living off the grid on these 120 acres will be much safer and more secure than living in the city.

"I've got an independent water well and a backup solar-powered generator system in case the city's electrical grid goes down. We could plant a large garden to feed the entire Tribulation Force congregation. Plus, the longhorn steers I raise are bound to taste much better than the synthetic meat and mealworms the climate change demagogs wish to force down our throats!

"Furthermore, Jesus warned that earthquakes will strike in various places. If one does strike Hideaway Falls, you'll be much safer here than at your house because this log home is classified as earthquake-resistant. Each of the log's tongue and groove design absorbs the earth's vibrations like car shocks absorb road bumps. So this home may still be standing when others in the city have collapsed into a pile of rubble!

"Well, Macy, what do you think?"

Macy adjusted the pillow under her head as she lay on the bed pondering Jack's proposition. "Jack, I would love to live here—but those mirrors on the ceiling got to go!"

Jack smiled as he picked up the remote off the nightstand and handed it to Macy, "See that red button on the left; press it."

Macy's eyes widened as the silver reflection faded to black, "That's cool!"

"Press it again," Jack said.

Macy giggled like a schoolgirl, "Good heavens, it will be like sleeping under a star-filled night sky."

Macy stood, giving her brother a hug and a peck on the cheek. "Jack, I'm sold on the idea! Let's go tell the boys—they'll go positively crazy!"

"You discuss it with the twins, I'll be in the living room."

"Okay, Jack, see you in a few."

Ten minutes later, Macy and the smiling twins entered the living room. Jack was watching TV and laughing. "What's so funny?" Macy asked.

Jack grinned, "Guess what happened to the Mayor who outlawed talking about Jesus in public? He was riding his bicycle at the County Fairgrounds when a pickup truck hit a big mud puddle and drenched the Mayor with mud and water. The reporter asked him if he got the license plate number. He said, 'Are you kidding? My glasses were covered in slimy mud. I was lucky I didn't crash!'

The twins high-fived one another, and Macy giggled, "Who says God doesn't have a sense of humor?"

Chapter Twelve

The Samson Option

Dusty Rhodes and his reporting team were onboard the World News Network Company Jet, destination Jerusalem, Israel. Sergius Alexander had invited Dusty to a top-secret summit to meet with Israel's Prime Minister and Israeli Defense Force Commanders. It was a twelve-hour flight, providing time to watch a movie, take a snooze, and shoot the breeze.

Mike got out of his seat and approached Dusty. "Hey Dusty, remember when I offered to research the Continuationists versus the Cessationist controversy?"

"Yeah, what did you find out?"

Dusty slid over a seat, and Mike sat next to him. "Well, I discovered some fascinating details about modern-day apostles and prophets. First, according to Acts 1, verses 21 to 26, to qualify for the office of apostleship. One must have lived at the time of Jesus. Starting with the baptism of Jesus by John and then had been an eye-witness of His death, resurrection, and ascension." So, if today's self-proclaimed apostles aren't at least 2,000 years old, they are liars and deceivers."

Dusty chuckled, "Yeah, there are a lot of windbag preachers on the television and YouTube, but I don't think any of them is windy enough to blow out 2,000 birthday candles!

"You know, Mike, Jesus did warn that many FALSE APOSTLES and FALSE PROPHETS would arise in the last days. The number of them that have come on the scene this past decade is astounding."

"Mike nodded, "Isn't that the truth!

"I also discovered that of the hundreds of self-proclaimed prophets on TV, the internet, and in churches. Most, if not all, do not pass the biblical test of a true prophet. According to Deuteronomy 18, verses 21 to 22, the test of a true prophet is a 100 % success rate. Anyone who claims to be a prophet of God but whose predictions fail to come to pass, even once, is a false prophet!

"Dusty, if you remember when Donald Trump ran for President for the second time. Nearly every self-proclaimed prophet and apostle predicted he would win the election again and become the 46th President of the United States. No doubt they figured it was a shoo-in, but guess what? Every one of them was wrong! Trump had to vacate the White House to make room for the new President.

"The truth of God's Word is that no apostles and prophets exist today because they are no longer needed. God's Word tells us that Christianity is "built upon the foundation of the apostles and prophets, Jesus Christ himself being the chief cornerstone" (Ephesians 2 verse 20). Anyone familiar with construction knows that a FOUNDATION IS LAID ONLY ONCE. There is no second-floor or third-floor foundation.

"Furthermore, according to 2 Corinthians 12 verse 12, the proof of apostleship is the ability to perform MIGHTY SIGNS, WONDERS, AND MIRACLES. Unquestionably, no one today can perform the signs, wonders, and mighty deeds as did the first-century apostles. And unlike the modern-day apostles and prophets in the New Apostolic Reformation and the Charismatic and Pentecostal churches. The biblical apostles didn't require a raised stage, special mood-setting music, lighting, or sound effects to perform those miracles.

"Plus, unlike today, everyone who received healing stayed healed, and no one was ever sent back home in their wheelchair!

"I'm not saying that God doesn't heal today; God does answer prayers. I'm saying that God doesn't heal through those charlatans, deceivers, and liars. It's remarkable that even though the predictions made by these self-proclaimed apostles and prophets seldom come to pass. Tens of thousands of deceived Christians give millions to support their ministries and mansions!"

Dusty turned to Mike with a concerned look, "Mike, I can see you did your homework, but let's continue this conversation later. I'm concerned about Alan. He hasn't said anything since we left New York ten hours ago."

Dusty squeezed past Mike onto the aisle and approached Alan Qasim, his teammate. "Is it okay if I sit beside you for a while?"

"Suit yourself," Al said while mindlessly staring at the floor.

"Al, I'm surprised you didn't chime in on the conversation; that's unlike you. Is everything okay?"

Alan hesitated momentarily, "Well, to tell the truth, Dusty, things right now are not good. I spoke to my mother on the phone last night and told her I became a born-again believer in Jesus Christ, and that I know beyond a shadow of a doubt that I will one day live in paradise. I told her that she and the family could have that same assurance if they placed their faith in Jesus.

"My mother started crying and then screaming at me, saying I was a disgrace to the family. I heard my father say, 'Tell my son that if he's a Christian, he is no longer my son! He has dishonored his family's good Muslim name. Tell him never to return home unless he is willing to renounce Christ!

"I told my mother that I will never deny Christ—No matter what!

"My father grabbed the telephone from her and cursed at me. Telling me that he will kill me if he ever sees me again. He said I should have counted the cost before converting to Christianity. He said, 'Don't you dare come home unless you first renounce Jesus

Christ and repeat the Shahadah: 'There is no god but Allah, and Muhammad is his prophet.' Then he hung up the phone."

Dusty swallowed, "Do you think your father would really attempt to kill you?"

"Yes, I do, it's called an "honor killing. He believes that it is his religious duty to kill me, but I'm not worried because my family lives far away."

"Alan, who would your father be honoring in killing you?"

"The god of Islam, Allah!"

Dusty shook his head, and his brow creased, "Alan, you did nothing worthy of death. You're not an evil criminal. You are an innocent person."

"Dusty, you don't understand. In Islam, if you are a non-Muslim, you are not considered innocent. You are the worst of sinners.

"Do you remember when the Hamas terrorists dragged civilian victims behind motorcycles and paraded the murdered bodies through the streets in pickup trucks while sitting on top of them?"

"Yes, that was disgusting and gruesome; why did they do that?"

"For the same reason, deer hunters show off their prize kill and mount the animal's head on the wall. To the Islamist, killing an infidel is not murder, but a trophy."

Dusty raised his brow, "But I thought that Muslims believed in the Ten Commandments of God. You know, "Thou shall not lie, steal, murder, covet another man's wife, etcetera?"

"Muslims believe that Allah revealed the Ten Commandments to Moses on Mount Sinai and are virtues shared by all three Abrahamic faiths, Judaism, Christianity, and Islam. Radical Islam, however, believes that the latter Quranic war verses abrogate the earlier peace verses concerning infidels. Therefore, the Ten Commandments (or similar commandments in the Quran) pertain to how Muslims should treat other Muslims, but it does not apply to non-Muslims.

"This radical Islamic ideology is why so many young Muslim men desire to wage jihad against non-Muslims. They have been brainwashed into believing that God wants them to plunder, rape, and kill infidels. The females kidnapped during jihad are the reward of the jihadist, to be humbled sexually as often as he desires.

"Furthermore, jihadis are taught that if he is killed in battle against the infidels, seventy-two virgins and rivers of wine await him in Paradise. And their martyr's death guarantees their family will also be granted Paradise!"

Dusty shook his head, "That is quite the incentive, but it amazes me how anyone can be so gullible as to believe that God wants them to rob, rape, and kill people! I'm surprised more Muslims don't defect from the faith."

"Dusty, I think people would leave Islam by the droves if the penalty for leaving Islam wasn't death!"

"Well, Alan, I would rather take my chances of being killed than end up in hell. Jesus said, "Do not fear those who kill the body but cannot kill the soul. But rather fear God who can destroy both soul and body in hell."

A tear spilled from Alan's eye, and his voice quivered, "I love my family, and that is why I told them about Jesus!"

Dusty swallowed, "I'm so sorry to hear that your family has disowned you, but don't forget you have a second family right here on this plane. And in case you haven't noticed, someone on this plane has a crush on you!"

Alan lifted his gaze from the floor and glanced at Dusty, "Do you mean Olivia?"

"That's right, brother."

Alan smiled slightly and said with an upbeat voice, "Perhaps I will ask her to sit with me on the flight back. Now that I'm not a Muslim, I can date whenever and whomever I wish, and besides, I think Olivia is sweet, smart, and attractive."

The World News Network Company Jet circled the Ben Gurion Airport, and a few minutes later, the sound of screeching tires touching down on the tarmac echoed through the Jet. The team exited the plane and then were shuttled to the King David Hotel in Jerusalem.

Dusty located his room, swiped the key card, and entered his luxury suite. He unpacked, showered, and lay on the bed watching iTV 24 Evening News. Six hours later, Dusty woke to the buzzing sound of his phone. He glanced at the clock on the end table; it was Monday, Seven O'clock AM, "Hello, Dusty Rhodes speaking."

"Mr. Rhodes, this is Amir Tavor. I am head of the Israeli Secret Service. A security team will be at your door in exactly five minutes. They will be dressed in light blue coveralls and wearing a cap that says Apex Plumbing. They will escort you to the meeting. That is all for now, goodbye."

Knock, knock.

Dusty opened the door and invited the two agents in. They flashed Dusty their Secret Service identification and handed him matching apparel. Dusty slid the blue coveralls over his shirt and pants and put on the Apex Plumbing cap.

The agents escorted Dusty down the elevator, past the restaurant, and out of the hotel exit. A nondescript white service van pulled up, and the three entered through the sliding side door. Dusty was greeted by Amir Tavor, blindfolded, and driven to an undisclosed location. The van took several turns to ensure no one was following and then pulled into an underground garage and the blindfold was removed.

Dusty was escorted to a high-security conference room and introduced to the Israeli Prime Minister and Defense Force Commanders: Army General Abrams, Navy General Herzl, and Air Force General Lavine.

Ten minutes later, Sergius Alexander walked through the door. Dusty sucked in a sharp breath and released it when he noticed that Sergius's pyromaniac partner, Eli Isaa, wasn't with him. Sergius walked to the table, "Mr. Prime Minister, it is nice to see you again.

Generals, please take a seat. Thank you for meeting with me on such short notice and at such an early hour. I will get right to the point.

"What I wish to share with you concerns your national security and, quite possibly, your national survival. My position as the Superior General of the United Nations Security Force has provided me with an international intelligence-gathering network that is the best in the world. I have undercover operatives in every nation. A trusted source has informed me that the citizens of Israel are in imminent danger of an all-out attack from a confederation of radical militias coming from Iran, Iraq, Yemen, Lebanon, Syria, and terrorists living in Israel.

"Presently, the opposition has an arsenal of 150,000 rockets and missiles ready to fire at a moment's notice. Syria recently acquired 10 Russian-made Game-Changer Mobile Missile Launchers and 200 Iskander missiles. The Iskander missiles can strike any city in Israel with near-pinpoint accuracy. Each missile is fitted with thermobaric warheads that will be launched from Damascus targeting dozens of the most populated cities in Israel."

Army General Abrams rose to his feet, "Mr. Alexander, I must interrupt you for a moment?"

Sergius's eyes narrowed as he stared at General Abrams, "Say your peace, General."

"The Israeli Defense Force is keeping a close watch on the terrorist groups and is well aware of the gathering storm in Damascus. I don't know where you get your intel, but Israeli intelligence is unaware of any thermobaric missile system acquisition!"

Sergius's eyes narrowed even more in unspoken arrogance, *How dare the General question me! Who does he think he is?* He cleared his throat, "General Abrams, I am fully aware that Israeli intelligence is among the best in the world, but it is not all-knowing—it is not God. My position as the Superior General of the United Nations Security

Force provides exclusive access to connections and insider information that no one else has.

"The Game Changer Mobile Launchers and Iskander Missiles were acquired over the past three years. They were shipped piecemeal in inconspicuous boxes, crates, and containers to avoid detection and then reassembled in buildings that resemble three-story apartment buildings, not military facilities.

"It is a secret operation that the terrorists have dubbed *Operation Lightning Strike*. Israeli intelligence, perhaps, is not as intelligent as you think!"

Dusty raised a hand, "Sorry to interrupt, but I have a question."

"Yes, Mr. Rhodes."

"What is a thermobaric warhead?"

The Prime Minister glanced at General Herzl, "Would you please address Mr. Rhode's question?"

"Yes, sir, Mister Prime Minister. Mr. Rhodes, a thermobaric weapon, is a two-stage munition. The first-stage charge distributes an aerosol cloud of carbon-based fuel particles. A second charge ignites that cloud, creating a massive fireball, a huge shock wave, and a vacuum as it sucks up all surrounding oxygen. The blast wave lasts significantly longer than a conventional explosive and can vaporize humans. It is not as powerful as a nuclear weapon, but it is the closest thing to it!"

Sergius Alexander looked at the Prime Minister, "May I continue?" He nodded affirmatively, and Sergius continued, "The attack will consist of a land, sea, and air assault ambushing Israeli citizens and engaging in gun battles with Israeli forces. The lightning-quick attack will include militants in motorboats and paragliders storming Israeli beaches and civilian neighborhoods. A coordinated ground attack by jihadis on dirt bikes and ATVs equipped with anti-tank RPGs will attack Israeli ground forces. Simultaneously, an aerial assault will commence with dozens of attack drones (UAVs) striking Israel's Air Force bases, and thousands of rockets and missiles will be fired from several locations into Israeli cities.

"The barrage of rockets and missiles will continue until the Iron Dome and David's Sling Defense Systems are exhausted. Then, with no defensive interceptor missiles left, several waves of Russian Iskander thermobaric missiles will be launched from Damascus. If everything goes as planned, hundreds of thousands of Israeli citizens will die, dozens of Israeli cities will be ablaze, and the Syrian forces will have recaptured the Golan Heights. From there, the Syrian Arab Army, consisting of one hundred thousand soldiers, will invade Israel!

"Since Israel is only 290 miles long and 85 miles across at the widest point, such an attack will be devastating. I suspect that your nation's only hope of surviving such an onslaught is to do something you have never done before, and that is to employ the Samson Option!"

The Prime Minister turned to Dusty, "Mr. Rhodes, just in case you are unfamiliar with the Samson Option. You should know that in a scenario that threatens Israel's existence, we have warned its enemies that, if necessary, Israel will use the Samson Option, which includes nuclear weapons!"

The Prime Minister turned his attention to Mr. Alexander, "Considering your military and political background, I appreciate your assessment, Sergius. Israel, however, does not have many friends as it is. The nations get upset with just a few civilian casualties. Imagine the world's reaction if we employ the Samson Option on Damascus, a city of over two million!"

Air Force Commander General Lavine got up and stood beside the Prime Minister, "Mr. Alexander, with all due respect, the Samson Option is a last resort option. We've had great success in defending our nation using conventional weapons. Within minutes of the first missile launch, Israel's Air Force fighter jets and bombers will be on their way to Damascus. The Air Force's advanced radar system will detect the location of the thermobaric missile launching sites and destroy them."

"Thank you, General Lavine, for your assessment. I realize that strategy has been effective in the past, but it will not work this time," Sergius explained. "The thermobaric missile attack will come in waves of ten missiles. Each of the ten Game-Changer truck-mounted launchers accommodates two Iskander missiles that can be launched in under 60 seconds. Immediately after the missile launch, the second wave of ten missiles will be fired. After each firing, the mobile launchers will be driven to an undercover reload facility. Providing little time for the Israeli Air Force to detect, locate, and respond. This fire-and-hide strategy will be repeated over and over until all 200 thermobaric missiles are launched at Israeli targets.

"Furthermore, the Game-Changer Mobile Launchers have been placed in civilian neighborhoods throughout Damascus to ensure success. The enemies of Israel have witnessed the extreme measures Israel often takes to avoid civilian casualties. Therefore, they are gambling the Israeli Defense Force will not use the Sampson Option for fear of worldwide criticism."

Sergius Alexander refocused his attention back to the Prime Minister. "I realize that Damascus is home to over two million people, but Israel is home to almost nine million. No doubt, two million people are a lot of casualties, but you will be killing tens of thousands of the world's worst terrorists!

"Furthermore, I'm sure the world can be convinced of the necessity of using nuclear weapons. In fact, it's the reason I insisted that Dusty attend this meeting. Dusty and his team will be reporting live as the attack occurs. The world will not believe the Israeli account of this battle, but they will believe World News Network's most trusted reporter, Mr. Dusty Rhodes."

Sergius stood and then walked around the table, tossing a large envelope in front of the men. "Gentlemen, inside you'll find photos and a flash drive video of Iskander Missiles being loaded onto the

Game Changer Mobile Launchers in Damascus. Dusty will air the pictures and video during the attack, leaving no doubt of the necessity of Israel using nuclear weapons.

"You must, however, not strike preemptively. Your response must be one of a defensive posture to justify the use of nuclear weapons. Northern Israel cities will undoubtedly suffer casualties from Hezbollah's missile assault from Lebanon, but most of Israel will be spared.

"That is all I have to say, gentlemen. The ball is in your court!"

The Prime Minister rose from the chair, shaking Mr. Alexander's hand, "I'm curious as to the reason you're giving us this heads-up warning. I mean, what's in it for you, Sergius?"

"Mr. Prime Minister, I can see that you haven't yet figured out who I am. Perhaps you should ask your Rabbis about me. People are not always who they appear to be. The Muslims believe I am on their side, and I am to a degree. However, I am not on the side of radical Islam. The Quran and the Hebrew Scriptures reveal that God desires world peace. World peace, however, will not come about as long as radical Islamists misinterpret the words of the Quran and believe that Allah wants them to wage jihad against everyone who does not follow their militant version of Islam.

"The terrorist groups participating in *Operation Lightning Stike* are opposed to the *Covenant of Land-for-Peace Treaty* I brokered between Israel and the Muslim nations. Insisting that the entire 35-acre Temple Mount area belongs to the Muslims. Therefore, they are intent on preventing the construction of the Jewish Temple and, thus, must be eliminated!"

"I can't argue with that," the Prime Minister said. "The world certainly would be far better and safer without terrorists. No one knows that better than Israel. I appreciate the heads-up. The Generals and I will carefully consider and evaluate everything you shared in determining the best way to protect Israel from the coming storm."

Sergius walked to the door, then turned, facing the Prime Minister and IDF generals. "I do have one final word of warning, gentlemen. The attack will commence in two days."

General Lavine's eyes widened, "Two days! That doesn't give us much time to prepare."

"Yes, General, two days. The surprise attack was scheduled to start in 10 days, but minutes before my arrival, I was notified that *Operation Lightning Strike* would commence at 1800 Hours MST, 6 PM, Wednesday evening."

Sergius motioned to Dusty, "Mr. Rhodes, may I speak to you in the hall?"

"Sure."

Sergius Alexander and Dusty exited the conference. "Thank you, Dusty, for attending. I have an area adjacent to the Temple Mount reserved for you and your team to report from. It is close to a bomb shelter, just in case. Here is the name and phone number of the person who will assist you and supply your needs."

"Thank you for the opportunity, Mr. Alexander."

"You're welcome. Goodbye, and good luck!"

Amir Tavor approached Dusty, handing him the blindfold. "The agents will escort you back to the Hotel, are you ready to go?"

Dusty slid the blindfold over his eyes, "Yes."

The Prime Minister and the Generals discussed the situation in the conference room. Finally, all agreed that the Sampson Option was on the table if the attack began at 6:00 PM and went down as Sergius Alexander predicted. The Prime Minister dismissed the Generals with these words: "Gentlemen, pray for peace, but prepare for war!"

Dusty and the two Secret Service agents returned to the King David Hotel. They exited the van and strolled by the Hotel restaurant on the way to Dusty's room. Dusty stopped and peeked inside the door, expecting to see his team. He scanned the area left and right. He didn't see his team but noticed God's two witnesses eating breakfast. Dusty's voice rose excitedly, "There's Moses and Elijah. I got to talk to them!"

The Secret Service agent grabbed Dusty's arm, "Sorry, Mr. Rhodes, but our orders are to escort you back to your room. You can talk to your friends some other time, but right now, the only place you are going is to your room."

The agent tightened his grip, "Come on, let's go!"

"Okay, okay, don't get so excited," Dusty mumbled.

The two agents escorted Dusty to his room and watched him enter. Dusty closed the door and quickly dialed Mike's number, it rang two times.

"Hey, Dusty, what's up?"

"Moses and Elijah are in the restaurant! Get the crew and meet me there, pronto."

Dusty hurried back to the restaurant, hoping to meet and interview God's two witnesses. He entered and surveyed the tables. "Shoot, Moses and Elijah are gone—stupid Secret Service agents!"

The team arrived minutes later, and everyone sat at the corner table. Mike laughed and asked, "Dusty, did you get a new job?"

Dusty looked curiously at Mike and then remembered that he was wearing blue coveralls and the Apex Plumbing cap. Dusty removed the cap and looked to his left and right, ensuring no one was close enough to listen in. He spoke softly, telling his team about the upcoming battle and that Damascus may get Nuked.

Alan's eyes widened, and his countenance fell as he stared at Dusty. "Al, what's wrong? You look like you've seen a ghost."

Alan covered his face with his hands and shook his head, "My family lives in Damascus!"

Dusty swallowed hard, "Call your family and tell them to pack their suitcases and get the heck out of there!"

"I can't, Dusty. My family has disowned me and has blocked my phone calls and text messages. Even my sister, who usually texts me daily, will not speak to me. I have no way to contact them. They will all perish and end up in hell."

"Olivia stood and placed her hand on Alan's shoulder, "Don't worry, Al, all of us will pray and ask God to intervene."

Everyone, even Nicole, bowed their heads and prayed. "Please, God, don't let Alan's family perish!" The team opened their eyes, and Dusty said, "Alan, I've got an idea! Come with me."

"Where are we going?"

"To the Temple Mount to talk to Moses and Elijah. It's less than a mile from here. I'm pretty sure that is where we will find them. Let's go."

Dusty and Alan dashed out of the King David Hotel and sprinted to the Temple Mount. Ten minutes later, they slowed to catch their breath. Dusty pointed, "There they are! They're talking with Misty Carmichael."

"That pretty blonde reporter?" Alan asked.

Dusty rolled his eyes, "Yes, Al, that's the one. Come on, let's go talk to them."

Misty looked up, "Dusty, what a pleasant surprise. You're not here to replace me, are you?" She asked with her fingers crossed behind her back.

"No, Misty, you're doing a great job. I need to speak to Moses and Elijah."

Moses glanced at Dusty, "No autographs."

"It's nothing like that, Mr. Moses. Please allow me to explain."

"We're all ears, son. Speak your mind."

"Misty, would you please excuse us? It's personal."

"Sure."

"Mr. Moses and Mr. Elijah, My name is Dusty Rhodes, and this is my friend and coworker, Alan Qasim. Alan is a recent Christian convert from Islam. His family lives in Damascus, and there is a good chance the city will be wiped off the map soon!"

Elijah interrupted, "No, Mr. Rhodes, your wrong. There is not a good chance that Damascus will be destroyed—its destruction is certain!"

Dusty looked curiously at Elijah, "I just came from a top-secret meeting about the upcoming battle. How in the world do you know about it?"

"I have a prophet friend in Heaven that goes by the name Isaiah. Perhaps you heard of him?"

Dusty's brow creased, "Do you mean Isaiah, the Old Testament prophet?"

"Yeah, that's the one," Elijah answered. "Isaiah wrote about the destruction of Damascus in the book that bears his name about 2700 years ago. It's the topic Moses and I will be preaching about on the Temple Mount over the next few days."

Moses smiled and placed his hand on Alan Qasim's shoulder, "Misty told us that our Temple Mount debut went viral. Everyone thought Elijah and my performance was pretty cool and that World News Network expects the entire world to be tuned in to the next broadcast. So, don't worry, brother, your family will be warned. What your family members do with that warning is up to them, but they will be warned."

Alan wiped away an escaped tear, "Thank you so much!"

Moses stood, "Gentlemen, please excuse me. I wish to continue conversing with Misty Carmichael—she is one fascinating lady!"

Dusty gave Elijah a quizzical look, "Did Moses say, 'Misty Carmichael is fascinating?'"

Elijah rolled his eyes, "Yeah. Go figure?"

Chapter Thirteen

Grand Opening!

The big day had arrived. The Grand Opening of the Tribulation Force Freedom Center. Macy hung the WELCOME sign on the entrance door as she watched the parking lot begin to fill. Jack informed the twins that only those with an invitation and their guests should be allowed entrance as a security precaution. The twins stood at the entrance to greet the left behind congregation, and Jamie's eyes grew as wide as his smile when he saw that one of the guests was Sierra McFarland.

Everyone took a seat and Macy switched on the microphone, "I'm so happy to see you again, and welcome guests. In a moment, my brother Jack will speak. Jack is a former Army Ranger Combat Instructor. He is an expert in hand-to-hand self-defense techniques, electronic surveillance, survival techniques, and various weapons.

"After Jack's presentation, my Son Jason will answer any questions you have about water baptism. We are having a baptismal service today, so it's important that you understand its purpose and significance. So, without further ado, please welcome my brother Jack."

Jack walked onto the platform and raised the microphone stand, "Hello, everyone, and welcome to the Tribulation Force Freedom Center. Before I begin my presentation, I want you to know that this place is not just a training center but a refuge, a sanctuary, and a mission center. Your safety and well-being are a priority. Enjoying the service is difficult if you're always looking over your shoulder, wondering if an evil or deranged person may walk through the door and start shooting. Don't worry; the doors are locked during service, and I'm always armed. So, please sit back and enjoy the service.

"Okay, let's get started. Everyone, do me a favor and raise your hand if you use any of these services: Microsoft Text Messenger, Google, Gmail, Hot Mail, Twitter X, Facebook, and the Metaverse. From the raised hands, it appears that about 90 percent of you use what I like to call "gotcha" services.

"Now raise your hand if you think that it's a good idea to let strangers know what you believe, where you live, where you go, the websites you visit, the things you purchase, the podcasts you listen to, the subject of your text, email, and phone conversations, and who your Christian friends and relatives are?

"I don't see any hands raised, so I assume you and I are on the same page. Instead of using those "gotcha" apps and services, I prefer to remain incognito as long as possible, and so should you. I suggest you ditch those "gotcha" services and switch to ones that don't track you.

"I recommend using the BRAVE WEB BROWSER or DUCK DUCK GO as the search engine. Switching to a private text messenger app such as SIGNAL and a private email server such as FASTMAIL. You can also add an extra layer of privacy by using a VPN to hide your IP address while searching the internet. These apps and services are FREE or inexpensive, and none track or spy on you. There are several private communications apps and services available. Whichever ones you choose, read the privacy info carefully and often.

"In my opinion, the 'gotcha' services can benefit the Christian in just one way. To confuse the enemy and lead them down the rabbit hole. It's easy to do. Just use the "gotcha" messaging apps to occasionally say something good and positive about Sergius

Alexander, the World Economic Forum, the United Nations, the New World Order, etc. The idea is to keep the surveillance hounds off your electronic trail whenever and wherever you tread.

"Whatever form of communication you use, remember that some words throw up red flags. Never use the words bomb, gun, bullets, unconstitutional, Antichrist, and especially not MAGA. The New World Order politicians are not interested in MAKING AMERICA GREAT AGAIN—THEY WANT TO DESTROY IT!

"Instead of communicating with words that may trigger a red flag. Substitute those words and phrases with less obvious ones, and encourage your friends and family to do so. For example, you can substitute the words,

Son of God *to* Son of Man.
Christian *to* Fisher-of-men.
President *to* Potato Head.
White House *to* Nut House.
Congress *to* Hell's Kitchen.
Deep State *to* Deep Blue Sea.
Guns and bullets *to* Hammer and Nails.

"The first-century Christians didn't have the technology we have to contend with, but they often lived under the threat of persecution. That's why the Christian "fish" symbol was invented. It was like a secret handshake, used to determine friend or foe. Of course, everyone knows what the fish symbol stands for today. So, if you have a fish emblem on your car, I suggest you remove it pronto. It will do nothing to win souls for Christ but will make you a target!

"Also, don't trust anyone just because they identify as a born-again believer. Make them earn your trust. The sign of a true believer, according to Jesus, is their love for Him will be greater than their love for friends, family, and even their own life. Don't forget Jesus' warning,

"Think not that I am come to send peace on earth: I came not to send peace, but a sword. For I am come to set a man at variance against his father, and the daughter against her mother, and the daughter in law against her mother in law. And a man's foes shall be they of his own household. He that loves father or mother more than me is not worthy of me: and he that loves Son or daughter more than me is not worthy of me. And he that takes not his cross, and follows after me, is not worthy of me. He that finds his life shall lose it: and he that loses his life for my sake shall find it." (Matthew 10 verses 34 to 39).

"If someone wishes to please their friends or family more than obey Jesus, it's a good indicator that they are not true believers. Don't forget that.

"Learning how to defend yourself has never been more critical than it is today. Especially important if the Jackass Party gets its way in revoking the Second Amendment Right to keep and bear arms. Every Sunday, I will teach one self-defense fighting technique that is easy to learn. The first self-defense technique I want to share with you is the Cross-eyed Duck. It's a corny name, but it is an effective defensive weapon.

"Please, everyone, hold up your hand, palm facing me. Now, fold your fingers so your hand looks like a duck head, and your fingers form the duck's beak. And slightly spread your fingers. Now, you're ready to defend yourself with quick jabs to the attacker's eyes. It causes instant pain and vision problems, giving you time to run and escape—that is the goal.

"Of course, if you have pepper or bear spray, use that instead. Just be sure you don't spray it into the wind. Unless you think your attacker will die from laughing so hard when the pepper spray blows back in your face!

"You don't want the attacker to see it coming, so practice the *Cross-eyed Duck Technique* using a quick draw, like Sheriff Matt Dillon in a Gun Smoke Western!

"Speaking of Sheriffs, the County Sheriff has incredible power. No one, not the Governor or even the President, can make the Sheriff enforce laws that he deems unconstitutional. So encourage Christians to run for Sheriff and then get out and vote!

"That's it for now. Next week, I will present a list of essential survival items to include in your Bug Out Bag and another self-defense technique. Now it's time to hear from the Son of the Preacher Man, my Nephew, Jason Rhodes.

"HOORAH!"

The Doctrines of Men – Verses – the Word of God!

"Thank you, Uncle Jack. I'm anxious to try out your Cross-eyed Duck self-defense technique. Can I get a volunteer? I'm joking. I probably would poke myself in the eye. So, I better stick with what I know best. I'm sure most of you are aware of the confusion and debate within Christendom over the purpose and significance of water baptism. I've studied the topic extensively and am here to answer any questions you may have. So, if you've got a question, please raise your hand."

Six hands went up, and Jason's eyes fell on the young lady with the long red curls. "Sierra McFarland, it's so nice to see you. Before you ask your question. May I ask you one first?"

"Sure, I guess."

"Sierra, my brother Jamie was wondering if you are still single and available. To tell the truth, Jamie never actually said that, but I'm pretty sure that's what he's thinking!"

Sierra smiled and blushed a little, "Yes, I'm single, and you can tell Jamie for me that I think he's cute!"

Jamie had a crush on Sierra since Junior High. He had planned on asking her out on a date, but something about her caused him to become tongue-tied in her presence. Perhaps it was because she had a reputation for refusing to date some of the best-looking jocks in school, and he figured that he'd be turned down as well. Whatever the cause of Jamie's shyness, Sierra's remark about his cuteness, apparently cured the problem. Jamie was sitting up straight and smiling like a lovestruck teenager.

Jason cleared his throat and snugged his necktie. "Sierra, since Jamie and I are identical twins, I suppose you must think I'm pretty cute too."

Sierra's red curls swung as she shook her head, "No. I always thought you were sort of a nerd!"

Everyone laughed.

"Ouch!" Jason said as he loosened his necktie. I guess I deserved that for putting you on the spot. Let's start over. Sierra, what's your question?"

"Well, Jason, I was raised as Lutheran and was baptized as an infant. Now that I'm a born-again believer, must I get baptized again?"

"Thank you for your question, Sierra.

"The reason Lutherans baptize infants is the same reason Catholics do. Both have a fundamental misunderstanding of Original Sin. They believe the consequence of Adam's disobedience caused all people to die both *physically* and *spiritually*. Lutheranism teaches that even though babies appear cute and innocent, they are nevertheless sinful creatures in need of forgiveness! That, however, is not what the Bible teaches about infants and young children.

"Concerning the original sin of Adam, God's Word states:

> "Wherefore, as by one man [Adam] sin entered into the world, and death by sin; and so death passed upon all men, for that all have sinned: For until the law sin was in the world: **but sin is not imputed when there is no law**. Nevertheless, death reigned from Adam to Moses, even over them that had not sinned after the similitude of Adam's transgression, who is the figure of him that was to come" (Romans 5, verses 12 to 14).

"From these verses, we learn that when Adam (the representative and progenitor of the human race) sinned, physical death passed upon all men, for all have sinned. *Universally, all die: Sinless infants, moral people, religious people, equally with the depraved.* So, Adam's sin is the cause of physical death, but it is not the cause of spiritual death because **'sin is not imputed when there is no law.'**

Since infants and little children are too young to understand the Ten Commandments of God, they are not under the law because Scripture states that *sin is not imputed when there is no law*. Therefore, since infants have never transgressed God's law, they do NOT need to be reborn spiritually because they have never died spiritually!

"Universal sin is responsible for physical death, and personal sin—the breaking of the Ten Commandments—is responsible for spiritual death. The apostle, John, confirms this truth in 1 John 3 verse 4: 'Whosoever committeth sin transgresses also the law: *for sin is the transgression of the law.'*

"Commenting on this, the apostle Paul stated: "I was alive once without the law, but when the commandment came, sin revived, and I died" (Romans 7 verse 9). So, it is with us! We all are alive *once* without the law. That is, from the day we are born until we are old enough to comprehend sin, righteousness, and judgment (John 16 verses 8 to 11).

"Theologians refer to this age as the Age of Accountability. It is the age when our conscience starts to accuse or excuse our thoughts and actions in light of God's laws written in His Word and upon our hearts (Romans 2 verse 15). At that time, sin revives, and we die spiritually, and henceforth, are in need of spiritual rebirth.

"This misunderstanding of original sin concerning infants and young children is why Catholics and Lutherans invented infant baptism. Lutheranism teaches that baptism is a means of grace through which God forgives sins and gives saving faith to the infant. In an attempt to justify the doctrine biblically, they declare that Jesus Christ mandated infant baptism in the Great Commission of taking the Gospel to the whole world:

"Go, therefore, and make disciples of all nations, baptizing them in the name of the Father and of the Son and of the Holy Spirit, and teaching them to obey everything that I have commanded you." (Matthew 28 verses 19 to 20).

"Lutheranism contends that these verses teach that people, including infants, can become Christians through baptism. The problem with this interpretation is twofold. First, notice that the passage does NOT say, *Go therefore and baptize all nations, making them disciples.* It says, *'Make disciples of all nations, baptizing them.'* In other words, if preaching the Gospel results in Salvation, that person is to be baptized—not the other way around!

"The Great Commission recorded in the Gospel of Mark confirms that conversion must precede water baptism:

"Go into all the world and preach the gospel to every creature. He who believes and is baptized will be saved; but he who does not believe will be condemned" (Mark 15:15-16).

"Notice again the order of the Great Commission: Preach the Gospel to every creature, then baptize those who believe. Also, notice that the person that Jesus says "will be condemned" is not the one who is not baptized, but the one who does not believe!

"If the Lutheran interpreters can read infant baptism into the Great Commission, then I suppose that Jesus' command to preach the Gospel *to every creature* means that we should also preach the Gospel to *squirrels, rabbits, and cows!* "I'm being facetious because infant baptism is just as unbiblical and ineffective as preaching the Gospel to squirrels, rabbits, and cows.

"The second problem with this interpretation is that the Great Commission doesn't teach that water baptism can save the soul of anyone, regardless of age! It is believing the Gospel that saves the soul, not baptism. That is what Scripture teaches and why you will not find one example of infant baptism in the Bible—not one! Every instance of Christian baptism recorded after Jesus' death and resurrection was performed only on those who had first believed and confessed their faith in Christ.

"One such example of this is found in Acts chapter 8. Here, we read about Philip the evangelist's encounter with the Ethiopian eunuch. The Ethiopian man was sitting in his chariot reading the prophecy in Isaiah but didn't understand it. So, the man desired Philip to explain the passage to him. Phillip joined the man in the chariot, explaining that it was a prophecy about Jesus, and preached the Gospel to him.

"As they traveled, they came upon a pond, so the man said, *"See, here is water. What hinders me from being baptized?"* Philip responded, "If you believe with all your heart, you may. And the man answered and said, *"I believe that Jesus Christ is the Son of God.* So, he commanded the chariot to stand still. And both Philip and the eunuch went down into the water, and he baptized him." (Acts 8, verses 36 to 38).

"We learn four things from Philip's encounter.

1. It is believing the Gospel that saves the soul, not baptism.

2. Christian baptism is to be done to those who understand the gospel message, believe it with all their heart, and confess their faith in the Son of God.

3. Baptism should be done soon after conversion.

4. Baptism is to be done by immersion, not sprinkling.

"Immersion is important because it represents the believer's union with the Savior. Jesus died, was buried, and rose again. In like manner, Christians, too, have died to sin (pictured by being submerged under water) and then arise to walk in the newness of life (illustrated when rising out of the water).

"You'll not find one instance of infant baptism in God's Word because Christian baptism has nothing to do with Salvation but everything to do with the Christian walk.

"Know ye not, that so many of us as were baptized into Jesus Christ were baptized into his death? Therefore we are buried with him by baptism into death: that like as Christ was raised up from the dead by the glory of the Father, even so we also should walk in newness of life. For if we have been planted together in the likeness of his death, we shall be also in the likeness of his resurrection: Knowing this, that our old man is crucified with him, that the body of sin might be destroyed, that henceforth we should not serve sin" (Roman 6 verses 3 to 6).

"Water baptism is the Christian's first act of obedience in putting off the "old man" and putting on the new man. When you repent and believe the Gospel, you become a Christian. When you are baptized, you become a disciple of Christ, empowered by the Spirit to walk in the newness of life.

"All the confusion is eliminated when one's doctrine is built upon the truth of God's Word, rather than the traditions and doctrines of men. The doctrine of infant baptism is an unbiblical doctrine that has deceived millions into believing that they are on the straight and narrow. In reality, they are on the wide road leading to damnation!"

"So, the answer to your question, Sierra McFarland, is that your infant baptism counts for nothing. To be born of water, without first being born of the Spirit, is nothing more than a bath!"

Jason looked at the clock on the wall. "I have time for one more question."

One hand went up. It was Geraldine Moore. At 87 years old, Geraldine is the oldest member of the congregation. She is a tough old bird, lives alone, shovels her driveway in the winter, and mows her lawn with a non-motorized push mower in the summer. She says the reason she outlived her latest husband, Lester Moore: 'Is a shot of whiskey every day. No Less, No Moore.'

"Geraldine, what's your question?"

"Well, Jason, I was wondering if you are single and available because I kinda like nerds!"

Everyone laughed, and Jason stepped away from the microphone, shaking his head.

When the laughter finally subsided, and the redness faded from Jason's face. He returned to the microphone, *"Geraldine, thank you, but I think you're just too much for me to handle."*

Jason lifted his gaze, "Okay, everyone, listen up! My mother, Uncle Jack, Jamie, and I will all be baptized today, and so should you if you have become a born-again believer. The baptismal pool is full of warm water, and baptismal robes are hanging in the changing rooms, so you won't have to wear wet clothes on the way home.

"So, who wants to get baptized?"

Twenty hands went up!

The Tribulation Force Freedom Center Grand Opening was a success story in the making. It was fun, exciting, and educational. Surprisingly, out of the 50 Faith Calvary Chapel members left behind at the rapture, 38 showed up, and everyone brought one or more guests. Two people were saved, and twenty got baptized. Among those baptized was Sierra McFarland, which made Jamie's day. Even old lady Geraldine Moore took the plunge—giving Jason a wink as she rose from the water!

Chapter Fourteen

Operation Lightning Strike!

It's Wednesday in Jerusalem, Israel. World News Network reporter Dusty Rhodes and his team are preparing to broadcast *Operation Lightning Strike*, scheduled to commence at 1800 Hours MST. Moses and Elijah had just walked up the temple mount stairs and were about to speak. The camera zooms in as Moses waves his staff over the crowd.

Moses shouts, "Silence!"

The crowd listens intently. "You citizens of Israel that fear God, and you enemies of the Jewish state, harken unto the words of Isaiah, the prophet of the Most-High."

> Look, the city of Damascus will disappear! It will become a heap of ruins. The towns of Aroer will be deserted. Flocks will graze in the streets and lie down undisturbed, with no one to chase them away.
>
> The fortified towns of Israel will also be destroyed, and the royal power of Damascus will end. All that remains of Syria will share the fate of Israel's departed glory, declares the Lord of Heaven's Armies.
>
> In that day Israel's glory will grow dim; its robust body will waste away. The whole land will look like a grainfield after the harvesters have gathered the grain. It will be desolate, like the

fields in the valley of Rephaim after the harvest. Only a few of its people will be left, like stray olives left on a tree after the harvest. Only two or three remain in the highest branches, four or five scattered here and there on the limbs, declares the Lord, the God of Israel.

Then at last the people will look to their Creator and turn their eyes to the Holy One of Israel. They will no longer look to their idols for help or worship what their own hands have made. They will never again bow down to their Asherah poles or worship at the pagan shrines they have built. Their largest cities will be like a deserted forest, like the land the Hivites and Amorites abandoned when the Israelites came here so long ago. It will be utterly desolate.

Why? Because you have turned from the God who can save you. You have forgotten the Rock who can hide you. So you may plant the finest grapevines and import the most expensive seedlings. They may sprout on the day you set them out; yes, they may blossom on the very morning you plant them, but you will never pick any grapes from them. Your only harvest will be a load of grief and unrelieved pain.

Listen! The armies of many nations roar like the roaring of the sea. Hear the thunder of the mighty forces as they rush forward like thundering waves. But though they thunder like breakers on a beach, God will silence them, and they will run away. They will flee like chaff scattered by the wind, like a tumbleweed whirling before a storm.

In the evening Israel waits in terror, but by dawn its enemies are dead. This is the just reward of those who plunder us, a fitting end for those who destroy us (Isaiah 17, NLT).

"The prophecy I quoted will be fulfilled this day! Northern Israel will suffer casualties, and many villages will be set ablaze. BUT WOE

UNTO YOU BLASPHEMERS: ENEMIES OF THE GOD OF ISRAEL. SOON YOU WILL BE DEAD, AND DAMASCUS WILL BE NO MORE. The Grim Reaper is coming, and Hell is opening its mouth to receive you!"

Moses handed Elijah the microphone. Elijah's gaze fell upon Alan Qasim. "Mr. Qasim, please come up here. I believe you have something to say."

"You heard him, Alan. Go warn your family," Dusty said.

Moses lowered his staff, and the crowd made way for Al Qasim. He climbed the stairs, and Elijah handed him the microphone. Al said a silent prayer and then began to speak.

"What Isaiah the prophet wrote concerning the destruction of Damascus will happen. I know this because Isaiah made many prophecies, and everyone has come to pass just as predicted. The most famous of his predictions was the foretelling of an event that changed the world 2,000 years ago and continues to change lives today. These are the words of Isaiah.

> Therefore the Lord Himself will give you a sign: Behold, the virgin shall conceive and bear a Son, and shall call His name Immanuel.
>
> For unto us a Child is born, Unto us a Son is given; and the government will be upon His shoulder. And His name will be called Wonderful, Counselor, Mighty God, Everlasting Father, Prince of Peace.
>
> Of the increase of His government and peace, there will be no end. Upon the throne of David and over His kingdom, to order it and establish it with judgment and justice. From that time forward, even forever. The zeal of the Lord of hosts will perform this!" (Isaiah 7 verse 14, and 9 verses 6 to 7).

"Isaiah foretold that this child would be unlike any child ever born. He declared that a virgin would conceive and give birth. Who has ever heard of such a miraculous thing? A virgin becoming

Veloci-Rapture

pregnant and giving birth! Then Isaiah foretold that this person conceived of a virgin would be called *Wonderful, Counselor, The Mighty God, The Everlasting Father, The Prince of Peace, and Immanuel, which means God with us!* This was no ordinary child; this child was God incarnate!

"One hundred and nine biblical prophecies about this person's miraculous birth, ministry, miracles, rejection, crucifixion, death, burial, resurrection, and ascension were foretold hundreds of years before the child's birth. According to oddsmakers, the chance of anyone fulfilling all those prophecies is equivalent to picking the winning Powerball numbers three million times in a row! Only one person in history has fulfilled those prophecies, and that man is Jesus Christ!

"Why am I telling you this?

"So, you may believe that Jesus is the Son of God, the Savior of the world. And that the Bible is the true Word of God. What has been prewritten will be fulfilled just as Isaiah has proclaimed. The destruction of Damascus is at hand. Believe and escape with your life, or stay and die in your sins. The choice is yours!"

As soon as Al Qasim finished his speech, sirens began blasting throughout Israel, warning civilians to take shelter. The camera zoomed in on Dusty, "Hello, everyone. I'm Dusty Rhodes, and this is a World News Network breaking news report, broadcasting live from the Temple Mount in Jerusalem, Israel.

"I've been informed that radar has detected rocket launches from dozens of locations north of Israel. The Iranian-backed terrorist organization Hezbollah reportedly has an arsenal of 150,000 rockets and missiles. The Iron Dome, David Sling, and Israel's New Laser Defense System have been activated, and the Israeli Defense Force has scrambled jet fighters, helicopters, and attack drones to mitigate the onslaught coming from land, air, and sea.

"Please, friends, family, and viewers, don't worry about my safety. I'm wearing a bulletproof vest, and armed guards surround my team. Plus, a bomb shelter is close should things get too dicey. Also, don't worry about Moses and Elijah. The book of Revelation tells us they are invincible until their work on Earth is finished."

The night sky glowed as the Iron Dome intercepted rocket after rocket, and gun battles echoed through the streets of Jerusalem. Shwooofp, Hoooosh, BOOM! The ground shook, and a cloud of debris ascended as the police station a block away took a direct hit and burst into flames!

Dusty announced nervously, "The voice in my earpiece just informed me that the Shwooofp, Hoooosh sound followed by loud BOOM was not from an incoming rocket but a shoulder-launched rocket-propelled grenade (RPG). It appears that the terrorist group Islamic Martyrs Brigade is responsible and is on the move inside Israel."

Several more explosions and the rat-a-tat-tat sound of gunfire indicated that the enemy was getting closer and closer. Camera 5 zoomed in on a dozen motorcycle riders with handle-bar mounted rockets and machine guns approaching the Temple Mount. POP-POP-CRACK-CRACK-POP!

Dusty's voice rose, "The gunfire is getting close, I've been told to take shelter. The broadcast will resume when it is safe to come out." The team turned to run to the shelter. Shwooofp, Hoooosh, BOOM! The front of the shelter was blown to pieces. There was no place to hide, nowhere to run.

Moses and Elijah watched as the motorcycle warriors stormed the Temple Mount. One rider fired a rocket at God's two witnesses. The rocket flew between Moses and Elijah and hit the Dome of the Rock, blowing a massive hole in the golden roof. When the jihadist saw what he had done, he pulled his pistol from his holster and shot himself in the head.

Another rider drove his motorcycle up the Temple Mount stairs and confronted Moses and Elijah. He got off his cycle and pointed a strange-looking device at them. The device had a hose that ran over the man's shoulder and connected to a pack on his back.

It was a flame thrower!

The terrorist smiled sinisterly, "Which of you wants to be cremated first?"

Elijah pointed at Moses and said, *"Age before beauty!"* The man pointed the flame thrower at Moses, "Say your prayers!"

Moses lifted his staff, "Mr. terrorist, I will make you a trade. My staff for my life. I parted the Red Sea with this staff and performed many miracles with it."

The man extended his hand and commanded, "Give it to me!" Moses tossed the staff onto the ground, and it became a Cobra! The hissing snake slithered toward the man, stopped, and raised its head three feet off the ground. The Cobra displayed its deadly fangs—the terrorist's eyes bulged—the Cobra hissed and spit venom into the man's eyes. He screamed, rubbing his eyes, and stumbled backward, falling off the Temple Mount.

Moses grabbed the Cobra by the tail, and instantly, it transformed back into a wooden staff.

Elijah smiled, shaking his head, "Moses, that was awesome! I heard about spitting cobras, but I never saw one before."

Moses wiped the sweat from his brow, "That flame-thrower dude had me worried for a moment. The last time I transformed the staff into a viper was when I confronted the Pharaoh of Egypt in 1491 B.C."

Elijah laughed.

Meanwhile, the security guards protecting Dusty and his team were battling the motorcycle jihadis. They killed four of the twelve bikers, and the enemy killed four of the six guards. The team crouched behind a large stone as the rat-a-tat-tat sound of bullets ricocheted off the stone wall behind.

The eight bikers disappeared down the street and came charging back with guns blazing. The two guards were outnumbered and outgunned. The terrorist opened fire, the machine gun's full-metal jacket bullets penetrated the guards' vests, and their blood splattered Olivia's face and clothing. She coughed and gagged, almost throwing up.

"Olivia, are you okay?" Alan asked as he pulled her hair from her face. "No, I'm not okay, I'm scared to death." Alan used his sleeve to wipe the blood off her face, "Don't worry, Olivia. If the terrorists kill us, it will be a promotion. Unlike the terrorists, Heaven is our home, and our God is real."

The motorcycle gang surrounded the team and dismounted the bikes. The soldiers zip-tied the team's hands behind their backs. Then, he separated Dusty from the rest. The plan was to take Dusty hostage and kill the others.

The leader commanded that Alan, Olivia, Mike, and Nicole kneel before him. He slowly walked around the defenseless team and stopped in front of Nicole. He put his finger under her chin and lifted her head, "You're a pretty little thing, aren't you?"

Nicole smiled and then chomped down on his finger…

"Ouch!"

He drew the pistol from his holster and pressed the gun barrel against her forehead. Nicole's eyes widened, and she released her bite. He shook his hand, trying to relieve the pain, and then grabbed Nicole by the hair and dragged her alongside Dusty.

Nicole sprung to her feet and spit in his face. He slapped her hard, pulled a handkerchief from his back pocket, wiped off his face, and shoved it into her mouth. He smiled as he stared into Nicole's eyes, "*My comrades and I will take turns having fun with you before I kill you!*"

The man started the video recorder and stood before Alan, Olivia, and Mike. His men stood behind the reporting team, pulled knives from their sheaths, and pressed the cold, sharp steel against their throats.

Dusty's eyes widened, and a tear ran down Nicole's cheek. They knew what was coming next. The evil men were about to behead their teammates!

Dusty pleaded with the terrorists, but they snickered and laughed.

Dusty screamed, *"Please, God, rescue us!"*

Suddenly, a terrifying roar startled the terrorists. They looked up just in time to see a pride of lions leaping from the roof with claws extended and mouths snarling!

The lions pounced on the men, ripping out throats and tearing away flesh. Dusty and his team watched the Lions chase down the last two terrorists. They ran, trying to escape the bloodthirsty lions, but to no avail. It was a tug-of-war between the lions. The men screamed as the ferocious maneaters tore them limb from limb.

Soon, the screaming stopped, and the lions turned back, blood dripping from their jaws!

The lions approached, looking intently at the reporting team. The female lions stopped, but the large male lion walked closer and closer and closer. It opened its mouth wide, displaying its four-inch fangs, and let out a loud, blood-curdling roar!

The team trembled at the thought of being eaten alive. Moses and Elijah stood on the Temple Mount, hands raised, praying to the God of Heaven. Suddenly, a supernatural wave of peace and serenity flooded the team's souls, and the big cat's tail wagged.

The team looked into the eyes of the lion and, in unison, calmly said, "Thank you!"

The big lion turned back to the pride, and the lions walked away, dragging their prey with tails wagging.

Dusty scooped up the terrorist's knife and cut loose his and his teammate's zip-tie handcuffs.

His phone rang. It was the Prime Minister, "Dusty, are you and your team okay?"

"Yes, Mr. Prime Minister, but you'll not believe what happened."

"Dusty, I saw it all; we have cameras everywhere around the Temple Mount. I would never have believed it if I hadn't seen it with my own eyes. Those lions escaped from the Jerusalem Zoo yesterday! We can talk more about this later, but we have a war to win right now."

"Yes, Mr. Prime Minister, please update me so I can inform the world?"

"Well, Dusty, since the attack began, the IDF has destroyed multiple launch sites in Lebanon and killed hundreds of terrorists, but the rocket barrage continues. The Iron Dome and David's Sling defense systems intercepted 97 percent of the 4,900 missiles fired. Several towns and villages in northern Israel have been hit, so we have casualties.

"I just got off the phone with Syria's President. I told him the IDF is aware of his recent acquisition of the Russian-made Game-Changer Mobile Missile Launchers and the Iskander thermobaric missiles. I warned him to stay out of the conflict, and if he didn't, the Syrian Capital City would suffer unimaginable consequences."

"What was the President's response?" Dusty asked.

"The President said two words, 'Allahu Akbar!' Which means Allah is the greatest. Then he hung up on me. Can you believe it? The lives of two million of his citizens hang in the balance, and all he had to say to me was, Allahu Akbar!"

"Mr. Prime Minister, that sounds like a declaration of war, a religious war if you ask me!"

"It can mean nothing else, Dusty. We are prepared to use the Samson Nuclear Option if necessary. Stealth bombers are already in the air, heading for Damascus. We anticipate Syria will not initiate the attack until they believe the Iron Dome and David Sling interceptor rockets are exhausted. I've instructed General Lavine to drop the nuclear payload when the Iskander thermobaric missile launches are detected out of Damascus. We can tell if the missiles launched are equipped with thermobaric warheads by the massive airburst when intercepted.

"Thanks to Sergius Alexander's heads-up, the IDF has retained enough interceptor rockets to shoot down the first two waves of missiles. Once it is determined that the missiles launched are indeed thermobaric, then, and only then, will the nuclear payload be dropped on Damascus. Let's hope and pray that it doesn't come to that, but I am afraid it will!

"When you hear the Nuclear Advance Warning Sirens, which pulsate at a high pitch, that will be your cue to air the pictures and video that prove Syria's evil intentions. It will be time to expose Syria's plan of striking Israeli cities with weapons of mass destruction, justifying Israel's necessity of implementing the Samson Option."

"Mr. Prime Minister. I want you to know that you are doing the right thing. The Hebrew Scriptures tell us that God blesses those who bless Israel and curses them who curse Israel. Unfortunately, Islam doesn't believe in the God of the Bible, but many will become believers after Damascus falls. Muslim's faith in Allah will be shaken to the core when the God of the Bible defeats the god of Islam in this battle!"

"Thank you, Dusty. I do have some good news. IDF satellite videos reveal that tens of thousands of civilians have fled and are still fleeing from Damascus. Evidently, Moses and Elijah's warning speech had an impact."

"Thank you, Mr. Prime Minister. That is wonderful news."

Dusty downed a Coke and resumed the live broadcast. "Ladies and Gentlemen, I just spoke with Israel's Prime Minister. He stated that Israeli Intelligence obtained credible evidence that the Syrian Arab Armed Forces soon will enter the conflict.

"The Prime Minister is very concerned about Syria's entry into this war because Israeli Intelligence has learned that Syria now possesses 200 missiles equipped with thermobaric warheads capable of reaching every city in Israel. A thermobaric explosion is not as powerful as a nuclear explosion but is the closest thing to it. The explosion sucks oxygen out of the atmosphere, creating a massive fireball that can reach temperatures as hot as the sun's surface!

"The Prime Minister spoke with Syria's President, informing him he knew about his evil, clandestine plan, *Operation Lightning Strike*. Warning him to stay out of the battle, or the Capital City of Damascus would suffer inconceivable consequences.

"The Syrian President, however, is not backing down. He believes Allah will protect them, and Israel will be defeated once and for all. The Syrian Arab Army is on the march and is prepared to invade Israel immediately after the thermobaric missile attack.

"Live coverage of *Operation Lightning Strike* will resume after this special announcement from Israel iTV 24 News."

The Prime Minister looked steadfastly into the camera, "Citizens of Israel, please go to your local bomb shelter immediately. If a bomb shelter is unavailable, then stay at home. Close and seal your doors and windows as you have been trained, and hunker down until notified that it is safe to come out. Lastly, pray for God's favor and protection. Heaven knows we do not deserve His blessing or protection, but God is merciful, long-suffering, and faithful. His Word will be fulfilled just as the prophet Isaiah has declared it. Praise be to the God of Israel!"

An hour later, the Israeli Nuclear Advance Warning sirens were blaring. Dusty and the crew were advised to take shelter but continued the live broadcast under the Jerusalem night sky. Dusty surmised that the Temple Mount was an unlikely Syrian missile target since it is the holy site for Jews and Muslims.

At eleven o'clock, the night sky gave way to the thunderous sound of massive airbursts as the Iron Dome began intercepting one Iskander thermobaric missile after another. The Iskander missiles were launched ten at a time. Dusty started counting after the interception of the first wave, "That's five, Kaboom; six, Kaboom; seven, Kaboom."

Seven Iskander missiles were destroyed, creating massive, brilliantly bright airbursts. Three more missiles of mass destruction to intercept. Dusty continued counting as he watched the night sky, "Kaboom, that's eight; Kaboom, that's nine. One more to shoot down…"

Dusty watched and listened intently, but the sky remained black and silent. No interception, no airburst explosion. The Iron Dome had intercepted nine of the ten Syrian thermobaric missiles, but one evaded interception. A few moments later, the Israeli sky west of Jerusalem glowed an ominous and eerie orange. The Israeli city of Rehovot had taken a direct hit!

The reporting team knew what to expect next. The World News Network Satellite Camera zoomed in on the city of Damascus. Dusty swallowed hard, and his voice quivered as he witnessed the nuclear explosion. The brilliant flash of light produced by the atomic blast was almost blinding. The camera video revealed a giant mushroom-shaped cloud forming over the city of two million. The Damascus skyline quickly faded from velvet black to a hellish fiery red as it gave way to the destructive force. Minutes later, the blast's shockwave vibrated the earth below the reporting team's feet, and a hot wind blew through Jerusalem.

The nuclear blast incinerated everything within 35 miles of the Syrian Capital, including 100,000 Syrian soldiers amassed near the Israeli border. Soon the rat-a-tat-tat sound of small gunfire and distant explosions that had permeated the atmosphere fell silent, and the sirens ceased.

"He that touches you, touches the apple of My eye. Saith the Lord God of Israel."

Several hours later, the Israeli news media informed the nation's citizens that Israel was victorious and that it was safe to come out of the bomb shelters as the winds of heaven had dispersed the radioactive fallout.

Unfortunately, the victory was not a time of celebration but a time of mourning. The terrorist militias had murdered hundreds of civilians, and several Israel communities were decimated. The thermobaric missile that evaded the Iron Dome Defense System exploded in Rehovot, a city of 160,000 residents. The total number of Israeli lives lost was too soon to determine, but Israeli citizens were assured that Israel was doing everything possible to extinguish the fires and rescue any survivors.

The war was over, and Damascus, Syria, the world's oldest continuously inhabited city, was no more.

Chapter Fifteen

A Tale of Two Cities

Dusty and his team decided to meet for breakfast at the King David Hotel restaurant to celebrate Israel's victory and God's miraculous intervention. The Company Jet wasn't scheduled to fly back to Babylon, New York, for a few days. So, they had time to relax and perhaps visit a few Holy Land tourist sights.

Dusty closed his hotel room door, walked into the elevator, and pushed the lobby button. His phone rang. It was the Prime Minister. "Hello, Dusty. I'm calling to congratulate you and your team on a well-done job and tell you how blessed Israel is to have friends like you and Sergius Alexander.

If you remember, Sergius suggested I ask the Rabbis about him, so I did. The Rabbis told me they believe Sergius Alexander may be Israel's long-awaited Messiah. I know you are familiar with the Old Testament Prophets and Scriptures. So, I want to get your perspective on Mr. Alexander."

Dusty had to bite his tongue to avoid divulging Sergius Alexanders' true identity. He was no friend but Israel's archenemy. He pretends to be on Israel's side because he wants the Temple rebuilt so he can be worshipped in it! The time will come to reveal his evil intentions, but it was too soon.

"Mr. Prime Minister, you should ask Moses and Elijah that question!"

"That's a good idea, Dusty. If you've got a minute, I have a few more things to tell you."

"Sure, I'm walking to the restaurant right now, but you keep talking, and I will keep listening…"

The elevator door opened, and Dusty walked into the King David restaurant. The team noticed Dusty and waved him over to the table. Dusty finished the phone conversation and then took a seat. "Sorry, I'm late. I just got off the phone with the Prime Minister. He is so deceived. He thinks Sergius Alexander is manna from heaven and may even be Israel's Messiah."

Mike shook his head, "Man, Israel is in for a rude awakening!"

"You got that right," Dusty said. "According to the biblical prophets, Israel will not recognize Jesus Christ as the Messiah until the end of the Tribulation after the Antichrist and his armies have slaughtered two-thirds of the Jews, dashed their children into pieces, plundered their homes, and ravished their wives."

Nicole rolled her eyes, "Guys, can't we talk about something less depressing?"

Dusty smiled, "Sure. I do have some good news to report. Guess what, the Lions are back in the Zoo."

"That's great. Where did they find them?" Mike asked.

"At the Zoo, waiting for it to open! Can you believe it?"

"Talk about the providence and sovereignty of God. First, the lions escaped from the Zoo and then happened to show up at the right place and time to save our lives. And when the Lion's job was done, they returned home to the Zoo!"

Mike grinned, "That is crazy news. Especially considering that God's Word tells us in the book of Revelation that the only person able and worthy to open the end of the world scroll and break open its seals was Jesus, the Lion of the tribe of Judah!"

Nicole about fell off her chair, "Seriously, Jesus is called the Lion of the Tribe of Judah. That's remarkable."

Olivia stood, "Please pardon me for switching the subject, but I'm worried about Alan. I called his phone several times, but no answer. It's not like him to keep everyone waiting. Has anyone seen him?"

Everyone shook their head, "Not since last night."

"I'm going to go find him," Olivia said. She walked past several tables and was about to exit the restaurant when a tall, dark-skinned man suddenly grabbed her arm and spun her around. She looked up. His dark, piercing eyes revealed who he was. "Oh my goodness, it's you! Alan, you look amazing," Olivia said as she stood on her toes and kissed him on the cheek.

Alan was late because he had a head-to-toe makeover. His bushy black beard was transformed into a tight stubble beard. The thobe robe was replaced with blue jeans and a V-neck polo shirt. And the Muslim skull cap was gone, revealing his thick black hair.

"Come on, Al. Everyone is waiting."

Alan and Olivia approached the table. Olivia tilted her head toward Alan, "Hey, team, look what the cat drug in!"

Everyone did a double take.

Nicole was the first to comment on Alan's new look. "Congratulations, Alan, you no longer look like a freak!"

Dusty chuckled, "Al, all you need is a cowboy hat, and you'll look just like Dustin Lynch, the country-western singer."

Alan smiled, "Yeah, that's the name of the guy I pointed out in the magazine. I told the hairstylist I wanted to look just like him. She said, "It won't be easy, but I'll do my best."

"Kudos to the stylist, Alan. She did a good job."

"Thanks, Dusty, but I'm unsure if the stylist was a she. She looked like a lady but sounded like a guy. She said when she dated guys, her friends called her Jackie, but now that she dates girls, her friends call her Jack. I'm unsure which pronoun to use—it's so confusing!"

Everyone laughed.

The waitress approached, "Are you ready to order yet?"

"Order whatever your heart desires. I'm buying!" Al said.

Nicole's eyes widened, and eyebrows raised, "You gotta be kidding. Uncle Scrooge is buying breakfast."

"Yes, I'm buying. Order whatever you want—as long as it's under 10 dollars—it's celebration time! My mother called me this morning. My brothers, sister, and father are all alive. They're staying with relatives in a village a few hours' drive from Damascus. And guess what? They want to know more about Jesus!"

"Alan, that is great news. I'm so happy for you," Nicole said.

Everyone looked at Nicole with raised brows, "What are you blockheads staring at? I can be nice sometimes!"

"Nicole, I like that side of you," Mike said.

"Yeah, well, don't get used to it!"

Dusty placed his order and then rose from the table. "Hey guys, I'm going to call home; I'll be back in a minute." Dusty exited the restaurant and hit the speed dial on his phone. Macy answered.

"Hi, Mom, it's me."

"Dusty, I was just thinking about you. I was so worried. Is everyone okay?"

"Yes, everyone is fine. I can't wait to tell you about Moses and Elijah's exploits and the man-eating Lions. It was a mind-blowing experience!"

Mom raised her brow, "Did you say man-eating LIONS?"

"Yeah, six ferocious lions! The team and I are about to eat breakfast. So I will tell you about it later. How is everything at home?"

"So far so good. The boys and I are moving in with Uncle Jack today. It will be safer, and his place is out of this world. Wait till you see it.

"Oh, and guess what? Jamie is going on a date with Sierra McFarland."

"Well, it's about time. He was in love from the moment he laid eyes on her."

"Mom, tell everyone to be cautious. It is getting crazy everywhere. I got an email from Samantha's Pastor, Joshua. He said that ever since Sergius Alexander's speech at the United Nations, the enemies of Christ think it's open season on anyone who shares the Gospel.

Several churches in Joshua's town have been burnt to the ground. Some creeps even followed one of Joshua's church members to his home. Forced their way in, hog-tied him and his wife, and made them watch as they raped their daughter and sodomized his son!"

"Oh, my goodness, that's horrible. It sounds like the second horseman of the apocalypse has begun to ride!"

"I think you're right, Mom. It's starting to get nasty, fast.

"I gotta get going. I will call you later, Mom."

"Okay. Love you!"

"Love you too, goodbye."

A Walk in the Park

Jamie walked to the kitchen and kissed his mother on the cheek. "See you later, Sierra and I are going to Enchilada Momma's restaurant for lunch."

"Okay, Jamie, but keep your head on a swivel. The news reported that random crime in America has skyrocketed. Robberies are up 3000 percent, and violent crime is up 2000 percent. Plus, your Uncle Jack said that the President's refusal to secure the border has resulted in over 100 nations dumping their prison and insane asylum population on America's doorstep. Tens of thousands of notorious criminals, gang members, and crazy people will soon be roaming America's streets."

Jamie glanced sideways at Mom, "I don't think you need to worry about an illegal alien invasion in Hideaway Falls; the Southern border is a long way from Wisconsin."

"I hope you are right. Just be careful and tell Sierra hello for me."

"Hey, Jamie, tell Sierra the Nerd says hello too!"

"Jason, Sierra doesn't think you're a nerd. She just said that because you embarrassed her."

"Thanks, Jamie, I appreciate that. I was starting to get one of those nerdy inferiority complexes."

Jamie pushed the remote start on Mad Max. "I will be home in a few hours to help load the U-Haul trailer."

Moving day had arrived. The twins and Macy were thrilled about the move to Uncle Jack's Luxury Ranch. It was a perfect location to ride out the approaching tribulation storms. One hundred and twenty acres of pristine farm and wilderness land. There is plenty of room to grow a garden and go fishing in the creek and the trout-stocked pond. And since Jack's land bordered the county forest, it was the ideal location for hunting squirrels and rabbits, quail and pheasants, and deer and bear.

Jamie pulled out of the driveway and headed for Sierra McFarland's home. Sierra and her sister, April, lived with their parents when the rapture happened, but now the sisters have the house all to themselves. Jamie parked along the curb in front of the two-story home. Sierra walked out the door dressed in slim blue jeans and Western boots. Her long red hair was accented by a waist-length button-down white blouse, blue eyes, and a bright smile.

Jamie put on his sunglasses to hide his staring eyes, then rolled down the window. "Hi, Sierra."

"Hi, Jamie. Let's walk, the weather is lovely. The restaurant is less than a mile away if we cut through Central Park."

"Sounds good to me." Jamie jumped out of the truck, and the two lovebirds strolled down the sidewalk. Enchilada Momma's restaurant was one of the few thriving joints still serving authentic Mexican food made from real meat, cheese, and flour tortillas. It was expensive but worth it.

"I haven't been to Central Park since I was a kid," Jamie said.

"Really, I jogged through the park a couple of weeks ago. I like to feed the ducks." Sierra said as she snapped her fingers, "Oh, shoot, I forgot to bring some bread crumbs."

Jamie bent down to tie his shoe, "We can get some breadsticks at the restaurant and feed the ducks on the way back."

Sierra smiled, "Okay, Jamie, the last one to the duck pond has to buy lunch!"

Jamie looked up to see Sierra sprinting down the sidewalk. He shouted, "You got a headstart, that's not fair."

Sierra slowed to catch her breath as she approached the duckpond. She inhaled sharply but almost gagged from the stench of urine and body odor. Tents of homeless people lined both sides of the sidewalk and encircled the pond. She took a few more steps and stopped, waiting for Jamie. A man standing nearby grabbed his crotch and made an obscene gesture. *"Hey baby, I've got a present for you."*

Sierra glared at the man, *"In your dreams, scum bag!"*

Jamie caught up to her, "He's a druggie, just ignore him and keep walking."

A few seconds later, a slim, tall man, around 25 years old, approached speaking in a foreign language. Jamie shrugged, "I can't understand anything you're saying." The man rubbed his belly and then held up three fingers.

"I think he's trying to tell us that he hasn't eaten in three days," Sierra said.

Jamie pulled his wallet from his back pocket and reached for the *Gift Certificate* he had planned to use at Enchilada Momma's restaurant. The man grabbed the wallet and bolted across the grass and around several tents. Jamie took off after the thief, chasing him halfway around the duck pond. The man lost his footing on the slippery slope, almost sliding into the pond. He sprung to his feet, and Jamie tackled him.

The two struggled, rolling around on the ground. Jamie ended up on top and raised his fist. The man covered his face and screamed, *"Please, don't hit me!"*

Jamie grabbed the wallet, resisting the temptation of giving the thief a knuckle sandwich. "I thought you couldn't speak English. Get out of here while you still can!"

The thief took off, and Jamie heard someone scream, *"You stinking perverts, let me go!"* The voice was unmistakable—it was Sierra's. Jamie ran as fast as he could to Sierra's rescue. He circled back around the duck pond, hurdled the park bench, and rounded the corner, sliding onto the sidewalk. The rage and worry that swirled through his mind quickly faded when he saw Sierra step onto the sidewalk.

"Sierra, are you okay? I thought I heard you scream?"

"I'm fine, but I don't think the two guys behind those bushes will feel too good when they wake up!" Jamie looked behind the bushes, "What on earth happened to them?"

Sierra wiggled her left boot and then her right boot. "I introduced them to thunder and lightning!"

Jamie tilted his head curiously, "You kicked the daylights out of those two guys by yourself?"

Sierra smiled, "Well, yeah, but they deserved it.

"When I was watching you chase the thief, the perverts snuck up behind, grabbed me by the hair, and dragged me behind the bushes. So, I did what any good Christian girl would do. I screamed, *You stinking perverts, let me go!*

"The ugly one twisted my arms behind my back, and his buddy pulled out a switchblade and held it to my throat as he undressed me with his eyes. He lowered the switchblade and cut the top button off my blouse. He grinned and was about to cut off the second button. So I kicked him where it hurts most. He dropped to one knee but still held onto the knife. So I kicked him under the chin, and it was lights out!

"I threw my head back, smacking the other pervert's nose, and elbowed him in the solar plexus. I broke free, turned to face him, and was startled by his appearance. *His facial tattoos, vertical eye pupils, and forked tongue made him look like Godzilla!*

"He wiped his bloody nose on his sleeve, then in a voice that sounded like a man possessed, said, *'My enemies call me DRAGON, do you know why?'*

"I answered, Because of your breath!

"My answer must have ticked him off because he snarled, 'I'm going to kill you!'

"He tried to grab me again. So, I used Uncle Jack's *Cross-Eyed Duck technique* and twice poked his eyes. I could tell it hurt and that he couldn't see very well. So I delivered a roundhouse kick to the side of his head. He didn't even see it coming—what a loser!"

"Sierra, you never cease to amaze me," Jamie said as he attempted to hug her. She extended her arm, stopping him, "Not so fast, big guy! You've got duck poop on your shirt." Sierra said with a giggle.

Jamie grabbed her hand. "Let's get out of here."

Sierra nodded, "Let's go back to my place. I'll get you a clean shirt from Dad's closet, fix sandwiches, and introduce you to my sister."

The two exited the Park and walked across the street onto the sidewalk. Sierra's house was just a few blocks down the road. "Sierra, may I ask you a question?"

"Sure."

"Where did you learn to fight like that?"

"I have a second-degree black belt in Karate. I thought you knew that. I planned to open a Martial Arts Dojo, but the Rapture interrupted the plans."

Jamie looked at her with a gleam in his eye, "Sierra, the Tribulation Force Freedom Center would be the perfect location for your Martial Arts Studio. Your Karate skills and Jack's military self-defense techniques will be an attractive and fierce combination. The Freedom Center will be the talk of the town."

"You think so," Jamie?"

"I know so. Mom, Jason, and Uncle Jack will love the idea!"

Sierra threw her arms around Jamie's neck, giving him a big hug. "Thank you."

"You're welcome," Jamie said as he stepped back, smiling and staring. He raised his right eyebrow, "Oh, and by the way, Sierra, that duck poop looks good on you!"

Sierra looked down at her duck poop-smeared white blouse, "Oh shit! I mean, shoot. Sorry, I guess old habits are hard to break."

Jamie laughed.

"Let's go in, and I'll introduce you to my sister, April. She's prettier than I am, so don't get any ideas."

"Prettier than you, Sierra? No way!"

"Thanks, Jamie, but she's gorgeous. I got my looks from Mom, and April got her looks from Dad. She has dark brown hair, hazel eyes, and a dark complexion. She's sweet and delicate. I bet your brother would like her."

Jamie shook his head, "Jason will not date anyone that's not a Christian. It's a biblical no-no."

"Well, I've been telling her about Jesus. Perhaps she will become a Christian. She's coming with me next Sunday to the Freedom Center meeting."

"Cool!"

After meeting Sierra's sister and eating a sandwich, it was time to head back home to assist with the move to Uncle Jack's ranch. Jamie pulled into the driveway. Jack, Mom, and Jason were busy loading the U-Haul trailer. Jamie exited his truck, "Man, O Man, you guys. You won't believe what happened. You were right, Mom; the alien invasion has come to town. There must be 200 tents of homeless immigrants camped out in Central Park."

"No kidding?" Mom replied.

"Yeah, and Sierra kicked the daylights out of two of them!"

"Sierra got into a fight?"

"Yeah, Mom, I could hardly believe it myself. Some homeless guy stole my wallet, and while I was busy chasing the guy, two perverts attempted to molest Sierra. She knocked both of them out cold! It turns out that Sierra has a second-degree black belt in Karate!"

Jack chuckled, "I wish I would have been there to see that! Perhaps I can persuade her to assist me in training the left-behind tribulation force."

"That's what I told her she should do!"

Mom handed Jamie a storage box, "Did you say 200 homeless families live in tents in Central Park?"

"Yes."

Mom pursed her lips, "That's a tough way to live, especially for the women and children."

Jamie rubbed his chin, and his brow wrinkled, "Come to think of it, I don't recall seeing any women or children. Most of them were young men."

Jack walked over to Jamie, squeezing his shoulder, "Young men, huh? As in military-age young men?"

"Yeah, I guess so."

Jack adjusted the brim of his hat, "That's not good. My friend, the border control agent, said that about 15 percent of the 120,000 illegals crossing the border every month in 2,023 were military-age men from the Middle East, former Soviet Republics, and China. In other words, they're from Islamic and Communist countries that hate America and want to destroy us!"

Macy looked sideways at Jack, "Fifteen percent of 120,000 times twelve months is 216,000, and that's just in 2023. The actual number of potential terrorists that have crossed the border since 2021 is likely much higher. *That is not immigration. It's an invasion!*"

"Yeah, Macy, and that's not even counting the 900,000 border crossing "got a-ways" that no one knows who they are or where they live!"

"Jack, what do you think these young men will do?"

"Well, Macy, if I was Satan and wanted to destroy America. The first thing I would do is fill the Congress and Senate with political operatives to ensure the border wall was not completed until a large contingency of America's enemies had crossed over.

"Second, I would undermine American citizens' Constitutional *Free Speech Rights* by introducing *Hate Speech Legislation* making it illegal to criticize the terrorist religion, "holy book," or its evil political and religious agenda.

"Third, I would pass *Gun Control legislation* to disarm law-abiding citizens so that when the city-to-city and the house-to-house takeover of America begins, Americans will be unable to defend themselves or their families."

Macy's brow wrinkled, "Jack, I have a question. The political party and its president, whose mascot is a Jackass, refused to finish the border wall, even though all the materials were bought, paid in full, and on-site. The Jackass Party is constantly pushing for more and more Hate Speech Legislation and Gun Control Laws. Do you think it's coincidental or sinisterly intentional?"

"Macy, you know what they say, *If it looks like a jackass, hee-haws like a jackass, and acts like a jackass. It's a jackass!* Don't forget many of America's politicians and their elite constituents are members of the World Economic Forum and agree with their Marxist New World Order agenda."

Jack pulled a piece of paper from his wallet and unfolded it. "I've got a copy of the globalists' utopian agenda right here. I will read it to you,

> *"You'll own nothing, and you'll be happy. Whatever you want, you'll rent, and it will be delivered by drone. The US won't be the world's leading superpower. A handful of countries will dominate. You will eat much less meat, an occasional treat, not a staple for the good of the environment. Polluters will have to pay, there will be a global price on carbon. You may be preparing to go to Mars…the start of a journey to find alien life."*

Jason laughed, "We will be happy owning nothing, riding the bus, living in a tiny rented apartment, and being thrown a piece of meat on special occasions. While the global elites live happier lives owning everything. Living in their million-dollar mansions, flying in their private jets, driving their fancy cars, and grilling out steaks on their yachts!"

"Isn't that the truth," Jack said. "There is one thing, however, that stands in the way of their globalist dystopian dream, and that is the United States of America! To accomplish their mission of "building back better," they must first destroy America's superpower status, Christian Foundation, and the Constitution."

"It wouldn't be the first time progressive socialists teamed up with Islamists to eradicate their perceived enemies. It is precisely what the German Socialist Nazi Party did in Germany when it exterminated 10 million of its citizens.

"Ironically, a large percentage of Americans think an open border, hate speech laws, and gun control legislation is a good idea. No wonder Adolf Hitler called those who voted for his Party "useful idiots!"

"Fourth, I would set off a nuclear bomb in a densely populated city, such as New York City. The dense population makes it the perfect terrorist target. Just one or two suitcase nukes will kill tens of thousands, and several located strategically throughout New York could kill millions."

Macy frowned, "Dusty lives just 35 miles from the Big Apple."

Jack pressed his lips together and nodded, "I know. I will warn Dusty and tell him what I think is in store for New York City."

Jack noticed Macy's watery eyes, "Do you want me to continue?" She nodded. Jack opened Mad Max's tailgate and sat on it. He took a deep breath and continued, "New York City is the ideal terrorist target because it is the world's premier global finance and banking hub.

"It is home to the World Trade Center, the New York Stock Exchange, and Wall Street. It's home to thousands of the world's wealthiest and most powerful individuals and corporations.

"Plus, New York Harbor is one of the world's largest and busiest deep-water shipping ports whose imports and exports supply Americans and feed the economy. Capitalism is the heartbeat of America. Destroy New York City, and America's heart will stop beating!

"Simultaneously, I would orchestrate a Nationwide Cyber Attack, causing a communications blackout from coast to coast. Under the cover of the blackouts, I would order the 200,000 anti-American operatives living in the United States to launch a surprise attack, invading cities, towns, and homes. Slaughtering Americans just as Hamas terrorists did when they attacked and brutally murdered innocent Israeli citizens in 2023.

"I fear it will be too late by the time Americans wake up. Americans don't understand the ethnic cleansing that has been taking place in Nigeria, where tens of thousands of Christians have been slaughtered by Muslim terrorists, is just the tip of the iceberg. Like the passengers on the Titanic, most Americans have no idea what's coming. The Islamists have a saying, *"First the Saturday people, and then the Sunday people. Little Satan and then big Satan."* In other words, first the Jews in Israel and then the Christians in America!"

A tear slid down Macy's cheek, "I remember reading an article about a man. I believe his name is Yossi Landau. Yossi was part of a volunteer team to recover victims in Israel Kibbutz Be'eri. The Hamas terrorists kidnapped twenty children and toddlers in the Kibbutz community. They zip-tied the children's hands behind their backs, and after abusing them, they piled them on top of one another. Poured gasoline on the crying and screaming children and burned them alive!

"How can anyone do such a wicked and demonic thing? The Jews and Christians would never treat Muslim children that way. Even the Nazis were not that evil!"

Jack rested his hand on Macy's shoulder, "God wrote a book, and Satan wrote a book. One book makes people good, and the other makes people evil. The terrorists shout praises to their God as they rob, rape, and kill men, women, and children. It's not that difficult to figure out which book Satan wrote."

Jamie swallowed hard, "Uncle Jack, Sierra, and her 17-year-old sister live alone two blocks from Central Park, which frightens me."

"Two young ladies living alone with potential terrorists just down the road, that's not good," Jack said with a concerned tone. "I'll tell you what, Jamie. Let's get you guys moved in. I will call and warn Dusty, and you can invite Sierra and April to my place. My old house is vacant and just down the road from the new home. If they wish, they can move in."

Jamie high-fived Uncle Jack, "That will be awesome!"

He glanced at his brother, "Jason, wait 'till you see Sierra's sister, April. She is gorgeous—but don't tell Sierra I said that!"

Jack handed Jason a box, "Come on, guys, are you gonna flap your jaws all day? Let's get moving!"

The twins saluted, "Yes, Sir, Uncle Jack!"

Chapter Sixteen

Destination Babylon, New York

Dusty looks out the Company Jet window as it circles the Israeli city of Rehovot. The thermobaric explosion reminds him of the 2023 Maui, Hawaii fire. Not a building was standing, and the area was littered with the metal skeletons of burnt-out automobiles.

The Jet picks up speed ascending above the fluffy white clouds. The pilot announces 12 hours to touch down, destination Babylon, New York. Dusty reclines his seat, "Hey Mike, do you recall our discussion on the trip to Jerusalem?"

"Yes, I was about to tell you what I discovered in my research about speaking in tongues. It was an eye-opening study that I can't wait to share with everyone."

"Well, Mike, you've got a captive audience. Go for it!"

Nicole was seated behind Mike. She scooted to the edge of her seat and said, "This should be interesting. I speak in tongues!"

Dusty glanced back at Nicole, "I never knew Catholics spoke in tongues?"

"Well, spiritual Catholics do. It's a gift of the Holy Spirit."

Mike rolled his eyes. "Nicole, if the Holy Spirit was in you. You would have been raptured."

"So you say, I told you before, Catholics don't believe in the rapture!"

"So, Nicole, you believe Sergius's Alexanders lie that the Christians were not raptured but swooned away to judgment?"

"Not really, but perhaps the disappearance was an alien abduction? Someone on the news said that he believes that is what happened."

"Earth to Nicole… Earth to Nicole," Mike's voice teased. "Think about it. There were about 465 million Christians and their children taken from the earth. If it was an alien abduction and each spaceship carried 250 passengers. It would take One Million, Eight Hundred and Sixty Thousand spaceships to transport that many people!

"Did you see even one alien spaceship, or alien, Nicole?"

Nicole tilted her head and thought for a moment, "No, I didn't see any spaceships, but perhaps that's because they were invisible!"

Mike pressed his lips together, "Nicole, I think you should recline your seat. Put on your headphones and listen to some music because I don't think you can handle the truth about what Scripture says about the gift of speaking in tongues!"

Nicole flipped her hair over her shoulder and slid closer to Mike. "You're lucky we are on this plane. Otherwise, I would kick your butt. I gave you a black eye once, and it can happen again!"

Mike frowned, "That's only because the guy you were swinging at ducked, and you punched me instead!"

Everyone chuckled.

"You know what they say, opposites attract," Olivia said.

"Are you kidding me? I wouldn't go on a date with Mike if my life depended on it!"

Mike chuckled, "Never say Never!"

Nicole snapped back, "In your dreams!"

Mike inhaled deeply and exhaled slowly. "You are a feisty one. I'll give you that much. Okay, Nicole, if you wish, you can participate in the conversation as long as you promise not to punch me."

"I promise!" Nicole said with crossed fingers.

Mike opened his laptop, "Okay, here goes. I discovered that the tongues spoken in Charismatic churches today are not biblical tongues. The gift of tongues that the first-century church experienced was the miraculous ability to speak fluently in an unlearned foreign human language. Listen as I read the account revealed in Acts 2, verses 1 to 11.

"When the Day of Pentecost had fully come, they were all with one accord in one place. And suddenly there came a sound from heaven, as of a rushing mighty wind, and it filled the whole house where they were sitting. Then there appeared to them cloven tongues, as of fire, and it sat upon each of them. And they were all filled with the Holy Spirit and began to speak with other tongues, as the Spirit gave them utterance."

"And there were dwelling in Jerusalem Jews, devout men, from every nation under heaven. And when this sound occurred, the multitude came together, and were confused, because everyone heard them speak in his own language. Then they were all amazed and marveled, saying to one another, "Look, are not all these who speak Galileans?

And how is it that we hear, each in our own language in which we were born? Parthians and Medes and Elamites, those dwelling in Mesopotamia, Judea and Cappadocia, Pontus and Asia, Phrygia and Pamphylia, Egypt and the parts of Libya adjoining Cyrene, visitors from Rome, both Jews and proselytes, Cretans and Arabs—we hear them speaking in our own tongues the wonderful works of God."

"This account reveals that, unlike the ecstatic utterances of unintelligible words spoken in Pentecostal and Charismatic churches today. The authentic gift of tongues given by the Holy Spirit was the supernatural ability to communicate in an UNLEARNED HUMAN LANGUAGE. We know this because the verse I quoted stated that all the people heard them speak the wonderful works of God in their own language!"

Nicole shook the back of Mike's seat, *"Who cares? I don't know why you are making such a big deal about it! So what if some people choose to worship God in unknown languages?"*

"The big deal, Nicole, is that millions have been deceived into believing they are born-again Christians because they speak in tongues. In reality, modern-day tongues are a blasphemous counterfeit of authentic biblical tongues that is no different from the unintelligible incantations uttered by the Shamans in Sudan, the Shango cult in Africa, the Zor cult in Ethiopia, and the Voodoo cult in Haiti. It is demonic and dangerous!

"Unfortunately, tongue-speaking deception is rampant and growing in acceptance. Listen to what the largest chain of Pentecostal churches in America, *The Assemblies of God (USA) Official Website,* states:

> *"When the early believers were filled, they spoke in other tongues; the same holds true today. Millions of believers worldwide share the exact testimony: When they initially were baptized in the Holy Spirit, they spoke in unknown tongues."*

"The problem with that statement is that the first-century church's early believers didn't speak in *unknown* tongues. Every instance of speaking in tongues recorded in the New Testament was a real human language—not unintelligible gibberish. There is not one instance of anyone possessing the ability to speak or pray in a so-called heavenly language or the tongues of angels."

Nicole pulled up the Bible App on her phone. "Why then did the apostle Paul, in 1 Corinthians 14 verse 2, say, 'For he that speaks in an *unknown* tongue speaks not unto men, but unto God: for no man understands him; howbeit in the spirit he speaketh mysteries.' See, it says right there that the tongue speakers spoke in unknown tongues!"

"Nicole, the word *unknown* is italicized in your Bible because the word is not in the original manuscript; the translators added it. When the apostle Paul addressed the Corinthian church, he wasn't addressing the church about them speaking in some unknown mystical language. Instead, he was upbraiding those who spoke in foreign languages when no interpreter was present. That is why Paul stated:

> "I thank my God, I speak with tongues more than you all: Yet in the church, I had rather speak five words with my understanding, that by my voice I might teach others also, than ten thousand words in an *unknown* tongue... But if there be no interpreter, let him keep silence in the church; and let him speak to himself, and to God" (1 Corinthians 14 verses 18 to 19 and 28).

"Then, a few verses later, Paul stated the purpose of the gift of tongues: *'Wherefore tongues are for a sign, not to them that believe, but to them that believe not.'* The gift of tongues was a SIGN TO UNBELIEVERS that the words spoken by the tongue speaker were of God because it is a miracle to speak the wonderful works of God in a language that the speaker was never taught. On the other hand, there is nothing miraculous in hearing someone speak unintelligible gibberish—even babies can do that!"

"I printed out an article by a Christian author that I think you'll find fascinating. Listen to what he wrote: "I remember my first experience speaking in tongues. At first, it was stimulating as I thought it would draw me closer to God and empower me to do more for His kingdom. One day, I was alone in my bedroom speaking in tongues...

> *Sha ba ba la so tora, so tora ba ba ba.*
> *Sodamora, sede sodamora, sede aya aya.*
> *Sunda la la la, baba, rendo shala, sunda la la la baba.*

"After about 15 or 20 minutes, I sensed a dark, evil presence enter the room. I stopped speaking immediately and dashed out of the room! It scared the H-E-double-hockey-sticks-out-of-me, but a few months later, I was convinced by a charismatic television evangelist to give it another try. So I went into my bedroom, kneeled alongside the bed, and began speaking and praying in tongues…

> *Kora bani, rendo shala, shala bani, kora mondi.*
> *Zabaru shala mashi, mondi la la lada, shala garo.*
> *Yara shala mashi, uno babuno, suda la baba, shala garo.*

"At the time, my wife was in the hallway dumping clothes down the laundry chute. The hallway that led to the bedroom was narrow. She thought I had accidentally brushed against her as she bent over, grabbing dirty clothes from the basket. She looked up, expecting to see me, but I wasn't there! I was in the bedroom, lifting my hands, speaking and praying in tongues, having a good old time.

"Suddenly, the same thing happened. I felt that same eerie evil presence enter the bedroom. A chill ran up and down my spine, and I dashed to the door. I couldn't get out of the room fast enough!

"I told my wife about my tongue-speaking experience, and she informed me what happened to her and that she, too, sensed the evil presence in the house. I never spoke in tongues again, and guess what? The evil presence left and never returned!"

Nicole twirled her hair between her fingers, "Well, Mike, how come I never sensed an evil presence when I speak in tongues?"

"Nicole, the invisible powers of this world are spiritually discerned. The natural man cannot discern spiritual things. I imagine you have never sensed the evil nature of speaking in unbiblical tongues because the Holy Spirit resides only in born-again believers. The desire of Satan and his demons is not to scare a person but to keep them deceived. As long as you are convinced that you are a Christian because you speak in so-called tongues, you'll never discover true Salvation.

"In my research, I came across a medical experiment that used brain scan technology to monitor the brain wave impulses of persons speaking in modern-day tongues. It revealed that the brain's frontal lobe (the region that controls thought, reason, and language) is active and lights up when speaking in human languages but substantially darkens when speaking in unintelligible tongues. The experiment demonstrated that the same brain wave impulses are duplicated when someone is under hypnosis, on certain drugs, or in a transcendental meditation trance.

"The danger is that anytime a person relinquishes self-control, whether from drugs, mind-emptying meditation, or unbiblical tongue speaking, it can open themselves up to demonic spirits. The more frequent and longer one speaks or prays in the tongues, the more prone one becomes to demonic influence and possession."

"Now the Spirit expressly says that in latter times some will depart from the faith, giving heed to seducing spirits and doctrines of demons."

Chills ran up and down Nicole's spine, and she shivered as she whispered to Mike, "Do you think I need an Exorcism? I watched the *Exorcist Movie*, and it freaked me out. I don't want my head to spin around backward and start projectile vomiting pea soup across the room!"

Mike could tell from her shaky voice that she wasn't joking. "Nicole, if you had refused to hear God's truth about tongues and got angry with me for expounding the truth. It would be a sign that you were under demonic influence, but since you haven't punched me, I don't think you have a demon. Just stop speaking in tongues, and you won't have to worry."

Nicole sighed, "Good!"

"Sorry Mike, please continue. I'm intrigued and want to know more."

"Okay, is everyone listening?

Everyone shouted, "Yes!"

"Undoubtedly, no one today has the genuine gift of tongues—the miraculous ability to speak fluently in unlearned foreign human languages. This is because God's Word foretold that PROPHECY WILL FAIL, TONGUES WILL CEASE, AND PARTIAL KNOWLEDGE WILL VANISH AWAY! Listen to what the apostle Paul said about it.

> "Love never fails: but whether there are prophecies, they will fail; whether there are tongues, they will cease; whether there is knowledge, it will vanish away. For we know in part and we prophesy in part. But when that which is perfect has come, then that which is in part will be done away.
>
> When I was a child, I spoke as a child, I understood as a child, I thought as a child; but when I became a man, I put away childish things. For now, we see in a mirror, dimly, but then face to face. Now I know in part, but then I shall know just as I also am known. **And now abide faith, hope, love, these three; but the greatest of these is love**" (1 Corinthians 13 verses 8 to 13).

"Notice that God's Word states that the gift of prophecy will fail, tongues will cease, and partial knowledge will vanish away. The question is, when will those three gifts—prophecy (the ability to foretell future events), tongues (the ability to speak and interpret an unfamiliar language), and partial (incomplete) knowledge—be done away?" It says, *'When that which is perfect has come, then that which is in part will be done away.'*

"The Continuationist Charismatic and Pentecostals churches claim that the phrase *when that which is perfect has come* refers to the time when Christians meet Jesus face to face, at which time the gifts of the Spirit will be done away, but faith, hope, and love, will abide forever.

"The Cessationist churches contend that the phrase *when that which is perfect has come* refers to the time when everything that God wanted us to know about Himself, Salvation, and the future had been revealed, then those things which were in part would be done away. In other words, those gifts would cease when the New Testament canon of Scripture—the perfect and infallible word of God—was completed.

"A careful examination of those Scriptures reveals that the passing away of the gifts of the Spirit cannot be referring to the time when Christians physically meet Jesus face to face because Scripture tells us that after they pass away, faith, hope, and love will abide (continue). The fact is that when Christians meet the Savior in person, the only one of those three that will continue is love, but faith and hope will not. Scripture states that *'faith is the substance of things hoped for, the evidence of things not seen...but hope that is seen is not hope; for why does one still hope for what he sees?"* (Hebrews 11 verse 1, Romans 8 verses 24).

"The faith and hope of the Christian is to receive our new supernatural immortal body and enter into everlasting life. Once we do, the redemption and resurrection of our body will no longer be the Christian's faith and hope—but a living reality! The only thing that will "abide" (continue forever) is "love" because God is love (1 John 4 verse 8).

"So, it is clear that the phrase when that which is perfect has come is not referring to Christ, but rather to the completed canon of Scripture. Therefore, the "face-to-face" part of the verse must refer to the Bible. This makes perfect sense because we are told in the first chapter of John that JESUS IS THE WORD OF GOD. So, when you read God's Word, it's as if Jesus is speaking with you face to face."

Olivia smiled, "It makes perfect sense to me, but Mike, I have a question. I remember hearing a preacher say that the passage in

Mark chapter 16 proves that the gifts of the Holy Spirit have not ceased but continue today. Are you familiar with that passage?"

"Yes, I am, Olivia. I'll read it so everyone will know what we're talking about.

> "And he [Jesus] said unto them, Go ye into all the world, and preach the gospel to every creature. He that believeth and is baptized shall be saved; but he that believeth not shall be damned. And these signs shall follow them that believe; In my name shall they cast out devils; they shall speak with new tongues; They shall take up serpents; and if they drink any deadly thing, it shall not hurt them; they shall lay hands on the sick, and they shall recover" (Mark 16 verses 15 to 18).

"The Pentecostal and Charismatic Continuationists use this passage in an attempt to provide Scriptural evidence that the gifts of the Spirit continue to be given in the 21st century. They point to the passage and say, '*See, it says right there that believers will* **cast out demons, speak with new tongues, and lay hands on the sick, and they will be healed.**'

"This is true, and that is precisely what the first-century believers did! They preached the Gospel everywhere (including foreign lands that required the gift of tongues to communicate the Gospel in foreign languages), baptized the believers, and established churches everywhere.

"This passage, however, is not a prediction that the gifts of the Spirit will be available to believers throughout the ages, but rather a confirmation that authenticated the truth that Christ had risen from the dead, as the two verses that follow confirmed.

> "So then after the Lord had spoken unto them, he was received up into heaven, and sat on the right hand of God. *And they went forth, and preached everywhere, the Lord working with them, and confirming the word with signs following. Amen."* (Mark 16 verses 19 to 20).

"The fact that the gifts of the Spirit were a first-century phenomenon was confirmed in the letter to the Hebrews written thirty-one years after the events recorded in the Gospels.

"God, who at various times and in various ways spoke in time past to the fathers by the prophets. Has in these last days spoken to us by His Son, whom He has appointed heir of all things, through whom also He made the worlds. Which at the first began to be spoken by the Lord, and was **confirmed to us by those who heard Him**, God also bearing witness both with signs and wonders, with various miracles, and gifts of the Holy Spirit, according to His own will" (Hebrews 1 verse 1 to 2, and chapter 2 verses 3 to 4).

"Notice that it says the gospel was "confirmed to us by those WHO HEARD JESUS." Who was it that heard Jesus? The answer, of course, is the first-century disciples who lived, walked, and talked with Jesus. How did the first-century believers confirm the gospel of Christ? It says, *"with signs and wonders, with various miracles, and gifts of the Holy Spirit."*

"If Christians today have the gifts of tongues, the power to cast out demons, and heal the sick. Then, the Pentecostals should also be able to **take up serpents and drink poison without harmful effects**, as stated in Mark. Yet, none of them dare do so because if they got bit by a viper or drank poison, they would swell up and drop dead! This is because those protective and miraculous gifts of the Spirit have passed away just as the Scripture foretold!

"Concerning the Charismatic and Pentecostal deception of the last days Jesus warned,

"Many will say to Me on that day, 'Lord, Lord, *have we not prophesied* in Your name, *cast out demons* in Your name, and *done many wonders* in Your name?' And then I will declare to them, 'I never knew you; depart from Me, you who practice lawlessness!" (Matthew 7 verses 22 to 23).

"This is the world we live in today, a time full of deceptions, manipulation, and the twisting of the truth. The purpose of the miracles of Jesus and the first-century believers was to authenticate who Jesus claimed to be. The sinless lamb of God and Savior of the World. Once all that God wanted us to know was recorded, the sign and revelatory gifts of the Spirit and the office of prophet and apostle vanished away.

"Even the apostle Paul, who had previously performed fantastic signs, wonders, and healing miracles, didn't heal his friend, *'Trophimus, but left him sick in Miletus.'* And he told Timothy *'to drink a little wine for his stomach's sake and his frequent infirmities.'* Indicating that the miraculous gifts of the Spirit were already vanishing away before the first century ended (1 Timothy 5, verse 23; 2 Timothy 4, verse 20).

"Nicole, Alan, and Olivia let me ask you a question. "What was the purpose of Jesus' healing miracles?"

The trio looked at one another and shrugged, "We're not sure."

"Well, team, Jesus gives us the answer in Luke chapter 5, verses 18 to 25. I will read it, it's enlightening.

> "And, behold, men brought in a bed a man which was taken with a palsy: and they sought means to bring him in, and to lay him before him.
>
> And when they could not find by what way they might bring him in because of the multitude, they went upon the housetop, and let him down through the tiling with his couch into the midst before Jesus.
>
> And when he saw their faith, he said unto him, Man, thy sins are forgiven thee.
>
> And the scribes and the Pharisees began to reason, saying, Who is this which speaketh blasphemies? Who can forgive sins, but God alone?

But when Jesus perceived their thoughts, he answering said unto them, What reason ye in your hearts?

Whether is easier, to say, Thy sins be forgiven thee; or to say, Rise up and walk?

<u>But that ye may know that the Son of man hath power upon earth to forgive sins, (he said unto the sick of the palsy,) I say unto thee, Arise, and take up thy couch, and go into thine house.</u>

And immediately he rose up before them, and took up that whereon he lay, and departed to his own house, glorifying God."

"The reason for Jesus' miracles is not what the—*Name It and Claim It,* and *Grab It and Blab It*—health and prosperity preachers teach. Jesus didn't perform miracles and heal people because he wanted everyone to be healthy and wealthy: ***but that you may know that the Son of man hath power upon earth to forgive sins!***"

"The purpose of the gifts of the Spirit and the miracles of healing done *after* Jesus' crucifixion by the first-century believers, prophets, and apostles was for the same reason. The miracles done *'In the name of Jesus'* proved that He had risen from the dead and was still in the business of forgiving sins (Acts 3, verses 1 to 16).

"Jesus and His apostles warned us that many false teachers, prophets, and apostles would arise in the last days, deceiving and being deceived. Don't be fooled; Satan and his minions come dressed as angels of light but are wolves in sheep's clothing."

"For such are false apostles, deceitful workers, transforming themselves into apostles of Christ. And no wonder! For Satan himself transforms himself into an angel of light. Therefore it is no great thing if his ministers also transform themselves into ministers of righteousness, whose end will be according to their works" (2 Corinthians 11, verses 13 to 15).

"So, the question is, Nicole, will you believe God's Word, or will you continue to deceive and be deceived?

"Well, Nicole, what's your answer?"

Nicole didn't say a word for a few minutes. Then, she quietly rose from her seat and stepped onto the aisle. Mike noticed Nicole in his peripheral vision and instinctively threw up a defensive arm covering his head and face.

"Put your arm down. I'm not going to slug you!" Nicole assured Mike. "May I sit next to you for a minute? I have something to say."

"Sure, Nicole."

Mike slid over one seat, and Nicole sat next to him. "Well, not that it's any of your business, but to answer your question, I believe God's Word. I promise I will never speak or pray in tongues again. Besides, I'm pretty sure that God can understand English anyway!"

Mike chuckled, "Yeah, I'm pretty sure you're right about that!

"Nicole, I'm sorry about what I said. You have proven that you can handle the truth."

"Thank you, Mike. Apology accepted."

"So, now that I know you can handle the truth, I've got one more thing to tell you before I close my eyes and enter dreamland."

"Okay, Mike, let me have it!"

"God's word says that you should call no man father!"

"Seriously, Mike, it says call no man father? Well, is it okay if I call him Dad or Papa?"

"Mike gave Nicole a quizzical look, "Not your biological father, screwball! It's fine to call your earthly parent father, but it dishonors God to call anyone on earth your spiritual father. Jesus said, 'Call no man your father upon the earth: for one is your Father, which is in heaven" (Matthew 23 verse 9).

"Comprende?"

"Well, yes and no," Nicole said with a confused look. "How, then, can I confess my sins in the Catholic confessional? The Sacrament of Confession always starts with the words, 'Bless me, Father, for I have sinned...'"

"That's another thing, Nicole. Your priest, the Pope, and even Mary cannot forgive sins. Not little sins, big sins, not any sins! God's Word states that there is 'ONE MEDIATOR BETWEEN GOD AND MEN, THE MAN CHRIST JESUS'" (1 Timothy 2 verse 5).

"So, Mike, you're telling me that even the Virgin Mary cannot forgive sins; are you sure about that?"

"Yes, Nicole. Mary was blessed to give birth to Jesus, but she was just like the rest of us, a sinner in need of a Savior. Mary told her cousin Elizabeth, 'My soul magnifies the Lord, And my spirit has rejoiced in God my Savior.' If Mary was sinless, she would not need a savior and never would have said that her spirit rejoiced in *God, her Savior!* Confessing your sins to Mary or a priest will not get you to heaven but will keep you out of it. There is one mediator between God and Men, the man Christ Jesus.

"The Catholic Church has its members confess sins to a priest because the Catholic hierarchy doesn't understand that when Christ died on the cross. The Old Testament Covenant, which included the priesthood, was replaced with the New Testament Covenant, whereby Jesus became our "High Priest," eliminating the need for priests.

"The Gospel of Matthew informs us that the moment Jesus died on the cross, the 'Veil of the Temple was torn in two from top to bottom' (Matthew 27 verse 51). The temple veil was a 60-foot-high thick curtain that separated the Holy of Holies—the earthly dwelling place of God's presence—from the rest of the temple where men dwelt. The fact that the veil was torn from top to bottom signified that God, not man, had ripped the curtain in two. Thereby providing a new and living way for humanity to enter His presence without the priesthood! Nicole, listen to what is written in Hebrews about it.

"Seeing then that we have a great high priest, that is passed into the heavens, Jesus the Son of God, let us hold fast our profession. For we have not a high priest which cannot be touched with the feeling of our infirmities; but was in all points tempted like as we are, yet without sin. Let us, therefore, come boldly unto the throne of grace, that we may obtain mercy, and find grace to help in time of need."

"Having therefore, brethren, boldness to enter into the holiest by the blood of Jesus, **By a new and living way,** which he hath consecrated for us, through the veil, that is to say, his flesh; And having a high priest over the house of God; Let us draw near with a true heart in full assurance of faith, having our hearts sprinkled from an evil conscience, and our bodies washed with pure water" (Hebrews chapter 4, verses 14 to 16; and chapter 10 verses 19 to 22).

"That's awesome!" Nicole said. "So, I no longer have to confess my sins to that nosey old goat or play ring around the Rosary. Instead, in prayer, I can go straight to the throne of grace to obtain mercy and grace."

"That's correct, Nicole."

"That's excellent news!" Nicole said excitedly. "I suppose next, you'll tell me that Purgatory isn't real or necessary!"

"I'm sure Dusty knows more about that subject than I do. "Hey, Dusty Nicole was wondering if purgatory is real or necessary. Can you answer that question for her?"

"Sure. Nicole, come sit with me."

Mike yawned, "Excuse me, Nicole, but I'm dead tired. Between the U.S. and Israel time difference and all the excitement over the past few days, I'm behind on sleep. We can talk later if you wish, but it's time for my beauty sleep right now."

Nicole pushed her hair from her face and looked into Mike's eyes. "Your beauty sleep hasn't worked in the past. What makes you think it will work this time?"

Mike pursed his lips and shook his head, "Good night, Nicole."

Nicole took a seat next to Dusty. "Nicole, my father preached on the topic of purgatory many times. You'll like what God's Word says and doesn't say about the subject.

"First, the Roman Catholic doctrine of purgatory is taught nowhere in Scripture. The word "purgatory" is not in the Bible. Even the concept of it is nowhere to be found. It was invented to accommodate Catholicism's denial of justification by faith alone. The truth of Scripture is that if you die in your sins, you will not open your eyes in purgatory but in the fires of hell. The good news is that you'll never have to worry about going to hell if you place your faith in Christ alone.

"Second Corinthians chapter 5 verse 21 tells us, *'For he [God] hath made him [Jesus] to be sin for us, who knew no sin; that we might be made the righteousness of God in him.'* In other words, if you receive Jesus Christ through faith in Him and His sacrificial offering on the cross. God views you spiritually just as righteous as Himself. It's the shed blood of God incarnate that purifies the sinner. Not the fires of purgatory.

> "Therefore being justified by faith, we have peace with God through our Lord Jesus Christ. In whom we have redemption through his blood, the forgiveness of sins, according to the riches of his grace" (Romans 5 verse 1 and Ephesians 1 verse 7).

"Nicole, the meaning of the word "grace" in that verse is *unmerited, unearned* favor. Therefore, Salvation has nothing to do with what we do, but what Jesus has done."

"So Dusty, let me get this straight. Jesus Christ is called the Son of God because God became flesh to save sinners from their sins. Since I'm a sinner, Jesus died for me! When I place my faith in Him, His righteousness—the righteousness of God—is imputed to me. Therefore, God in the courtroom of heaven can legally declare me innocent because Jesus paid for all my sins, past, present, and future.

"Sin can affect my fellowship with God, but can never condemn me because there is NO CONDEMNATION TO THOSE WHO ARE IN CHRIST JESUS. And since Salvation is a gift of God, I can never lose it because I never earned it in the first place!

"Is that correct, Dusty?"

"Nicole, I couldn't have said it better!"

Nicole got up, "Thank you, Dusty."

An hour later, Mike opened his eyes. Nicole was seated next to him. "What time is it?"

"It's 15 minutes to touch down."

Mike looked around. Dusty was checking his email, and Olivia rested her head on Alan's shoulder.

Nicole placed her hand on Mike's and looked into his eyes. "While you were sleeping, I thought about everything we've been through the past two weeks. The Rapture, the Antichrist and the False Prophet, Moses, Elijah, Isaiah's prophecy, Alan's speech on the Temple Mount, the war and the destruction of Damascus, your testimony, and our discussions. I've experienced and learned so much."

Nicole stood smiling, "I'll be right back."

She walked to the front of the plane and turned to face the team. "Everyone, guess what? I'm no longer a Catholic. I'm a born-again Jesus freak!

Chapter Seventeen

Wiley Coyote

"Ten minutes to touch down; fasten your seat belts," the pilot announces." Dusty slips on his shoes and checks his email. There is a message from pastor Joshua. He clicks it open.

Dusty, did you get home yet? I'm coming to town and thought I'd treat you to lunch. I hear Charlie's Hamburger Stand is still open.

Joshua, I love Charlie's burgers. How does One O'clock sound?

Perfect, I will see you then.

Dusty arrived home, showered, and glanced out the window just as Joshua's VW Bug pulled into the driveway—beep, beep! He waved and met Joshua on the driveway.

"Is that a 1962 Volkswagen Beetle?"

"It sure is. My father purchased it brand new, and it's been in the family ever since. It doesn't have the electronics like the new cars, and the top speed is only 72 miles per hour. But at least it will start if there is an EMP attack."

"Joshua, do you expect an EMP attack?"

"Who knows? I like to be prepared just in case.

"Well, Dusty, are you ready to roll?"

"Yeah, let's go."

Joshua started the Bug and took a left on Elm Street, "It's been a while since I've been to Charlies. I'm not sure if I remember the way."

"No problem I know how to get there. Take a right at the stop light. It's the quickest route."

Joshua came to a stop at the red light. An old couple walked across the street smiling and giving the thumbs up! Joshua returned the gesture with the horn—beep, beep!

"Do you get the "thumbs up" often, Joshua?"

"A lot, especially from older folks. I think this old Volkswagen Beetle brings back memories of a more peaceful and sane time."

The light turned green, and the VW Bug turned right onto Grand Avenue. A man standing at his mailbox gave the thumbs up and hollered nice wheels. Joshua's car smiled back—beep, beep!

"Joshua, do you know what the sound of your horn reminds me of?"

"Let me guess, the *Road Runner* cartoon?"

"Yep. I guess it's not the first time you've heard that."

"Nope. I hear that a lot. In fact, that cartoon inspired my wife, Jasmine, and I to name our baby boy Wiley Coyote Jackson. When our son was just a couple of days old, he got the hiccups, and every time he hiccupped, it sounded like the Road Runner's beep. So we named him after one of the Road Runner cartoon stars: Wiley Coyote."

"That's funny. Speaking of Wiley, I haven't seen him for a long time. How is he doing?"

"Dusty, you wouldn't recognize him. If I recall, the last time you saw Wiley was on his sixteenth birthday, and he was about your height."

"That's right," Dusty agreed.

"You're about 5 foot 11, right?"

Dusty stretched his neck, "Five foot eleven and a quarter inch to be exact."

Joshua smiled, "Okay, you were a quarter of an inch taller than Wiley 5 years ago. Well, he's 21 years old now and 7 inches taller than you."

"Are you kidding me? Wiley must be as big as Uncle Jack."

"No, he's bigger! He's 6 foot 6 and weighs 270 pounds, and he's as mean as he is big."

"Seriously, Wiley was such a nice young man."

"Not anymore!"

"A few years ago, Jasmine and I noticed that Wiley's cheerful attitude began to wane. Then, a few months later, he became restless and easily irritated. Then he got boosted with the third bee sting and soon became angry and mad at the world!

"Dusty, you do know what I'm referring to when I say bee stings? Joshua asked as he pressed his finger to his lips and then pointed at his phone. I must be selective in word choice because certain words can turn on the phone's microphone, enabling Big Brother to spy on us."

"Yeah, Joshua, I get it. I may have been born yesterday. But I wasn't born last night!" Dusty snickered. So, you're telling me that the bee stings affected Wiley's demeanor and personality?"

"Exactly! A few weeks before the Rapture, Jasmine confronted Wiley about his lousy attitude. He refused to listen, called his mother every nasty name in the book, and walked out the door. Three days later, Wiley walked in the front door with his head shaved and sporting a large Nazi, Swastika on his neck!"

"Man, O man, what did you do?"

"I kicked him out and haven't heard from him since!"

"I can't blame you!" Dusty said as they drove by the empty Walmart parking lot.

"Joshua, did you notice all the stores that have gone out of business on Grand Avenue?"

"Yeah, a bunch."

Dusty's voice rose excitedly, "Look at that! Walgreens is being looted right now, in broad daylight."

Joshua shook his head, "I told you, man, those bee stings are causing people to go crazy!"

Dusty nodded, "You don't need to convince me. I interviewed the Babylon police chief about the increase in vandalism and violence. He told me that home invasions, store looting, murder, rape, and every other crime skyrocketed soon after the implementation of the bee stings.

Unfortunately, after making that comment, the police chief was fired!"

Joshua turned the corner, "Well, it looks like Charlie's Hamberger Stand is still in business."

"Great!"

Dusty opened the car door, "Hi, Charlie!"

"Hello, I haven't seen you in a while. Great reporting, by the way."

"Thanks, Charlie, this is my friend Joshua. We'll have four burgers with the works."

"Coming right up!"

The grill had about 50 burgers cooking in a special juice that Charlie concocted, with a pile of onions marinating in it.

"How's business?"

"Better than ever!"

"It sure smells good. What's that special juice you cook the burgers in?" Joshua asked.

Charlie smiled, "I'd love to tell you, but then I'd have to kill you! That special juice is a family secret. It's what has made Charlie's Hamberger Stand famous. I've been offered lots of money for the juice recipe, but some things are more important than money."

"Here are your four burgers, fellas, that will be 40 dollars."

"Forty bucks; how do you keep the price so low?" Dusty asked.

"Not everyone can afford those 25-dollar burgers at the restaurants. If you can even find a restaurant that serves real beef. I raise my own Black Angus steers to keep the price down.

"The napkins and condiments are over yonder on the table."

"Okay, Charlie, see you later."

Dusty was about to sink his teeth into his second burger when two pickup trucks loaded with young men parked in front of Charlie's stand. Four men exited the cabs, and eight men jumped out of the truck boxes.

"Don't turn around, Joshua. I think Wiley and his skinhead friends just drove in. Let's see what happens."

"Charlie, cook us up forty hamburgers with the works."

"Sure, that will be 400 dollars."

"Four hundred dollars?"

"Yes, 10 times 40 is 400 dollars."

Wiley's eyes narrowed. "Charlie, are you getting smart with me?!"

"No, sir, I was just telling you how I arrived at the 400 dollar amount."

"I'll tell you what, Charlie. I will give you the 400 dollars, but you are going to tell me your secret juice ingredients and how to make it, or else!"

Joshua stood and turned around, "Wiley, what do you mean, "OR ELSE," are you threatening Charlie?"

"Well, fellas, look who's here if it isn't my Jew-loving father. He loves the Jews, even though they killed Jesus!"

"Listen, you big lunkhead. Jesus was a Jew, the apostles were Jews, Abraham, Isaac, Jacob, and all the patriarchs were Jews. You are right about the Jews participating in getting Jesus crucified, but the Romans are the ones who crucified Him. The real reason you hate the Jews is because God loves them, and you hate God!"

Wiley and his stooges raised their hand and arm as in a Nazi salute. Dusty stepped in between Wiley and his father. "Listen to me, Wiley. God has promised that those who bless the Jews, God will bless. Those who curse them, God will curse. You're on the wrong side—Adolph Hitler is in hell. Is that where you want to end up?"

Wiley pointed toward the sky. Dusty looked up to see what he was pointing at. Wiley brought his hand down hard and fast.

Slapping Dusty alongside the head, knocking him to the ground. "Stay out of this, little man. This is between me and my father!"

Joshua took a deep breath, his nostrils flared, and he pointed his finger at his son. "You are a real tough guy, aren't you? A big man when twelve of your buddies are backing you up!"

Wiley took a step closer to his father and put up his fists.

Joshua glared at his son, "What are you going to do, strike your own father?"

Wiley stepped back and lowered his hands as he considered what he was doing. A tear slid down his cheek. "No, pops, I'm sorry. I don't know why I get so angry.

Wiley turned, looking at Charlie, "Are those burgers ready?"

"Yes, bagged and ready to go."

Wiley turned to his buddy, "Butch, grab the burgers, let's get out of here!"

Charlie pushed the five bags of hamburgers across the counter. "The burgers are on the house!"

"Good, I wasn't going to pay for them anyway," Wiley said.

The skinheads began piling back onto the trucks. A police car pulled alongside and with lights flashing. The policeman exited the vehicle with his hand on his gun. "Is there a problem here?"

Charlie shouted, "No problem officer!"

The Officer nodded to the truck drivers. "You can leave." The skinheads laughed and shouted, "Heil Hitler" as they pulled away.

"Charlie, I'll have two burgers to go, no onions." The Officer looked at Dusty, "You're that famous news reporter, right?"

Dusty extended his hand, "Dusty Rhodes is my name."

"I'm Officer Harry Callahan."

Joshua chuckled, "Dirty Harry! You're more famous than Dusty! I love those old Clint Eastwood, Dirty Harry movies."

Officer Callahan smiled, "Same name, and I carry the same 44 Magnum firearm, but I don't live in a mansion.

"Listen, guys, "I've got a piece of advice for you. Stay as far away from those skinheads as possible. Wherever they go, there's trouble. The gang's leader, the big one, was arrested last week. He is one of the strongest men my officers ever encountered. It took three well-trained police officers armed with baton clubs, tasers, and Mace to take him down. I can tell you, it was quite the skirmish. The officers finally got him handcuffed, but all three of the officers needed medical attention after dealing with him."

The police officer wagged his head, "It's too bad such a brave young man is on the wrong side."

Joshua looked at Officer Callahan, "Bravery without wisdom is a car wreck waiting to happen."

The officer nodded, *"A brave bird, makes a fat cat!"*

"Why isn't he in jail?" Dusty asked.

"He was, but a few hours later, he was released. It's like a certain political party likes the violence and increased crime, but don't tell anyone that I said that. I need to keep my job!"

"Charlie, how much do I owe you?"

"Nothing, Officer, it is on the house."

"Thanks, Charlie."

The Officer got back into his squad car and left. Joshua paid for his son's burgers, and they headed back to Dusty's home. "Joshua, I'm so sorry. Losing your wife in the Rapture and seeing your son acting the way he does must be heartbreaking."

"Yeah, Dusty, it's very disappointing. Especially hearing my son and his stooges chanting the anti-Semitic slogan, *From the river to the sea, Palestine will be free.* The Jordon River runs the length of Israel on the western side, and the Mediterranean Sea sits on the eastern side. So, when people chant the slogan, they are, in essence, calling for the genocide of all Jews living in the state of Israel."

"Joshua, Wiley is not the only deceived young person. Tens of thousands of High School and College students have been deceived by their teachers and professors into believing that the land of Israel,

Jerusalem, and the Temple Mount belong to the Muslims. This is a total denial of the historical and biblical facts. The historical record confirms that the Jews are the indigenous people of Israel, not the Muslims.

"The Temple Mount is not called the Mosque Mount for a reason. Israel's King Solomon constructed the Temple Mount and the Temple that sat on it in 960 B.C., thousands of years before Islam became a religion. Furthermore, there are no historical records of a Palestinian government, no ancient Palestinian coins or artifacts that provide evidence that the modern-day Palestinian people have any rights to the land of Israel.

"The Jewish state of Israel is mentioned many times in the Quran, but *Palestine* is not mentioned even once. If there was such a historical land, the Arabs would never have named it *Palestine* because there is no "P" in the Arabic alphabet!

"More importantly, the biblical record tells us that God gave the land of Israel to the Jews. So, anyone that picks a fight with the nation of Israel over its land ownership is picking a fight with God, and that is a battle you cannot win!"

"You got that right, Dusty, but Wiley knows about Israel's heritage yet chooses to deny the truth. Like I said, those bee stings are causing people to lose their minds."

"Joshua, a conspiracy theory is circulating that claims the bee stings contain Graphene Oxide."

Joshua glanced at Dusty, "What's Graphene Oxide?"

"Well, Joshua, it is a liquid substance that works like an RFID (Radio Frequency Identification) receiver that can communicate wirelessly through 5-G cell phone technology. The Electro-Stimulated Graphene Oxide can activate dormant nanoparticles received in the bee sting.

"According to the theory, the millions of adverse reactions and thousands of deaths reported from the bee stings are the side effects, not the desired effect. The desired effect is to reduce the world's population by sending a G-5 signal to the host's cell phone that activates the bee sting, causing millions to die!"

"Dusty, it's just a conspiracy theory!"

"Yes, Joshua, it is, but that does not mean that it's not a real conspiracy. Before the bee stings, there was no such thing as *Sudden Death Syndrome*. Thousands of people of all ages, including physically fit young athletes, have died suddenly for no apparent reason. Something is causing those deaths!

"Yes, Dusty, but the people that died suddenly are in the thousands, not millions."

Dusty stroked his chin, "Yeah, that's true, but perhaps whatever is in those bee stings is not meant to kill everyone at once, but inconspicuously over time.

"Or maybe the *Sudden Deaths* are the side effect, but the desired effect is not to kill the host but to make them go crazy! I mean, look at all the senseless school and church shootings. Crime, violence, thefts, rape, and murder are off the charts. Even spectators and children marching in parades are not safe but have been run down, run over, and crushed beneath automobiles driven by insane murders. Perhaps when the button is pushed, it will cause millions to go crazy, and everyone will start killing one another!"

Joshua blinked away unshed tears, "Dusty, perhaps you're on to something. When Wiley and I stood eye to eye, I could see the evil, hatred, and rage in his eyes. If looks could kill, I'd be dead right now.

"If you are right about the G-5-activated bee sting ability to cause people to go insane. It's about to get real crazy, real soon! After all, millions of people from coast to coast have gotten stung two or three times, and everyone has a cell phone."

"Joshua, that's not the half of it. I got a call from Uncle Jack, and he told me that there are an estimated 200,000 criminals, insane people, and terrorists living in America that he believes will soon start a civil war—thanks to a particular political Party's open border policy.

"The war will begin with a Nuclear Explosion in New York City. It will be coordinated with a Cyber Attack, knocking out communication systems from coast to coast. Under the cover of the blackout, the terrorists will invade cities, towns, and homes, killing millions of unarmed citizens."

Joshua's eyes enlarged, "Oh my goodness, if the war goes down as Jack predicts, the citizens who supported *Gun Control Legislation* and willingly surrendered their *Second Amendment Rights* will soon discover they voted for the wrong Party. *It will be a bloodbath!*"

"It gets worse, Joshua. Jack believes that the politicians and complicit fake news media will blame the attack on the MEGA Patriots, Constitutionalists, and Bible-believing citizens as an excuse to round up and arrest the political dissidents. Hauling them off to deprogramming, re-education, and extermination camps. Effectively reducing America's population and at the same time establishing the globalist New World Order."

"Jeepers! Where did your Uncle Jack get his intel?"

"It's Uncle Jack's conspiracy theory, based on his expertise, military experience, and a movie."

Joshua glanced at Dusty, shaking his head, "A movie! What?"

"Yes, Joshua, a movie. My initial reaction was the same as yours, but it made perfect sense when Uncle Jack explained it to me. I'm sure you've noticed how the global elite often telegraphs what they plan to do before it happens!"

"Yeah, Dusty, I have noticed that. It's like they are so proud of their evil intentions and machinations that they can't keep their mouth shut but must brag about it! It's a catch-me-if-you-can mentality—believing they are so much more intelligent that the American people will never catch on until it's too late."

"Well, Uncle Jack said that the movie portrayed a similar terrorist plot to destroy and take over America, which confirmed his suspicion of the impending terrorist attack plan. I hope Uncle Jack is wrong, but if he's right. Like you said, Joshua. *It's about to get real crazy, real soon!"*

"And God saw that the wickedness of man was great in the earth and that every imagination of the thoughts of his heart was only evil continually. And it repented the Lord that he had made man on the earth, and it grieved him at his heart."

Joshua gave Dusty a quizzical look, "What was the movie's title, and who produced it?"

"Uncle Jack didn't tell me the name of the movie, but the movie's production company is owned by one of the leading advocates of the depopulation climate change cult."

"Who is that?" Joshua asked.

Dusty pressed his finger to his lips and pointed at Joshua's phone. He cupped his hand around his mouth, and whispered in Joshua's ear, his name is… "

To be continued…

Chapter Eighteen

Quick Thief

This chapter and the next two are EXTRAS, which I included to assist your understanding concerning the timing of the Rapture. Did you know that the name Velociraptor is Latin, meaning Quick Thief? That fact is what inspired the title of this book, *Veloci-Rapture*. Jesus said, *"Behold, I come Quickly! Like a Thief in the Night."* Like an attacking Velociraptor portrayed in the Jurassic Park movie, the Rapture will be QUICK, SURPRISING, AND TERRIFYING! Stealing away believers and leaving behind an unprepared world basking in the false sense of prosperity, peace, and security.

> But concerning the times and the seasons, brethren, you have no need that I should write to you. For you yourselves know perfectly that the day of the Lord so comes as a thief in the night. For when they say, "Peace and safety!" then sudden destruction comes upon them, as labor pains upon a pregnant woman. And they shall not escape" (1 Thessalonians 5, verses 1 to 3).

Jesus tells us that the Rapture will NOT happen during a time of tribulation but at a time of relative peace, security, and prosperity. It will happen when the world's citizenry will be enjoying life: *Eating and drinking. Marrying and giving in marriage. Buying, selling, planting, building, and planning for the future.*

"But as the days of Noah were, so also will the coming of the Son of Man be. For as in the days before the flood, *they were eating and drinking, marrying and giving in marriage,* until the day that Noah entered the ark, and did not know until the flood came and took them all away, so also will the coming of the Son of Man be.

Then two men will be in the field: one will be taken and the other left. Two women will be grinding at the mill: one will be taken and the other left. But know this, that if the master of the house had known what hour the thief would come, he would have watched and not allowed his house to be broken into. Therefore you also be ready, for the Son of Man is coming at an hour you do not expect" (Matthew 24, verses 37 to 44).

"Likewise, as it was also in the days of Lot: *They ate, they drank, they bought, they sold, they planted, they built,* but on the day that Lot went out of Sodom it rained fire and brimstone from heaven and destroyed them all. Even so will it be in the day when the Son of Man is revealed" (Luke 17, verses 28 to 30).

Just as it was in the *Days of Noah* and the *Days of Lot,* the same nonchalant, unsuspecting attitude will be commonplace at the time of the Rapture. In other words, the Rapture will happen when it's business as usual, but with increasing natural disasters and wars and rumors of wars. At a time, that pretty much describes our world today.

God removed the righteous believers before judgment fell in both the Days of Noah and the Days of Lot. The same, according to Jesus, will be true with the Rapture!

The consensus of prophecy students is that the Rapture will be a Pre-tribulation, Mid-tribulation, or Post-tribulation event. The Mid-tribulation Rapture theory places the Rapture at the mid-point of the

Tribulation. For the theory to be correct, the first half of the Tribulation must be a relative time of peace, safety, and prosperity—but that is just the opposite of what Scripture reveals about it!

During the Tribulation's first half, Jesus breaks the seals that unleash the Four Horsemen of the Apocalypse described in Revelation chapter 6, verses 1 to 8. Let's take a look at what happens when those seals are opened.

First Seal: The Antichrist

"Now I saw when the Lamb opened one of the seals; and I heard one of the four living creatures saying with a voice like thunder, "Come and see." And I looked, and behold, a white horse. He who sat on it had a bow; and a crown was given to him, and he went out conquering and to conquer."

The opening of the first seal introduces us to the rider on a white horse that most expositors believe represents the Antichrist. The Antichrist will debut on the world stage as the man with the answers to the world's dilemmas. He will quickly rise to fame, fortune, and power through diplomacy, mighty signs and wonders, and armed conflict.

Second Seal: Peace Taken from the Earth

"When He opened the second seal, I heard the second living creature saying, "Come and see." Another horse, fiery red, went out. And it was granted to the one who sat on it to take peace from the earth, and that people should kill one another; and there was given to him a great sword."

The Second Horseman brandishes a Great Sword. His horse is fiery red, indicating it will be a time of rage, ruin, and bloodshed. This rider will usher in a time of violence, murder, and revolution. He represents not only nation rising against nation and kingdom against kingdom but also citizen fighting against citizen and neighbor against neighbor!

Third Seal: Food Shortages and Economic Upheaval

"When He opened the third seal, I heard the third living creature say, 'Come and see.' So, I looked, and behold, a black horse, and he who sat on it had a pair of scales in his hand. And I heard a voice in the midst of the four living creatures saying, 'A quart of wheat for a denarius, and three quarts of barley for a denarius; and do not harm the oil and the wine."

The Third Horseman brings with him an economic collapse and severe food shortages. A denarius is a measure of money equivalent to a day's wages. People will have to work an entire day to earn enough money to purchase the ingredients needed to make just a couple of loaves of bread. Talk about inflation!

Fourth Seal: Widespread Death on Earth

"When He opened the fourth seal, I heard the voice of the fourth living creature saying, 'Come and see.' So, I looked, and behold, a pale horse. And the name of him who sat on it was Death, and Hell followed with him. And power was given to them over a fourth of the earth, to kill with sword, with hunger, with death, and by the beasts of the earth."

The Fourth Horseman's name is Death, and power is given to him to kill with sword, with hunger, with death, and by the beasts of the earth decimating one-quarter of the earth's population. As you can see, the first half of the seven-year Tribulation will not be a time of peace, safety, and prosperity—but a literal hell on earth!

You don't invite friends and family to a wedding when the church is burning. You don't start building a home and planning for the future when the economy is so bad and inflation is so high that you can't even afford a hammer and a box of nails. You don't plan a trip to Disney World when people are slaughtering one another, and lawlessness rules the day.

The Pre-Tribulation Rapture is also confirmed by the fact that the Christian church is mentioned in the first three chapters of Revelation (before the tribulation judgments begin) and not mentioned again until the end of the book (after the last judgment has passed). Indicating that the church will not be on earth during the entire tribulation period.

The Pre-tribulation Rapture is also foreshadowed in the first two verses of Revelation 4. Immediately after concluding the letter to the churches, John sees a door opened in heaven. He is told to "Come up hither" and is transported to heaven's throne room.

> "After this I looked, and, behold, a door was opened in heaven: and the first voice which I heard was as it were of a trumpet talking with me; which said, 'Come up hither, and I will show thee things which must be hereafter.' And immediately I was in the spirit: and, behold, a throne was set in heaven, and one sat on the throne." (Revelation 4 verses 1 to 2).

Notice that the voice said, "I will show thee things which must be hereafter." Hereafter what? After the church age! If the church was required to go through the first half of the Tribulation, as the Mid-tribulation advocates proclaim, the command to "come up hither" should have been given at the mid-point of the Tribulation—but such is not the case. The command was given before the first judgment seal was opened, indicating that the church was raptured before the beginning of the seven-year Tribulation!

The good news is that if you are a Christian or become one before the Rapture. God's Word promises that you'll be kept out of the Tribulation. In one of His messages to the seven churches, Jesus told them: "Because you have kept My command to persevere, I also will keep you from the hour of trial which shall come upon the whole world, to test those who dwell on the earth" (Revelation 3 verse 10).

Jesus' words make it clear that the persevering church (true born-again believers) will not go through the "hour of trial" (a reference to the Tribulation). The English word "from" in the above verse is a translation of the original Greek New Testament word "ek," which means "out of." Unlike other forms of hardship where God promises to be with us "through" those times of difficulty, believers are promised to be kept "out of" the Tribulation. If the church were destined to go through the Tribulation, the Greek word "dia," meaning "through," should have been used.

The first half of the Tribulation will NOT be a time to celebrate life: *Eating and drinking. Marrying and giving in marriage. Buying, selling, planting, building, and planning for the future.* Instead, it will be a time to mourn and bury the dead as the salvo of Tribulation Riders reduces the planet's population by TWO BILLION PEOPLE!

Jesus warns, "But take heed to yourselves, lest your hearts be weighed down with carousing, drunkenness, and cares of this life, and that Day come on you unexpectedly. For it will come as a snare on all those who dwell on the face of the whole earth!" (Luke 21 verse 34).

The Destruction of Damascus

You should also know that the destruction of Syria's Capital, Damascus, foretold by God's prophet, Isaiah, chapter 17, could happen *before* or *after* the Rapture. Scripture doesn't tell us when or by what means Damascus will be destroyed, but since its destruction happens in one day, it is assumed to be nuclear!

From a prophetic perspective, prophecy scholars believe that the destruction of Damascus will pave the way for the destruction of the Muslim nations mentioned in Psalm 83. Followed by the Gog and Magog invasion of Israel described in Ezekiel 38 and 39. This Russian-led multinational invasion will be covered extensively in the next Veloci-Rapture Novel!

Chapter Nineteen

Daniel's 70 Weeks Prophecy

People who believe the Rapture will happen sometime during or after the Tribulation do not understand Daniel's 70 Weeks Prophecy. According to Daniel, chapter 9, verses 24 to 27, the Tribulation will not begin until the church age comes to a close. Let's take a look at Daniel's prophecy.

"Seventy weeks are determined upon thy people and upon thy holy city, to finish the transgression, and to make an end of sins, and to make reconciliation for iniquity, and to bring in everlasting righteousness, and to seal up the vision and prophecy, and to anoint the most Holy" (Daniel 9:24).

A "week" in prophetic language is a "week of years," or seven years. Daniel's people are the Jews, and the holy city is Jerusalem. According to this prophecy given to Daniel by the angel Gabriel, Daniel's people have 70 weeks of years, or 490 years, to achieve these six objectives:

Finish the transgression.
Make an end to sins.
Make reconciliation for iniquity.
Bring in everlasting righteousness.
Seal up the vision and prophecy.
Anoint the most Holy.

Those six objectives have never been accomplished and will only be completed once the national chastisement of Israel during the Tribulation has ended and the nation is established in everlasting righteousness. The 70-week countdown started with the commandment to restore and rebuild Jerusalem.

> "Know therefore and understand, that from the going forth of the commandment to restore and to build Jerusalem unto the Messiah the Prince shall be seven weeks, and threescore and two weeks: the street shall be built again, and the wall, even in troublous times" (Daniel 9:25).

This decree to "restore and build Jerusalem unto the Messiah" came from King Artaxerxes of Persia in 445 B.C. and is recorded in Nehemiah 2. According to the Jewish calendar, the 490-year countdown that started in 445 B.C. should have ended in A.D. 40, but it didn't. Why? Because the angel Gabriel had something else to say about it. He said that during the first seven weeks (49 years), Jerusalem was to be rebuilt in troublous times. This was fulfilled as recorded in Ezra and Nehemiah.

Then Gabriel told Daniel that after the first "seven weeks" (49 years) was accomplished, another "three score and two weeks" (62 weeks = 434 years, for a total of 69 weeks = 483 years) would pass before the Messiah would arrive in Jerusalem. Guess what happened after the 483 years passed? Jesus the prophesied Messiah rode into Jerusalem on a donkey in A.D. 33. The exact year Daniel predicted that "Messiah the Prince" would arrive!

The Old Testament prophet, Zechariah also foretold about the event stating.

> "Rejoice greatly, O daughter of Zion! Shout, O daughter of Jerusalem! Behold, your King is coming to you; He is just and having salvation, Lowly and riding on a donkey, A colt, the foal of a donkey" (Zechariah 9 verse 9).

Even though Jesus fulfilled Zechariah's prophecy, the leaders of Israel refused to recognize Him as the Messiah, Savior, and King of Israel but instead desired his execution.

"And after three score and two weeks shall **Messiah be cut off, but not for himself**: and the people of the prince that shall come shall destroy the city and the sanctuary; and the end thereof shall be with a flood, and unto the end of the war desolations are determined" (Daniel 9:26).

Shortly after Jesus rode into Jerusalem on the donkey, He was "cut off"—from life, tried and crucified—"but not for himself:" *Not for His sins and transgressions, but for ours!* Precisely as Daniel had foretold.

Jesus testified that because of Israel's rejection, they would not see Him again until they acknowledged their offense, saying, "Blessed is he that cometh in the name of the Lord."

"O Jerusalem, Jerusalem, thou that killest the prophets, and stonest them which are sent unto thee, how often would I have gathered thy children together, even as a hen gathereth her chickens under her wings, and ye would not! Behold, your house is left unto you desolate. For I say unto you, **Ye shall not see me henceforth, till ye shall say, Blessed is he that cometh in the name of the Lord**" (Matthew 23, verses 37 to 39).

As part of Israel's national chastisement for rejecting Jesus Christ, the Messiah, Daniel stated that Jerusalem and the Jewish Temple would be destroyed: *"The people of the prince that shall come shall destroy the city and the sanctuary."*

The city's and the sanctuary's destruction happened just as Jesus foretold in the New Testament and Daniel predicted in the Old Testament in 70 A.D., when the Roman Legions led by Commander Titus invaded Jerusalem, destroyed the Temple, and slaughtered over a million Jews!

The *"prince that shall come"* is the future Antichrist, who will arise out of the area of the ancient Roman empire and will confirm a covenant with many for seven years but will break the covenant halfway through and set up the abomination that causes desolation in the rebuilt Temple in Jerusalem:

> "And he [Antichrist] shall confirm the covenant with many for one week [seven years]: and in the midst of the week he shall cause the sacrifice and the oblation to cease, and for the overspreading of abominations he shall make it desolate, even until the consummation, and that determined shall be poured upon the desolate" (Daniel 9:27).

Since the nation of Israel rejected Jesus Christ, God's dealing with Israel was put on hold and will not resume until the time of the Tribulation, the final week of Daniel's 70-week prophecy. So, God's offer of Salvation turned to the Gentiles as the apostle Paul testified in Acts 18, verses 5 to 6:

> "When Silas and Timothy had come from Macedonia, Paul was compelled by the Spirit, and testified to the Jews that Jesus is the Christ. But when they opposed him and blasphemed, he shook his garments and said to them, **"Your blood be upon your own heads; I am clean. From now on, I will go to the Gentiles!"**

So the start of the 69th Week of Daniel began with Israel's rejection of Jesus as their Messiah and Savior which in turn gave birth to the church age, which started on the day of Pentecost and will continue until the fullness of the Gentiles has come in: "For I would not, brethren, that ye should be ignorant of this mystery, lest ye should be wise in your own conceits; *that blindness in part has happened to Israel* **until the fullness of the Gentiles be come in**" (Romans 11 verse 25).

Notice that the verse says that *"blindness in part has happened to Israel."* There are Jewish believers in Jesus, called Messianic Jews, but as a whole, the nation of Israel will not believe in Jesus until the time of the end. At this time, Jesus will return in His Second Coming to rescue Israel from the invading armies, and the Jews will cry out: *"Blessed is he that cometh in the name of the Lord!"*

Until then, the church age will continue until the *"fullness of the Gentiles be come in."* There will only be a certain number of believers in the Christian church, and God knows that number. When the last person believes, making the church complete, the Father will tell the Son, *"Go get them!"*

After the church is removed via the Rapture, Daniel's 69th Week—the church age—will come to a close, and God's dealing with the nation of Israel will resume. Unfortunately, Israel will not recognize Jesus as their Savior, Messiah, and King until Daniel's 70th Week—the Tribulation period—runs its awful course.

So, as I said earlier, people who believe the Rapture will happen sometime during or after the Tribulation do not understand Daniel's 70 Weeks Prophecy. According to Daniel, the Tribulation CANNOT BEGIN until the church age (Daniel's 69th Week) ends. The Mid-Tribulation Rapture would mean that the church age must extend halfway into the Tribulation period (Daniel's 70th Week), but it cannot. The church age is not sixty-nine and one-half weeks. It's sixty-nine weeks—no less, no more!

"Watch, therefore, and pray always that you may be counted worthy to escape all these things that will come to pass, and to stand before the Son of Man!"

The Pre-Tribulation Rapture is the only plausible, sensible, and biblically correct possibility. It is the only one that fulfills Christ's depiction of a world: *Eating and drinking, marrying, buying, selling, planting, and building—unaware and unconcerned about the future that awaits them.* And the Pre-tribulation Rapture is the only one that doesn't violate Daniel's 70 Weeks of Years Prophecy!

Amazingly, those who promote the Mid-tribulation and Post-tribulation Rapture theories often ridicule and denigrate the Pre-tribulation teachers. It's as if their desire for Christians is not to escape the terrible Tribulation events but to be forced to endure them! For those of you who desire such a thing, God's prophet Amos has a word for you:

> "Woe unto you that desire the day of the Lord! To what end is it for you? The day of the Lord is darkness, and not light. As if a man did flee from a lion, and a bear met him; or went into the house, and leaned his hand on the wall, and a serpent bit him. Shall not the day of the Lord be darkness, and not light? Even very dark, and no brightness in it?" (Amos 5 verses 18-20).

Chapter Twenty

Six Mega Signs

In the second chapter of this book, I provided biblical insight explaining that it was NOT GLOBAL WARMING but GLOBAL INIQUITY that was causing natural disasters to become increasingly unnatural in frequency, intensity, and duration! This phenomenon is a mega sign that we are living in the last days. The unnatural disasters are birth pangs, harbingers of worse pain to come—the Tribulation!

Amir Tsarfati, the founder of Behold Israel, expressed the significance of this end-time sign.

> *ALL the boxes for the birth-pangs before the Tribulation are being checked. Each year is getting worse than the one before.*
>
> *Every single red line is being crossed and new ones are defined. Evil isn't ashamed anymore to be public and out in the open. This world is a mess.*
>
> *So why am I not depressed? Because none of the above are surprises to students of Bible prophecy.*

"These things I have spoken to you, that in Me you may have peace. In the world you will have tribulation; but be of good cheer, I have overcome the world." (John 16:33).

Mega Sign Two: Daniel's End Time Prophecy

"At that time Michael shall stand up, The great prince who stands watch over the sons of your people; And there shall be a time of trouble, Such as never was since there was a nation, Even to that time.

And at that time your people shall be delivered, Everyone who is found written in the book. And many of those who sleep in the dust of the earth shall awake, Some to everlasting life, Some to shame and everlasting contempt.

Those who are wise shall shine, Like the brightness of the firmament, And those who turn many to righteousness, Like the stars forever and ever.

But you, Daniel, shut up the words, and seal the book until the time of the end; many shall run to and fro, and knowledge shall increase" (Daniel 12 verses 1 to 4).

Daniel tells us that at the "time of the end," travel will increase exponentially, traveling "to and fro" like no other time in history. Traveling from coast to coast took weeks and even months a century ago, but today, it takes just hours to travel thousands of miles. And it isn't just the rich and elite that travel in Jet aircraft to distant lands, but as Daniel foretold, "many" shall run to and fro! Ordinary people, by the millions, travel the world for business and vacations in Jets and Ocean cruises daily. And if you can afford it, you can even travel into outer space or explore the deep blue sea!

Daniel also said that an explosion in knowledge would mark the time of the end. We are living in that world today. From lightning-quick Communication and Surveillance, Nanotechnology, Robotic Surgery, Genetic Engineering, Holograms, and Atomic Particle Colliders... To self-driving cars, Clones, AI Super Soldiers, UAVs, Exploding Dragonflies, ChatGPT, Metaverse, CBDC, Satellites,

Spaceships, Jets, Hypersonic Missiles, Transhumanism... and on and on!

Until 1900, human knowledge doubled approximately every 100 years. By the end of World War II, knowledge doubled every 25 years. A few years ago, knowledge doubled every two years. Today, the quantum computing technology called AI is taking the world by storm. Research that just a few years ago would take weeks can now be done in minutes, and human knowledge doubles every 24 hours or less!

Where is this high-technology MEGA SIGN taking us? To the time of the end, the rise of the Antichrist, and the Mark of the Beast!

Mega Sign Three: Psalm Chapter Two

"Why do the heathen rage, and the people imagine a vain thing? The kings of the earth set themselves, and the rulers take counsel together, against the Lord, and against his anointed, saying, Let us break their bands asunder, and cast away their cords from us.

He that sitteth in the heavens shall laugh: the Lord shall have them in derision. Then shall he speak unto them in his wrath, and vex them in his sore displeasure. Yet have I set my king upon my holy hill of Zion.

I will declare the decree: the Lord hath said unto me, Thou art my Son; this day have I begotten thee. Ask of me, and I shall give thee the heathen for thine inheritance, and the uttermost parts of the earth for thy possession. Thou shalt break them with a rod of iron; thou shalt dash them in pieces like a potter's vessel.

Be wise now therefore, O ye kings: be instructed, ye judges of the earth. Serve the Lord with fear, and rejoice with trembling. Kiss the Son, lest he be angry, and ye perish from the way, when his wrath is kindled but a little. Blessed are all they that put their trust in him."

This prophecy, written centuries before the birth of Jesus, foretold of His rejection by the nation's rulers at the time of Jesus and the apostles, but also a future time before the start of the Tribulation. The time when the governments of nations once known as Christian will desire to sever the ties of Christianity: *"The kings of the earth set themselves, and the rulers take counsel together, against the Lord and against His anointed, saying, "Let us break their bonds in pieces and cast away their cords from us!"*

Most of Europe's nations today have severed the cords that once tied them to Christianity and have become agnostic secular nations. The same thing is happening in our country. The United States of America was founded upon Judeo-Christian principles and virtues, but in less than 250 years, the nation born out of religious intolerance no longer tolerates its founder's religion in schools, government, and the public square!

What does God have to say about that?

"Now therefore, be wise, O kings; Be instructed, you judges of the earth. Serve the Lord with fear, And rejoice with trembling. Kiss the Son, lest He be angry, And you perish in the way, when His wrath is kindled but a little. Blessed are all those who put their trust in Him!" (Psalm 2, last verse).

The nations' severing of the cords of Christianity is a MEGA SIGN of the soon-coming Tribulation.

Mega Sign Four: Perilous Times and Perilous Men

"But know this, that in the last days perilous times will come: For men will be lovers of themselves, lovers of money, boasters, proud, blasphemers, disobedient to parents, unthankful, unholy, unloving, unforgiving, slanderers, without self-control, brutal, despisers of good, traitors, headstrong, haughty, lovers of pleasure rather than lovers of God." (2 Timothy 3 verses 1 to 4).

That description sounds awfully a lot like the characteristics of many of America's politicians and the constituents that vote for them. Don't you think?

Mega Sign Five: Sodom and Gomorrah

Scripture informs us that God included the account of the destruction of the ancient cities of Sodom and Gomorrah in the Bible to provide a historical EXAMPLE to future generations not to follow in their footsteps.

> "Even as Sodom and Gomorrha, and the cities about them in like manner, giving themselves over to fornication, and going after strange flesh, are SET FORTH FOR AN EXAMPLE, suffering the vengeance of eternal fire!" (Jude verse 7).

God's prophet, Isaiah, warns that the provoking of God's wrath occurs when a nation, state, or city demonstrates that it no longer fears God but instead legalizes, legitimizes, and celebrates abomination: *DECLARING THEIR SIN AS SODOM, THEY HIDE IT NOT* (Isaiah 3 verse 9).

According to the biblical prophet, it is one thing when immoral acts are done in a closet but quite another thing when acts of immorality against God are made public policy!

Reminiscent of the days when the man named Lot lived in Sodom. America no longer blushes or fears God but proudly hangs out its filthy laundry for the world to see! The United States of America has gone from being once known as the most Christian nation on earth to the world's leader in promoting and exporting abomination.

> *Lady Liberty is no longer the lady she once was. She has lifted her skirt. She has spread her legs. She has given*

> *birth to abominations that promise to bring judgment upon the earth.*
>
> *In every village, city, and state, the haunting voice of Sodom and Gomorrah can be heard. The voice that warns, the days of Lot have returned!*

What does God's prophet, Isaiah, have to say about such a nation? "Woe unto their soul, for they have rewarded evil unto themselves!" (Isaiah 3 verse 9).

The societal acceptance, promotion, celebration, and legalization of deviant lifestyles that God labels abominations is a MEGA SIGN that the Rapture and the Tribulation Judgments are just around the bend!

"Likewise, as it was also in the days of Lot: Even so will it be in the day when the Son of Man is revealed!"

Mega Sign Six: The Hosea Prophecy

I will return again to My place, till they acknowledge their offense. Then they will seek My face; In their affliction they will earnestly seek Me. Come, and let us return to the Lord; For He has torn, but He will heal us; He has stricken, but He will bind us up. After two days He will revive us; On the third day, He will raise us up, That we may live in His sight." (Hosea chapter 5, verse 15 and chapter 6, verses 1 to 2).

To understand this prophecy, one must consider the prophetic implications of the apostle Peter's statement, "That with the Lord one day is as a thousand years, and a thousand years as one day" (2 Peter 3 verse 8). In other words, "two days" equals 2,000 years, and "three days" equals 3,000 years.

Hosea's Old Testament prophecy foretold of a future time when the nation of Israel would reject the Lord. This was fulfilled in Jesus' first coming. Instead of receiving Jesus Christ as their Lord, Savior, and King, Israel rejected Him, and He was crucified. So, the Lord, through the mouth of the prophet, said, "I will return again to My place." This part of the prophecy was fulfilled when Jesus rose from the dead and, 40 days later, ascended to His place—Heaven!

Scripture reveals that it will take the terrible events of the GREAT TRIBULATION to awaken the nation of Israel. The time when Israel will be, as Hosea said, *"torn, stricken, and afflicted," and "in their afflictions, they will earnestly seek Me."*

Israel will finally realize that Jesus is who He said He is—the Messiah, Savior, and King of Israel—and they will say to one another: *"Come and let us return to the Lord; For He has torn, but He will heal us; He has stricken, but He will bind us up."*

When Israel finally acknowledges their offense, Jesus will return "after two days"—two thousand years after His ascension—to rescue Israel and forgive them. The Millennial reign of Jesus Christ will begin immediately after the Tribulation. At that time, Jesus will *"raise us [Israel] up, that we may live in His sight."* The time when the Jews and Christians will rule and reign with Jesus for 1,000 years—the third day!

The starting point for the 2,000 years began after the Jews of Israel rejected Jesus Christ, the Romans crucified Him, and He rose from the dead on April 6, A.D. 33. Then He was seen by over 500 eyewitnesses over 40 days, of which both biblical and secular history affirm.

> "For I delivered to you first of all that which I also received: that Christ died for our sins according to the Scriptures, and that He was buried, and that He rose again the third day according to the Scriptures, and that He was seen by Cephas, then by the twelve.

After that He was seen by over five hundred brethren at once, of whom the greater part remain to the present, but some have fallen asleep.

After that He was seen by James, then by all the apostles. Then last of all He was seen by me [Paul] also, as by one born out of due time" (1 Corinthians 3, verses 3 to 8).

So, adding 40 days to the April 6 resurrection date brings us to the date of Jesus's ascension into Heaven on May 16, A.D. 33. Two days—two thousand years—from A.D. 33 brings us to the year 2033. This means the Tribulation period will begin or end in 2033!

If Hosea's prophecy signifies the Tribulation begins in 2033, the pre-Tribulation Rapture will happen sometime between now and May 16, 2033. If Hosea's prophecy foretells that the Tribulation ends in 2033, the 7-year Tribulation must be subtracted from the 2033 date since Christians will NOT go through the Tribulation. This means the Rapture will happen between now and May 16, 2026. That's pretty close!

R.U. Ready? / 2026 – 2033

Chapter Twenty-One

Congratulations!

You have made it through the first few weeks of the Tribulation and are still alive! I hope you enjoyed the book, learned a lot, and had a few laughs. You may be interested in knowing that many things the Rhodes family experienced in this book are based on actual family events—from camping in the Wisconsin Northwoods to racing around in fast vehicles. The salvation account of Dusty, the News Reporter, is based on my own Salvation experience. The salvation account of the character Mike is based on my son's Salvation when he watched the Passion of Christ movie. Even the story about the demonic presence invading the home of the tongue-speaking Christian Author is an actual event that my wife and I experienced.

I wrote Veloci-Rapture as a Novel instead of a **Non-fiction** book because people whose shadow would never darken a church door or read Christian literature will read a Novel. My goal is not just to warn people of the Lord's imminent return and the tribulation but that they may be SAVED! *I hope that is your goal as well.*

Most people think people like Hitler deserve to go to Hell, but not them. The truth is there will be more unrepentant barbers, plumbers, school teachers, bricklayers, doctors, and nurses in Hell than murderers. While there are likely degrees of punishment, all who refuse, scorn, or neglect God's mercy must endure His wrath.

The good news is that you can do your part in fulfilling Christ's Great Commission by visiting Amazon's website and entering the number 9798866044153 in the search box. It will take you to the Veloci-Rapture order page, where you can order copies to hand out to friends and relatives.

If you prefer, you can have Amazon send the book as a gift to the addresses of your choice *with* or *without* letting the recipient know who gave the gift. Click the "Add to Cart" button and then the "Proceed to Check Out" button. Click the gift options link or the change address link and add the addresses before placing the book order.

Lastly, please write a review. A favorable review will help me as a new author and may result in the Salvation of a lost soul.

May God's face shine upon you, richly reward you, and bring you peace, comfort, and joy.

All the best,
Randel Ulysses Ready.

About the Author

I have a wonderful wife, four terrific children, and more grandchildren than fingers. I live in a small house in a small town but have a mansion in heaven. I haven't seen it yet, but I hear it's got a great view.

I've been a student of God's Word for 30 years and have the world's best teacher: *"But you have received the Holy Spirit, and he lives within you, so you don't need anyone to teach you what is true. For the Spirit teaches you everything you need to know, and what he teaches is true—it is not a lie"* (1 John 2:27 NLT).

My favorite song is by Casting Crowns called NOBODY! It's my favorite because the lyrics best describe who I am. Just a nobody trying to tell everybody all about Somebody who saved my soul.

Randel Ulysses Ready.
R.U. Ready

Printed in Great Britain
by Amazon